THE KISS

How an Innocent Gesture
Exposed the Racist Underbelly
of a Small Town

Advance Praises

THIS STORY OF 1960s racism in the American South allows a reader to enter the characters' historically conditioned attitudes, feelings, needs, vulnerabilities and overall humanness—white and black. While both "good guys and bad guys" exist in this hard-hitting story, Strickland shows how people are shaped into what they ultimately become. Without manipulating emotions, she illustrates how children's early exposure to racism, violence and humiliation can create perpetrators whose acts are nonetheless unconscionable, and how a devastating generational wheel keeps turning.

The Kiss kept me on edge, wondering what would happen next as the story took unexpected turns, sometimes breathtaking. Skillfully placed backstories revealed surprisingly interwoven threads of personal connections between some of the characters. Grave though the topic, and shocking some of the events, Strickland's wry wit had me laughing at times, warmed by moments of delight and tenderness, and strengthened in the belief that people can change. Great read!

~ Cheryl Warren
Retired Public Relations Manager/Editor

THE KISS, I started reading and thinking to myself, *I've seen this movie, or I've read a similar novel.* BUT, as I got into it, I was more and more intrigued and honestly, I started several times to rush to the end of the book to see what happened! I like it. It seems so real, because honestly similar, if not the very same things are happening today.

~ **Beverly Milam**
Retired Workers Compensation Corporate Claims Consultant
Canton, Mi

ACTION. MYSTERY. PERSONAL entanglement. Social ills. *The Kiss* contains all these elements. Sharon Hart Strickland wends through the lives of southerners in the eye of racial injustice, bringing to a head the worst items individuals can experience as they strive to make sense of a crazed world, based upon decades of behaviors rampant in the US during the height of civil unrest.

The author skillfully involves the reader in myriad events, which shaped our nation during the 1960's. The reader will certainly experience enlightenment as well as frustration from events both discussed and subtly hinted at, which form the basis of this compelling read.

The reader is spell bound when personal emotions and biases are exposed as readers traverse the entanglements which undoubtedly evolved during those troubled times.

This novel is of a quality that could certainly be used in collegiate level classes in sociology or psychology that might be determining factors governing bias or emotions.

~ **TR Stearns**, Ed.S.
Retired Public School Superintendent

Every page of *The Kiss* runs like a movie in front of my eyes. In her visceral soul search for understanding, Sharon Strickland never flinches at wrestling with the unspeakable issues. She says the hard words, because that's how the story gets told.

~ Ginny Greene
Author, *Song of County Roads*

Set in the South where historical and seemingly inviolate lines separate the lives of the white and black folk who live there. *The Kiss* shines a powerful light on what can happen when those lines are crossed While the result can lead to tragedy for some, other characters in the book are able to make surprising connections that ultimately lead to true redemption. As the novel makes it clear, racism is learned—and can be unlearned—not just in the South, but in us all.

~ Patricia Ann Helm
Former English Department Chair
Urbana High School
Urbana, IL

Racism is America's self-inflicted wound that never seems to heal. Sharon Strickland has written a powerful story of two Southern families, one white, one black, facing horrific challenges during the Civil Rights era. Twisted values of one generation are confronted as their children struggle to find a new path through a minefield of ingrained prejudice and violence. Be prepared for emotional impact!

~ Jeni Foster,
Former Chautauqua Lecturer with Oregon Humanities

Sharon Strickland has written a marvelous novel. I literally couldn't put *The Kiss* down and read it straight through. She has skillfully described an era and created a living history. The author writes wonderful dialogue and captures the vernacular of that day and age, when in America, black was black and white was white, and never were the two to be mixed.

~ **Doranne Long**, Physical Therapist
Author, *Your Body Book Guide to Better Motion with Less Pain*

***The Kiss* is** a walk through a time that many would like to forget existed. Sharon Strickland has written a powerful piece that shows us the underbelly of a not so distant past filled with hatred, violence, shame, and remarkably of bravery and survival. I was riveted and spellbound by the story she spun, felt as if I knew the characters, and could feel their pain and anguish as well as joy.

An important piece for all to read, so as to not forget and to keep us moving forward to a place of acceptance. In this time when racism seems to rear its head again, it becomes even more important a read.

~ **Holly Reynolds**, Ed.D.
Associate Professor Early Education
California State Polytechnic University, Pomona, CA

THE KISS

How an Innocent Gesture
Exposed the Racist Underbelly
of a Small Town

A Novel by Sharon Hart Strickland

Published by Rocky Rim Publishing

ISBN: 978-0-578-45393-4

Kindle Digital Version also available—ASIN: B07NW8RWDH

Published by: Rocky Rim Publishing, Gooding ID 83330

For general information on our other products and services please contact our Customer Care Department within the U.S. at 208 316 4229.

Rocky Rim Publishing also publishes books in a variety of electronic formats. Some content that appears in print may not be available in electronic books. For more information about Rocky Rim Publishing, its products and services, visit our website at:

http://sharonstricklandauthor.com

Published in the United States of America

10 9 8 7 6 5 4 3 2 1

Dedication

This book is dedicated to the brave men and women who marched, suffered beatings, arrests, church and home burnings, personal humiliations and even death for Civil Rights in the 1960s. And to the many who continue the fight for equality today in the face of modern-day racism, discrimination, and social injustice. May we find a way to honor one another's cultures and bridge the divides.

"There is no greater agony than bearing an untold story inside you."

~ Maya Angelou
(1928-2014)
American poet, singer, memoirist, and civil rights activist.

TABLE OF CONTENTS

PREFACE

IT IS HARD to look within ourselves, but necessary when we are truly soul-searching. I was raised by good, honest, kind, hard-working, Christian bigots.

As far as my father was concerned, no one could be trusted who wasn't white, Anglo-Saxon, or protestant.

As far as my mother was concerned, my father was always right.

As far as I was concerned, my parents were always right.

Until that fateful day of my high school graduation. As I stood in a circle of self-congratulating classmates after the ceremony, my father waiting just beyond, the brother of a black classmate came up beside us and kissed his sister on the cheek, then turned and kissed my cheek. Under the lights of the parking lot, I could see the blood drain from my father's face, as his mouth drew into that tight line of anger so easily recognized by his children. But he said nothing. Until the next day when he was leaving for work and kissed my mother and siblings good-bye. When he came to me, he asked which side of my face was kissed by that "nigger," because he didn't want to put his lips there. I told him not to bother and left the room.

That was my first epiphany, the first time I had ever questioned whether my parents might be wrong. And let's face it, even though I had black classmates that I liked, and my brother played sports with black classmates whom we all liked, I had to question whether I might be wrong, as well. I had laughed at the jokes, told the jokes, whispered the rumors, and feared the big, black boogeyman most of my young life. Yes, it was inherited, passed down through many generations, long before my father or me. And, yes, it was part of the culture and climate of the times in the sixties. But, to borrow a phrase, "the times, they were a'changin." And so was I, feeling that first pull toward independence and yearning to go into the world and find out who I was.

Through many years and miles on my journey, I've witnessed acts of discrimination and even been forced to participate indirectly. On one job, as a personnel assistant, I was told to underline with black felt pen the word "Application" on the form whenever the applicant was black, so that my boss could cull those applications as he saw fit before interviews. On another, I was told in a joking manner that we must be paying one employee too much, because "A Mexican shouldn't be able to afford a car like that." And what have I offered in response to these kinds of attitudes? Basically, head-shaking and a little lip service.

I thought I had overcome my own racism. Then one day, I arrived at the grocery checkout at the same time as a Hispanic woman, both of us with heavily laden carts. We smiled at each other and hesitated. Then it hit me: I *expected* this woman to defer to me, because she was brown, and I was white. That revelation hit me like a gut-punch, and I waved her ahead of me. Since that time, I've been even more aware of my own racial attitudes, not to mention the national and world-wide incidents of racism, classism, discrimination and even the ultimate atrocity of genocide.

I've been blessed with a good, kind, non-judgmental husband and we've created a family of children and grandchildren. I've kept my faith alive and been a spiritual seeker. My God calls me to be a better person and to love my neighbor. I've known for a long time that writing was part of that call. Even though I self-published one book several years ago, my priorities have always been raising a family and making a living with my husband. Story ideas have lingered in the background. But I never forgot the incident from my high school graduation, and it has been working its way out of me like a long-buried splinter.

I often wonder how my late father might have reacted to my biracial granddaughter, whom I love beyond words. Separating the man from his ideology, I like to believe he would have loved her with open arms. I like to think he knows better now, about a lot of things. My children will probably say the same about me after I'm gone, but hopefully, if there is one thing they have learned, it is to treat people of all races with dignity and respect.

In a nutshell, that's how this book came about. It is not an apology for my father's attitudes. To my knowledge, his racism never translated into any mistreatment of anyone, and he died believing he was right. I cannot speak for him, and I loved him with all this daughter's heart. This is a work of fiction, yet, there are pieces of me and people I have known, and pieces of situations I have known; pieces of history, and pieces of idealistic speculation. This story is told mostly from a white point of view, as I have no other vantage point. But through its telling, I have tried to walk in the shoes of blacks who suffered the indignities of racism in the arc of this book. In the end, this is a story from the imagination of an imperfect soul-searcher.

Acknowledgments

A story is rarely told without the support and assistance of others; *The Kiss* is no exception. I lovingly, and in deep gratitude acknowledge the following:

My family. Your love and support and are my bedrock.

Crystal: My BFF and patient photographer.

My *anam caras*—you know who you are. Thank you for your love and support from seed to printed page

Patrick Sipperly: I am so fortunate to have been introduced to your amazing talents in creating a cover I know will touch readers.

Arkansas State Archives: A treasure trove of state and national history.

The Eyes on the Prize Civil Rights Reader: Documents, Speeches, and Firsthand Accounts from the Black Freedom Struggle: General Editors Clayborne Carson, David J. Garrow, Gerald Gill, Vincent Harding, Darlene Clark Hine; published by Viking Penguin 1991.

Last, but far from least, my Literary Strategist, who kept me doing the right things, at the right time, and for the right reasons.

THE KISS

How an Innocent Gesture
Exposed the Racist Underbelly
of a Small Town

Chapter One

1963

The Kiss

"All things truly wicked start from innocence."

~ Ernest Hemingway (1899-1961)
American journalist, novelist, and short-story writer.

It happened on a warm October evening. The night began like any other Friday in Oakwood, Arkansas, a yawn of a town in Garland County, near the foothills of the Ouachita Mountains. Most of Oakwood's citizens had turned out for the high school football game. Whistles, chants, cheers and laughter wafted through the evening air. Players crashed together under the lights, as coaches yelled at referees. Fans shouted their joy and displeasure, while the pep band rallied the crowd with the school fight song. Just a typical autumn Friday night in any small town, USA. But this terrible night would leave death and despair in its wake.

Oakwood High School, an old, three-story building that sat among the oaks in the middle of town, had fostered the education of local residents for several generations. Its faded red brick façade had crumbled and been patched in corners. The third-floor windows had been nailed shut to avoid another unfortunate accident, like the one that left an unpopular teacher paralyzed, shortly after his lecture on Darwin's theory of evolution. When the first black students were bussed from across the beltline, Oakwood became the scene of angry protests. But the protestors settled down when they realized that only a few Negroes actually had the nerve to integrate their school, and especially after one of them became a star running back for Oakwood's anemic football team. The school had since enjoyed a fragile, uneasy calm.

The scoreboard showed that the Oakwood Hogs had just claimed victory. Cheering fans formed a gauntlet for the players, as they ran off the field. Fourteen-year-old Maggie Thorpe walked behind her parents, leaving the stands. She saw classmate Annalee Roberts approaching on her right at the foot of the stairs.

Maggie smiled tentatively. "Your brother played a good game tonite, Annalee."-

"Thanks. So'd yours," Annalee replied.

The girls were forced by the jostling crowd to walk side by side through the gate and into the parking lot. Willis Roberts ran up to his sister, full of adrenaline from the victory. He slipped between Annalee and Maggie, placing an arm around each girl's shoulder. Maggie stiffened.

"Hey, I'm glad to see you two being more friendly, girls," Willis said with a chuckle. "How 'bout that game, huh? Did you see that pass Michael threw me? Did you see that **RUN**? Man, we're good together!"

Willis kissed his sister on the cheek, then he turned and did the same to Maggie, before hurrying off toward the locker room. Annalee looked wide-eyed at Maggie, then uttered a hasty good-bye and rushed away. Maggie, however, stood frozen in place, staring blank-faced at her father, who had turned to look for her just in time to witness the kiss.

"Maggie! Go to the car with your mother! I've gotta tell Michael what time to be home. GO ON!"

"Daddy, I didn't do nothin'—he just came runnin' up and..."

Eddie Thorpe could barely contain his anger. "Do as I say. Go to the car. Now."

Maggie hurried off in humiliation, her face hot as tears brimmed in her eyes. Eddie looked around to see if anyone else had noticed. He spotted Jack Beauford, a co-worker he detested, in a group of men near the gate. With a smirk on his face, Beauford stared straight at Eddie.

Eddie caught up with Michael outside the locker room. "Son, you need to come home right after you change. I've heard there might be some trouble tonight and I want you off the street."

"But, Dad, I can take care of myself," Michael protested. "Everybody's goin' out to celebrate at Whistler's. I'll just grab a quick burger and RC and then come home, ok? Please?"

"Alright, but you listen to me. I want you home by 10:00 at the very latest. You hear me? And don't go nowhere else besides Whistler's. You got that?"

Michael ran off toward the showers. "Okay, I won't—thanks, Dad!"

Eddie watched his son trot off, then checked his watch. He turned as the family sedan pulled alongside him, with his wife, Irene, at the wheel. She stopped and slid over for Eddie to get into the driver's seat. Eddie climbed in, gave Irene a peck on the cheek and glanced at the backseat.

"Where the hell is Maggie?"

"She said you were mad at her about something and she wanted to ride home with Michael," Irene replied. "What's going on with you two, anyway?"

Eddie replied angrily, "Oh, nothin', she just let a nigger kid kiss her, that's all."

"Oh, Eddie, she wouldn't dare! Are you sure?"

"I know what I saw, Irene. That girl's got some explainin' to do. Why the hell did you let her go with Michael?"

Eddie put the car in gear and peeled angrily out of the parking lot.

Across the asphalt, under a tree and unnoticed, Maggie sat, crying softly. A car pulled to a stop beside her. She looked up, expecting to see the family car that she saw just a moment before. Instead, it was a dark blue Chevy full of teenage boys, with Billy Harper behind the wheel and Joey Beauford in the front seat. Before Maggie could react, two boys jumped out of the car, grabbed her, and dragged her into the back seat with them.

Billy Harper taunted her, "Relax, honey, we're takin' you to a party and your boyfriend's gonna be there, too."

Across town, a black pick-up pulled to a stop in front of a brick row house. Annalee Roberts heard a noise and peeked through the curtains.

"Shit! Those bastards done come for you, Willis! Why'd you have to go an' kiss that white girl anyway?"

Willis replied nonchalantly, "Oh, stop bein' such a scaredy-cat, Sis. I didn't mean nothin' and you know it. So's everybody else, too. You worry too much." He pulled back the curtain and saw the truck parked ominously in front of the house. His smile quickly faded.

"But, just in case, why don't you go on out the back door, while I have a talk with our visitors."

"Willis, don't you dare go out there! Just wait. Daddy'll be home soon and maybe they'll leave. Maybe they just wanna scare us."

"Annalee. Do as I say. Now."

Just then there came a light tapping on the door. Willis and Annalee froze and exchanged panicked looks. The door suddenly burst open and three hooded men came charging inside. Two of them tackled Willis, knocking him to the floor, tying and gagging him. The third grabbed Annalee, twisting her arms behind her back.

"Now just relax, little mammy," the man holding Annalee shouted. "It's him we want, not you. Don't give us no trouble and you won't get hurt."

Annalee flailed wildly, fighting and kicking. She screamed, but was punched to the floor.

"Bring her along," one of the men ordered.

Chapter Two

Six Years Earlier

Things are Changin' So Fast

"The past was erased, the erasure was forgotten, the lie became the truth."

~ George Orwell (1903-1950)
English novelist, essayist, journalist and critic.

It was another hot, sticky night, as Eddie Thorpe lit up a Lucky and drove his station wagon through the deserted streets of Oakwood. Heading to his suburban home after an evening shift at the Socony oil refinery outside of town, he rolled down the window, hoping to catch some air in the thick night. Instead, he swatted mosquitoes and cursed. A whistle screamed the approach of the midnight westbound train, just as Eddie turned the corner toward the double tracks on the edge of town.

"Shit!" Eddie said into the darkness. "Wouldn't you know I'd get caught by the damned train."

Just as he pulled up to the crossbuck, another car screeched to a stop across the tracks, coming from the opposite direction. Eddie could see human shadows in the reflection from the crossing lights, some sort of commotion around the other car. Loud voices, not distinguishable over the roar of the approaching train. Then the locomotive raced by and Eddie was left to speculate. In the brief gaps between boxcars, he could still see some shadows of activity around the car across the second track.

Probably just some kids out hootin' and hollerin', Eddie thought to himself. Keeping his foot on the brake, he put the car in gear when the caboose appeared up the track. Cautiously, he drove forward, making sure there wasn't an eastbound train on the other track.

Meanwhile, the car from the opposite side sped across the tracks, with young men hanging out the windows, shouting, cursing, laughing, holding up beer bottles, and pounding the sides of the dark sedan. Eddie gunned the engine, as they passed at the crossing. This provoked more shouts and laughter from the others, and Eddie was sure they were mocking him. Resisting the temptation to shout or gesture, he reminded himself that he was older and wiser than a carload of teenagers. He continued on his way, but only briefly, before slamming on the brakes. He was horrified to see a body lying on the road in front of him.

Eddie took the car out of gear, but left his motor running, his headlights illuminating the man on the road in front of him. He wasn't sure what to do. For several seconds, he stared at the man, playing mental ping-pong with himself. *Maybe the guy's dead, then I'm in the middle of somethin' for sure. But maybe he's not dead and he needs help. And again, I'm in the middle of somethin'. But I can't just leave him there, can I?*

In the midst of Eddie's deliberations, the man on the street slowly lifted his head. He shielded his eyes from Eddie's headlights. Slowly pushing himself up from the pavement to a sitting position, the man held his head in his hands. Then he rose, almost to standing. He stumbled and placed his hand on Eddie's hood to steady himself. Fear had two faces, as the Negro man's eyes locked with Eddie's for just a second. Then he was gone, disappearing into the locust grove alongside the road.

Eddie sat in his car, shaking. *What the hell just happened?* he wondered to himself. He opened the glove box and grabbed the bottle of Jim Beam that he kept there for emergencies. After two quick gulps, he returned the bottle and put the car in gear.

Eddie drove on through the night, puzzling over the incident, until he realized he was in his own driveway. Coming through the back door of his small frame house, still shaken from the events of the trip home, Eddie dropped his lunch pail on the kitchen counter. He stepped into the living room and pulled the knob on the television. Disgusted with the news of the day, he changed channels, only to find all three networks carrying the same story of the "Little Rock Nine" being escorted by federal marshals to attend Little Rock Central High School.

Eddie watched the report with disgust. "Thanks, Governor Faubus," he said to the television, as he ran his hand over his salt and pepper crewcut. "I voted for you and you can't even keep the coloreds out of our schools. Just don't know what this world's comin' to."

Eddie Thorpe was raised on a farm in the Arkansas delta. An only child, he worked hard alongside his father and the day-laborers hired to help pick the cotton. He loved baseball and fishing as a child, when there was precious time for relaxation. His mother doted on him, but his father was a harsh taskmaster. Eddie was never able to meet his father's expectations, be it on the farm, in school, or in sports.

Yet, Eddie knew, even as a child, that he was better than some. The belief was absorbed into his consciousness, practically from birth, that Negroes were the inferior race. They were there for the menial jobs, and to serve at the pleasure of whites. Didn't matter how you treated them, they always had to take it, because disrespecting a white person was tantamount to a death sentence. Often on the spot, at the end of a rope. These were the facts of life in rural Arkansas as Eddie grew up on the family farm.

When he went to high school, Eddie began to excel at athletics, especially baseball. He was the team's best hitter and a stellar outfielder. Even his father began to take some pride in him. Until the day that Eddie got in a fight after a victorious game.

Eddie had joined teammates who were headed for celebratory beers at the Stop 'N Sip on the highway. The boys were all under age, but one had an older brother who tended bar and looked the other way. Unaccustomed to the alcohol's impact, Eddie and his friends were soon boisterous and belligerent, looking for someone to fight.

As Eddie stepped out back to take a leak, he noticed a Negro emptying trash in the alley. He knew Finneas Lewis from the times he had helped pick their cotton, but he did not know Finneas worked at the bar.

"Evenin' suh," Finneas said as he passed Eddie. "You aughten to hang round these parts at your age, son."

Eddie decided to take the offensive and get his bluff in to keep Finneas from talking about who was as at the bar. "What'd you say to me, nigger?" Eddie spat.

"Beggin' your pardon, didn't mean no harm, son," Finneas replied with his head down, reaching for the back door.

"I'll teach you to disrespect me, nigger!" Eddie shouted. He jumped on the older man's back and began to punch him in the face. Finneas stumbled, but soon regained his footing and threw Eddie into a pile of wooden produce boxes.

"Don't mean you no harm, Mr. Thorpe. But I can't let you hurt me neither, cause I got this job to do." He turned to start for the door, when Eddie grabbed his ankles and pulled him down to the ground.

Eddie was drunk-mean, but far too impaired to take on a stronger man who had labored his whole life. Finneas had no choice but to throw the boy off him again. This time, Eddie landed against the block building and slowly slid to the ground, looking dazed and about to pass out. Job or no job, Finneas reasoned it best to disappear. He leaped over the fence behind the bar and ran for his life.

Bobby Ray Stevens, one of Eddie's teammates, saw the whole thing. He came through the back door, laughing and snorting at Eddie's defeat. "Man, you let that ol' nigger get the best of you, Thorpe!" He pulled Eddie up, shook him a couple of times, and dragged him back into the bar. "Hey, fellas, let's get some more beer in ol' Thorpe here—he just got his ass kicked by a nigger out back."

Eddie's ears were ringing, and he had trouble focusing his eyesight. Aware enough to know he was being humiliated, he shouted to his cronies, "That ol' nigger's a dead man!"

"Easy, hoss," Bobby Ray, cautioned him. "He done licked you fair and square from what I saw. But me and the boys here'll help you put some scare into him, ain't that right?"

A drunken chorus of agreement rose up from Eddie's teammates, as the boys headed for Bobby Ray's Oldsmobile parked outside. The new bartender picked up the phone and started to dial.

Halfway to Finneas Lewis' house, the group was intercepted by the sheriff at the old granary. Riding in the sheriff's car were Eddie's father and Coach Bishop.

"Where the hell y'all think you're goin', boys?" the sheriff drawled from his lowered window.

Herbert Thorpe came charging out of the car, calling for his son. "Edward Thorpe! You get your ass out here right now, boy!"

Amid snickers and whistles from his teammates, Eddie crawled out of the back seat and slunk over to his father.

"Ain't enough ya go out and get drunk with these boys, but you get in a brawl with one o' my pickers? I oughta kick your ass all the way home. Now git in the sheriff's backseat before I tear into ya right here." Eddie suddenly realized that he wasn't better than all Negroes after all, if his father needed their backs.

Walking to the sheriff's car, head down, and weaving precariously, Eddie suddenly stopped. He fell to his knees and vomited. His teammates laughed. His father cursed.

Sheriff Anderson addressed the others. "Now, your parents have all been called and they'll be here soon. You boys get outta that car and sit on the ground. Those that gotta urp, I suggest you do it before you see your parents. Bobby Ray, your daddy's ridin' with somebody else so's he can drive you home."

An audible group moan tumbled out of the car with the chastened boys. Coach Bishop addressed them as soon as they were on the ground. "I have never been so disappointed in a team in all my life. This is how y'all celebrate victory? For cryin' out loud, I thought y'all were better somehow. Ain't gonna be no practice tomorrow. Gonna be church and then laps, and I 'spect every one of ya to be there, ya hear me?"

"Yes, sir!" the group of forlorn boys chimed in unison. Except for Eddie, who was leaning out the back door of Sheriff Anderson's car, vomiting for the second time.

Now, Eddie shook his head, trying to dislodge the bitter memory, as well as the vision that still haunted him of the man in the road. He shut off the TV and sat on the couch with his evening paper. The headlines offered him more of the same. Racial unrest, with a little politics and Cold War uncertainty thrown in. He turned the pages, searching for the weather forecast, only to read that tomorrow promised to be another scorcher with hotter temperatures and higher humidity. He sighed and shut off the lamp. As he stretched and headed for the hallway, he noticed a sliver of light beneath the kids' bedroom door.

Eddie gently opened the door and peeked at his children. Eight-year-old Maggie was asleep in her twin bed with a Nancy Drew mystery open on top of her quilt, ten-year-old Michael fast asleep on the other side of the small room with a comic book beside his pillow. Eddie flipped off the light and headed down the short hallway, then stopped, turned back, and quietly opened the door again. He gazed at his children for a moment, as the hallway night light bathed them in a subtle glow. Eddie wished he could protect them from the world. He continued down the hall, muttering to himself, "Everything's changin' so damned fast."

In his bedroom at the end of the hall, Eddie slipped into bed, trying not to wake his wife. Irene rolled over and opened one eye, then patted Eddie's face.

"You're a little late tonite, aren't you? D'you have any trouble?"

"Naw, no trouble to worry you, just a long train. Sorry I woke ya," Eddie said. He gave her a quick kiss and turned his back to her, trying to get the images of his bitter childhood memories and the man in the street out of his mind.

CHAPTER THREE

1959

The Beltline

"Children are the most wholesome part of the race, the sweetest, for they are the freshest from the hand of God."

~ Herbert Hoover (1874-1964)
American engineer, businessman, and U.S. President.

MICHAEL AND MAGGIE Thorpe woke up with the sun on the last week of summer break. They jumped into their clothes, ate breakfast, and hit the back-yard running, not to be seen again until lunchtime. Still confined to a one-mile radius of home on parents' orders, they rode their bikes to the boundary, yearning to push it a little more each time.

One day, Michael asked for permission to take another route that extended the limit just a few blocks more. He told his mother that he wanted to say "hey" to a friend that had moved into the new subdivision.

Irene Thorpe gave in to Michael's pleas. "But do **NOT** go any farther, you two," she warned. "You know the beltline is only a few blocks beyond there, and you know better than to go that far."

Maggie was thrilled to accompany Michael on what she thought was the first trip beyond boundaries. Thrilled, that is, until they reached the end of Powell Lane, and Michael turned right instead of left.

Holy moly, Maggie thought, *he's headin' for the highway!* She hesitated for just a second before following him, more afraid of going home alone to Irene's questions, than of following her brother to parts unknown.

They rode alongside the highway only a short while before Michael turned off on a side road. In a matter of fifteen minutes they were in territory unfamiliar to Maggie. Michael cut through alleys and unknown side streets, slowing only to let Maggie catch up. This part of town was run down, with boarded-up businesses and empty houses sitting in weed patches growing hip-high. Maggie began to get scared. She shouted at Michael to hold up.

"Where are we? And where we goin'?" she asked when he pulled alongside her.

"It's just a little farther," Michael said. "Trust me."

Michael took off and Maggie followed, to where she didn't know, but she had no choice at that point. They rode up a dirt road with a slow incline for a few hundred yards.

Then Michael turned on a path that paralleled the railroad tracks. He motioned for Maggie to walk her bike. Soon, they were almost invisible in tall weeds.

They came to a side track where an old boxcar sat rusting in the sun. Michael stashed his bike underneath and hopped up into the car. Maggie did the same. Michael motioned for her to lie on her belly beside him and look out the other side.

Stretched out for several blocks in front of them was the land across the beltline. Maggie knew it only as "Niggertown," a place she'd seen from the railroad overpass, coming home from trips.

"How'd you find this place?" Maggie asked.

"I got a friend in Little League that lives down there. I give him a ride home on my handlebars after last week's game. Daddy was workin' and Mama was at women's auxiliary."

"What's his name? Where's he live?"

"His name's Willis. He lives in that third house from the right on the next street over, the one with the sheets on the line in the back yard."

"Why'd we come here, Michael?"

"I dunno. I just like to look down there. It's like a different world from where we live. But it's folks, goin' bout their business, just like we do."

"Ain't you scared of 'em?"

"Naw, I don't see why. None of 'em was mean to me when I took Willis home. Rode right up to his house and passed a couple of men and a lady on the way, and they just smiled at me and said 'hey' to Willis."

"But everybody says there's mean ones and lazy ones. And that they're gonna sneak in and steal all our stuff."

"Maybe some are like that. Heck, some whites are like that, too."

Maggie thought for a minute. "You know we'll get spanked if Mama finds out we were here. We'd best get home, doncha think?"

"Yeah, I guess..." Michael looked intently at Willis' house, hoping to catch a glimpse of his friend's sister. She chewed him out for not knowing his place when he dropped Willis off. She also intrigued the pre-pubescent boy. He'd never seen anyone like her before. Beautiful, mahogany skin, flashing black eyes and full red lips. He'd since had dreams about her. But, of course, he couldn't tell Maggie that was the real reason for this excursion into forbidden territory.

Chapter Four

Play Ball

"On matters of race, on matters of decency, baseball should lead the way."

~ A. Bartlett Giamatti (1938-1989)
American professor of English Renaissance literature, the president of Yale University, and the seventh Commissioner of Major League Baseball.

Little League baseball games were played at the Oakwood Grade School, just a few blocks from the high school. The single diamond on the north side of the school caught some shade most of the day, and there was a small bleacher area for spectators.

Michael was excited that Grandma and Grandpa Thorpe planned to visit from the farm and attend his last ballgame of the season. He had practiced his swing and pitching each afternoon of the week. When he saw his grandfather's old pick-up roll to a stop outside the backstop, he ran to greet them.

"How's my Mikey-Boy?" Granny Ruth asked, as she wrapped her grandson in a big bear hug.

"Good, Granny. I'm really glad you come to my game!"

Grandpa Thorpe came around the front of the truck and shook hands with Michael. "Where's your old man, son?"

"He'll be along soon, sir. He said he'd get here at game time cause he don't wanna sit in the bleachers no longer than he has to."

"Humph," Grandpa returned. "If me and Granny can do it at our age, it ain't gonna hurt your old man. He always was kind of a weaklin', ya ask me."

"Oh Herbert, don't talk like that about your only son," Granny shamed him. "He's a hard-workin' boy and always has been."

"Aw, you always did take up for him, even when he left the farm for city life."

"And you never forgave him for that, did you—you old coot?"

Michael had heard this harmless bickering before. He said cheerfully, "I got a couple special places saved for ya over here. Follow me."

Just as Michael led his grandparents to their seats, his teammate Willis walked by, all suited up and ready for the game.

"Wanna play some catch to warm up, Michael?" Willis asked as he passed.

"Sure, just give me a minute," Michael replied.

Grandpa Thorpe was incensed. "What the hell? You mean to tell me you're playin' with niggers, Michael? Dammit, I taught your old man better than to let his kids run with coons. You work 'em and hire 'em when ya need to, but ya don't let 'em on your ball teams."

Michael was embarrassed and ashamed at the same time. He looked at Willis, who had turned toward the dugout. He couldn't say anything to his grandpa. He couldn't apologize to Willis. He wanted to do both, but he didn't have a voice.

Eddie walked up, after overhearing the whole thing. "Michael! Come here!" he shouted, as Michael was heading for the dugout.

Michael slowly walked to his father, sulking and cringing at what might come next.

"You didn't tell me you had coloreds on your team," Eddie said accusingly.

"Willis is the only one, Daddy. And he's good, too."

"You didn't tell me cause you thought I wouldn't let you play, ain't that right?"

Michael hesitated, looking at his shoes. "Yeah, I guess," he finally said.

"Well, it's a good thing it's your last game, cause I'd put my foot down otherwise, and you know it. Go on now, while I try to calm down your grandpa."

Eddie sat down by his folks, as Irene and Maggie approached with popcorn and sodas. Maggie hugged her grandparents and Irene nodded to each.

"Thought you'd like some refreshments," Irene said, handing out the drinks.

"Thanks, dear, that was right thoughtful of you girls," Granny Ruth smiled.

"D'you know he was playin' with coloreds?" Grandpa Thorpe pounced on Eddie accusingly.

"Naw, I haven't been able to make a game yet this year cause of work."

"Well, ain't you gonna do nothin' about it?"

"Aw, hell, Dad, it's the last game. No use makin' a fuss about it now."

Irene piped up cheerfully, "Michael said that little Willis is one of the best players on his team."

"Oh yeah, they're all good at sports, ya know," Granny added.

"They oughtta have their own damned teams," Grandpa declared. "Ain't fittin for our boys to have to share locker rooms and showers with 'em, ya ask me."

Eddie shook his head. "Dad, they don't even have locker rooms or showers at this age. I guess they gotta integrate the teams like they're integratin' the schools. Hell, over in North Carolina, they're even tryin' to get fed at the lunch counters. I don't like none of it, but we can't do nothin' about it cause it's the law now."

"Well, I'd do somethin' about it, alright," Grandpa continued. "I'd march right up to that little nigger and tell him to get back across the beltline where he belongs. Ya let one in, the rest'll follow. Just wait and see."

"Okay, Dad, you made your point. Now, for Michael's sake, can ya please just let it go?"

"Humph," Grandpa snorted, as he settled back with his arms crossed over his chest.

Michael wanted to say something to Willis, but he wasn't sure how to begin. Willis sat in the dugout, on the end of the bench all alone. Usually the only player that had anything to do with Willis, while the other boys just ignored him, Michael slowly approached and sat down next to him.

"Willis, if you heard my grandpa, I'm real sorry you did. He's got old ideas and sometimes he's rude about spoutin' off."

"S'ok," Willis said without looking at Michael. "Your granddaddy ain't the only one round here with those ideas."

"Well, anyhow, I'm sorry if he hurt your feelins'. He don't mean nothin' by it, he just says too much sometimes. An' I can' say nothin' course, cause he's my grandpa an' all."

"I ain't holdin' it gainst you, Michael, but my daddy says they mean it, alright. He don't like me playin' ball over here, but he knows it's the only way I can. If he wasn't workin', he'd be here to watch me."

"Well, maybe it's best he ain't, since Grandpa's here," Michael replied. "An' I can't give ya a ride home today with them here and all."

"S'ok, I understand. My sister's gonna meet me at the tracks just to make sure I'm okay."

"Well, maybe I could give ya a ride that far, if we started out from behind the snack shop," Michael offered, hoping to catch a glimpse of Willis' sister again.

"Naw, that's okay, Michael. Annalee don't feel too friendly toward you after you brought me up to the house that time. Thinks you don't know your place. That's kinda funny, ain't it? How'd your grandpa like that?" Willis snickered and poked Michael in the shoulder.

Michael just grinned, while he silently repeated a name over and over in his mind, *Annalee. Annalee Roberts.*

Chapter Five

1961

Alabama Eye-Opening

"If not us, then who? If not now, then when?"

~ Frequently attributed to John Lewis (1940)
American Politician and Civil Rights Leader.

Maggie strapped on her white patent shoes over lace-edged anklets. She wore the navy dotted-Swiss dress that her mother recently bought her. Irene took Maggie to visit her parents in Tennessee every summer, but this year, their trip would take place in springtime and they were going to Alabama. Irene's aunt had a stroke, so they planned to visit her, where Irene's parents would meet them.

Irene smoothed her brown traveling suit and placed a matching pillbox hat on her carefully styled French roll. She checked herself in the mirror, grabbed her purse and rushed toward Maggie's room.

Eddie carried the suitcases to the car and opened the door for Irene.

"Gonna miss you gals, ya know," he said with a grin, as he settled into the driver's seat.

"Oh, Edward, you'll enjoy havin' no women in the house and you know it," Irene teased. "You and Michael can put your feet on the coffee table and eat in the livin' room and all those other things you guys probably do when we're gone."

"Yeah, like walk around in your underwear," Maggie giggled.

"Alright, young lady, that's enough," Irene scolded Maggie. "I hope you'll remember your best manners around Nana and Papa, specially under the circumstances."

Eddie winked at Maggie in the rear-view mirror. "And that's why your brother and I never get to go, ya know."

After checking the bags at the station, Eddie embraced his wife and daughter. "Now don't get in no trouble, cause I ain't gonna come with bail money," he said to Irene as he gave her a peck on the cheek. He mussed Maggie's hair. "You do what your Mama says, young lady. I'll see you girls in a couple weeks."

Once settled on the bus, Irene removed her gloves and took Maggie's hand. "You know, I think this is gonna be a good trip, Mags. You're gettin' so grown up that you'll appreciate the family relationships. Nana an' Papa will be delighted at what a nice young lady you're becomin'. An' hopefully you'll get to see Aunt Margaret before she passes."

Maggie smiled at her mother. "I know you named me after her. Am I like her?"

"You've got the same twinkle in your eye that she always had. She was fun, like you. A little too opinionated sometimes, but she was always my favorite aunt."

"What d'ya mean? Was she always spoutin' off or somethin' like Daddy and Grandpa Thorpe?"

"Not hardly. She was very mannered and respectful. Except when she thought she saw an injustice. That's when she took to her soapbox, usually against the grain of her family."

"Like what? Gimme an example," Maggie prodded.

"Well, contrary to your Grandpa Thorpe, your Great Aunt Margaret was always takin' up for the Negroes. She defended Grandmother's maid, Lila, when Grandmother accused her of takin' some jewelry one time. Grandmother fired Lila and was about ready to ship Aunt Maggie off to boarding school. Turns out Margaret was right in that case, though, cause Grandmother found the missing jewelry, right in the toe of her shoe, where her niece Dora stuck it. Mama's cousin Dora was a spoiled brat, from what I hear, and nobody was really surprised that she was the culprit."

"What'd my grandma do?" Maggie wanted to know.

"You mean Mama? Well, nothin', she just followed the rules and never made much trouble, from what I hear. They always called her 'the good one,' if that tells you anything."

"Does kinda fit, don't it? I can't imagine Grandma ever rockin' the boat or causin' any trouble. Sounds like you got a little bit of both in you, Mama. You go by the rules, but I've seen you get your dander up a time or two."

Irene patted her daughter's hand. "Not very often, Mags, probably not as often as I should, truth be told."

Irene woke from a fitful nap, just as the bus passed the Anniston, Alabama, city limit sign. It had been a long, tiring trip, as the 400-plus miles included bus stops in just about every small town along the way. Irene gently shook Maggie awake. "We're finally here, sweetheart."

Maggie stretched and looked out her window. She saw a small town passing by—a little larger than Oakwood—but much the same in makeup: small businesses, churches, schools, a few parks. The downtown sidewalks were full of pedestrians and a few men in Army green. A sign announced a turn-off to Fort McClellan. They circled the block and arrived at the bus terminal, where they disembarked amid blowing debris and diesel fumes.

"I'm gonna call Papa to pick us up," Irene said. "Wait for me at the counter and order us a soda while we're waitin'." She handed Maggie fifty cents and headed toward the pay phones.

Maggie sat at the counter and placed her overnight bag in the next seat to save it for Irene. She ordered two RC Colas™ from the friendly waitress, a bleached blonde woman in her forties, whose name tag identified her as Ida.

"Y'all just passin' through?" Ida asked as she placed the drinks and straws before Maggie.

"We're visitin' my great aunt. She had a stroke an' ain't doin' too well."

"Oh, I'm sorry, hon, hope she gets better. Just a word o' warnin', y'all hadn't better stay around here too long at the station, cause I hear there's trouble brewin' with the coloreds. Best drink your sodas and get on to where ya goin'."

Irene sat down beside Maggie in time to hear Ida's warning. "Well, it'll only take Papa a few minutes to get here, Mags, so drink up and we'll be on our way." She laid a quarter on the counter, with a smile and nod to Ida.

Aunt Margaret's home sat on the edge of town, near the Appalachian foothills. An older area that used to house large estates in years past, the properties were later chopped up out of economic necessity and sold off for single-family dwellings. Margaret's house was an old, two-story, wood-sided house with chipped paint, crumbling foundation corners and a few cracked windows, set in among long-neglected willows and a few scrub pines.

After a week, the visit was strained. Irene and her mother, Olivia, had always had a tense relationship. Her father, Bernard, went along to get along. Aunt Margaret's health was deteriorating rapidly, but her personality was still feisty. She watched television and shook her shriveled right arm at reports of Freedom Riders being beaten and arrested for trying to integrate the bus lines and use whites-only public facilities. Irene and her mother tried to keep Aunt Margaret calm, to little avail. When the news announced expected trouble at the Anniston depot, the old woman's agitation only increased.

"Go th!" Margaret declared from her sick bed. "Go f' m'," she demanded in her stroke-impaired speech.

"Now, Aunt Maggie, you just calm yourself down," Irene warned her. "You'll be havin' a heart attack next. I'm gonna turn off that television if you keep this up, you hear me?"

"No use tryin' to talk to her," Olivia, said. "She'll go to her grave defyin' everybody just like she's done her whole life. We wouldn't even **BE** here in Alabama, if she hadn't married that worthless do-gooder that left her nothin' but this tumble-down house and a load of debt. Give her a sleepin' pill, even if it isn't time yet."

Irene didn't like her mother's tone, but she couldn't bring herself to openly challenge Olivia. Instead, she walked across the room and sat down on her aunt's bed. She said soothingly, as she stroked Margaret's hand, "You need to calm down, Aunt Maggie. Okay? Just settle down and you'll feel better."

The old woman looked beseechingly into Irene's eyes. With her good left hand, she squeezed Irene's. "Go f' m'," she said again. "Ree g' f' m'."

"What?" Irene asked. "What are you sayin', Aunt Maggie? You want me to go downtown and see for myself what's goin' on?"

Aunt Margaret squeezed her eyes shut and managed a crooked smile. A tear rolled down her cheek as she tried to nod.

Irene sighed, wondering if she could fool her aunt by agreeing. "Okay, now take your pill, Aunt Maggie, and get some rest. I'll let you know what I find out when I return."

Olivia accosted Irene once outside the bedroom door. "Were you just humoring her, or do you actually intend to go to a riot, for cryin' out loud?"

"Mama, I was just humorin' her, but the more I think about it, the more I think I'll go. She just wants confirmation that somebody's doin' what she'd be doin' if she could. I'll just go take a quick look, nothin' else."

"And are you takin' your daughter with you?"

Maggie had stopped in the hallway, listening to the conversation between her mother and grandmother.

"Take me where? What's goin' on?"

Irene sighed, then faced her daughter squarely. "Maggie, there is something goin' on down at the bus station and I told Aunt Margaret I'd check it out and let her know what's happenin'. That's all."

"I wanna go with you," Maggie pleaded.

"No, Mags, it ain't a place for a young girl. These are adult issues and it might not be safe for you."

"Mama, you said yourself that I'm becomin' grown up. Well, then, I need to know what's goin' on in the world around me. And I'm Aunt Margaret's namesake, so I need to be there for her, too. Besides, you can't go by yourself."

Olivia took Maggie by the shoulders. "Just because your mother has apparently lost her head, doesn't mean you need to as well, young lady. Now, if she's determined to follow through on this foolish plan, you need to stay here with me and Papa."

"Where is Papa?" Maggie asked. "I bet he'd be all for this. Mama says Aunt Margaret and Papa are like two peas in a pod."

"Yes, well, that may be," Olivia answered, "but he still knows better than to send a child into harm's way. Irene, are you going to stop this foolishness, or do I have to wake your father from his nap?"

Irene looked from her mother to her daughter. She remembered the time in her sophomore year of high school when Lila's granddaughter, Nell, looked them up in Tennessee and went to work as Olivia's maid, and how the girl was mistrusted from the beginning. Olivia hid her jewelry in a locked drawer and never left Nell alone in the house. The worst part was, Olivia always insisted on polishing the silverware herself, because, as she put it, "After all, those utensils go in our mouths."

"Maggie, you may come with me," Irene began, "but you must do exactly as I say. Mother, you can tell Father where we've gone when he wakes up, just in case he wants to join us."

Irene caught her breath, as she turned the key in Aunt Margaret's old Studebaker. She exhaled deeply when the engine turned over. Maggie reached out her hand.

"I'm proud of you, Mama."

"I'm proud of you, too, baby. Let's just hope neither one of us comes to regret this."

"Mama, you're a grown woman. You shouldn't have to agree with your mother all the time anymore."

"Oh, it's not just my mother, Maggie. You know how your father and his father feel about these things, too. I just don't know what to feel sometimes. But if I can do somethin' for that poor old woman that I've loved my whole life, then I'm gonna do it."

They drove toward the bus station. On the way, they heard a loud explosion and saw smoke rising in the sky just outside of town. Irene braked instinctively.

"Don't stop, Mama, we gotta see what's goin' on now!" Maggie urged.

When they arrived at the bus depot, they found only a small crowd of people milling about outside. No buses were in sight. There didn't appear to be any problem. They entered the station to see only a small, calm group of people. Puzzled, Irene turned to the waitress Ida, who had walked up beside her.

"What's happened? Can you tell us what's goin' on?"

"Oh, they chased those niggers right out o' town!" Ida replied. "The bus slowed down, and somebody slashed its tires. Then they took off again. Buncha guys went after 'em in cars. Sounds like somebody threw a bomb at 'em!"

Irene embraced her daughter, trying to turn her around. "Maggie, let's go, this is no place for us."

Maggie stayed put and brushed off her mother's arm. "Why, Mama?"

"Maggie, we need to go NOW," Irene said. "We can't do or say nothin' about this. It ain't our fight. Whatever is goin' on isn't for us to meddle in."

"But I don't understand, Mama," Maggie pleaded. "Why are they chasin' and bombin' Negroes?"

Bernard Wilson entered the terminal, searching for his daughter and granddaughter. He spotted Irene waving him over. He looked quizzically at his daughter.

"What is it? What's happened? Has Maggie been hurt?" he asked.

"No, Daddy. Not physically. She seems to be havin' an emotional reaction to all this stuff."

Bernard placed his arm around his granddaughter's shoulder. "Maggie, my dear, whatever is goin' on here, it ain't the fight of a twelve-year-old girl."

"You mean a twelve-year-old WHITE girl, Papa. If I was a Negro, I couldn't even be here, could I?"

Bernard sighed and squeezed Maggie's shoulder. "Ah, my dear child, you seem to have inherited your namesake's social awareness, which isn't a bad thing. But sometimes, you have to accept the way things are, not the way you'd like 'em to be."

Irene gently tugged Maggie's arm. "Let's go see Aunt Margaret, Mags. Papa will take the television out of her room when we get back, and we'll tell her only that the bus got out of town safely. It may be a little fudging of the truth, but it will bring her comfort and that's what she needs right now. A person deserves to die in peace."

Die in peace Aunt Margaret did, as they returned to find that she had slipped away in her sleep while they were gone.

Olivia, Bernard and Irene were relieved that her long decline had ended. Maggie was glad that she didn't have to tell Aunt Margaret something less than the whole truth… something she didn't even understand herself.

Chapter Six

1962

GED and KKK

"In so many ways, segregation shaped me, and education liberated me."

~ Maya Angelou (1928-2014)
American poet, -singer, memoirist, and civil rights activist.

At the end of his afternoon shift, Eddie Thorpe was punching his timecard, when something posted on the bulletin board caught his eye. The community college flyer announced a class for students interested in a General Education Degree. Now in his early forties, Eddie had always been a little self-conscious about not finishing high school. He would have graduated, had it not been for the whole baseball victory celebration-drunken brawl-father's ass-kicking event. After that, he briefly ran away from home to Little Rock. There he panhandled for a few months, until another ass-kicking in an alleyway one night made him reconsider the comforts of home.

Eddie looked around and surreptitiously wrote down the phone number from the poster, then stuffed the scrap of paper into his pocket. Suddenly, he was slapped on the back and he turned to see Jack Beauford.

"You gonna sign up for them classes, Eddie? Best be getting' that education now for sure. Can't let those coloreds get smarter than us, huh? They want our jobs now, ya know. We gotta keep one step ahead of them niggers all the damn time."

Eddie said over his shoulder, "Yeah, I gotta go, Jack. Gotta pick up the kids."

"Well, I'll be seein' ya, Eddie," Jack replied. "Maybe in school," he added with a sinister chuckle.

Jack sucked on a toothpick and watched Eddie leave. Another man, Leland Harper, walked up beside him and looked in the same direction.

"I don't like that guy. He sure seems to keep to hisself," Leland offered.

Jack threw down his toothpick and smiled. "Eddie's got a boy and girl around Joey and Billy's age. I'm thinkin' he'd make a good recruit."

"Yeah, well, the way things are goin', we're gonna need all the help we can get. You sure you can trust him?"

"No, but we'll watch him for a while, so's we can see where his loyalties lie. Man's got two kids, he can't be happy with the way things are goin' in the schools."

In her small yellow kitchen with its red gingham curtains, Irene Thorpe bustled about with last-minute dinner preparations. Her brown hair flecked with gray tied back with a blue ribbon that matched her shirtwaist dress, Irene was the picture of domestic efficiency. Eddie and the children were already seated at the table. With an amused twinkle in his eye, Eddie watched Michael, now fifteen, and Maggie, now thirteen, greedily grab the bowls of food as soon as they were placed on the table. Irene surveyed the spread for a final check, then seated herself across from Eddie.

"You know," Irene began, "it'd be nice if we started supper by sayin' grace, instead of just diggin' in."

Michael hastily repeated the words he knew his mother despised, "Good food, good meat, good grief, let's eat!"

Maggie chuckled at her brother's joke. Irene just shook her head and scowled at her son. Eddie gave Michael a playfully disdainful look.

Eddie reached for the potatoes, casually announcing, "You know, you two aren't gonna be the only students in the house pretty soon. Your old man's gonna start night school."

Maggie and Michael looked at him in surprise. Irene smiled proudly at her husband.

Michael shook his head. "How come? Don't know why anybody'd go to school that don't have to!"

"Just tryin' to get ahead, son. Who knows what's gonna happen, with things changin' so fast? If I ever expect to get ahead at work, I gotta get a diploma. May take me a while, with my work schedule, but I gotta do it."

"Gee, Daddy, that's great!" Maggie said." Let me know if you ever need any help with your homework."

Everyone laughed at Maggie's little joke. The red wall phone beside the dinner table interrupted their laughter, and Eddie reached out to answer it.

"Hello? Oh, yeah, Jack, yeah, I remember, but I ain't sure I'm gonna go along... well, it's just not... I don't wanna... okay, Jack, okay, but just to see what it's all about. Yeah, okay, see ya then. 'Bye."

Eddie hung up the phone and gave Irene a knowing look, then returned his attention to dinner.

Irene seemed upset. "Honey, I wish you wouldn't get mixed up..."

Eddie interrupted her. "Irene, shush. Ain't no subject for the dinner table."

"Who was that, Daddy?" Maggie asked." What subject?"

"Ever hear the expression that kids should be seen and not heard?" Eddie replied. "Eat your dinner, kiddo."

Three nights later, a big, black sedan without lights rolled to a stop on a dirt road in the woods. Jack Beauford got out of the driver side and stretched, then headed over to the passenger door and opened it. Eddie climbed out, removing a blindfold and rubbing his eyes.

"We'll go on foot from here," Jack stated. He reached into the trunk of the car and pulled out a white robe and hood, plus what looked like a flour sack. "You're an invited guest tonight, so you can come along in this." He handed Eddie the sack with eye holes cut out." Next time, you'll have the right outfit."

"I told you before, Jack, I ain't sure there'll be a next time."

"Aw, come on, Eddie. You want them coloreds takin' over? That's what they want, ya know. Equality my ass! They want what we got. Hell, you got a daughter, Eddie. You know what those niggers do to a white girl if they get her alone? Just a matter of time 'til somethin' happens at school, I'm tellin' ya."

"Yeah, well, I ain't so sure this is the way, Jack. But then I ain't sure of much these days."

The two men stepped through the trees to a clearing where a rally was in progress. A large fire crackled in the center of a circle of men wearing white robes and hoods. Jack advised Eddie to keep quiet and stay by his side.

They advanced into the group. Hooded men nodded their heads at them and made room. Then one man moved to a makeshift podium and raised his hands to quiet the crowd. The man wore a robe and hood and spoke in a booming voice that startled Eddie.

"BROTHERS, we all KNOW why we are here. To STEM THE BLACK PLAGUE! To PROTECT our wives and daughters from the NIGGER SLIME that creeps EVEN NOW at their heels! Brothers, they are IN OUR MIDST and PUSHIN' US ALL THE TIME! We must send those coloreds a MESSAGE: KILL THE NIGGERS!"

Worked into a frenzy, the crowd picked up the chant: "KILL THE NIGGERS! KILL THE NIGGERS!"

The head Klansman shouted, "FRIDAY NIGHT AS USUAL. WE MEET BACK HERE AT MIDNIGHT, MY BROTHERS!"

The crowd's repeated chants only grew louder as they waved their flags and shouted into the night, "KILL THE BLACK MAN! KILL THE NIGGERS!" The blazing fire crackled and shot sparks sinisterly into the air, as though feeding on the evil at hand.

Eddie was unnerved by the whole experience. He determined on the spot that he would never accompany Jack Beauford again.

Chapter Seven

School Dazed

"The secret of education lies in respecting the pupil."

~ Ralph Waldo Emerson (1803-1882)
American essayist, lecturer, philosopher, and poet.

Racing around the corner in the high school hallway, Maggie Thorpe ran into a girl she knew only by name, Annalee Roberts, coming from the opposite direction. Books flew everywhere, and both girls stooped to pick them up. Maggie handed Annalee some books, as a group of teen boys strolled by.

"Look at the nigger-lover helping her chocolate friend," taunted Billy Harper.

Maggie shouted back, "Shut up, you idiot! We just collided, that's all. I ain't no..." Maggie looked at Annalee and handed her the last book, as the boys went down the hallway, snickering.

"Sorry. I didn't mean no harm." Maggie started to walk away, when Annalee spoke up.

"Well, thanks for nothin', white girl who ain't no nigger lover." She marched on down the hall, leaving Maggie stunned and shaking her head.

Maggie entered the hot, crowded lunchroom and searched for her two best friends. Linda Franklin and Rosie Jackson saw her, beckoned, and made room for her at their table. She sat down in the middle of their conversation.

"Well, I heard that he had the nerve to ask Rhonda out. 'Course, she just tried to ignore him," Linda said.

"Who you talkin' about?" Maggie asked.

Rosie answered, "Willis Roberts, that colored football player that's so good. He thinks just because he's an athlete, he can date white girls."

"He is kinda cute, for a colored boy," Linda whispered.

All three girls giggled, as though sharing a naughty joke.

Rosie continued, "His sister, Annalee, is in my social studies class, and she thinks she's somethin', too. Uppity niggers, anyhow."

"Oh, I think that's who I just run into in the hallway," Maggie said. "I helped her pick up her books, but she acted like it was all my fault or somethin'. Her brother used to play Little League with Michael an' he seems nicer."

Rosie leaned in toward the others. "Well, my daddy says some of 'em just gotta be put in their place."

The girls heard a scuffle in the hallway and ran to see what was going on. Rosie shouted, "Maggie, it's your brother!"

Maggie and Rosie pushed their way through the crowd for a better view. Maggie reported over her shoulder, "Yeah, it's Michael alright, and that colored kid we were just talkin' about, that Willis Roberts. But they're helpin' each other up."

Linda came running up to them breathlessly. "I was just over there talkin' to Rhonda, and she said that Billy Harper and his pals jumped Willis, and Michael tried to pull 'em apart and then Billy and the others turned on him, too."

"Holy moly," Maggie said. "This ain't good. Daddy always tells us not to take sides. He sure won't like Michael helpin' a colored boy."

"Billy Harper's always lookin' for somebody to fight, but Michael shoulda just stayed out of it, that's for sure," Rosie added.

"But it don't seem fair to gang up on Willis that way," Linda said. "Even if he is colored. Sounds like Michael was just trying to stop it, not take sides."

"Yeah, I guess," Maggie answered. "Still, Michael better watch it for sure. He'll be called a nigger-lover for no good reason."

Annalee Roberts separated from the crowd when she overheard Maggie's comment. "So, what's a **GOOD** reason, white girl?"

Maggie turned and realized that she had offended Annalee again, without meaning to. "Oh, lookit. I didn't mean nothin'. You must have your feelings stuck out all over you. And besides, my brother just helped out your brother, so that ought to make you appreciate us a little more."

Annalee fired back in an exaggerated accent, "Oh, yessum, I surely do 'preciate all the nice things you white folks does for us darkies!"

Willis Roberts appeared suddenly and took Annalee's arm. "Come on, Sis, we need to get home." To Maggie, he explained, "Miss Thorpe, you'll have to excuse my sister. She's not always as courteous as you or your brother."

Willis steered Annalee down the hallway and toward the exit. Maggie stared after them with a perplexed look on her face. Annalee turned just before the exit, then marched into the heat waves with her head held high.

Seated at the kitchen table, Eddie had books and papers spread out before him. He scratched his head and looked at his wife, as Irene filled his coffee cup.

"I don't know, Reeny. This is a lot tougher than I thought it'd be. Maybe I ain't smart enough to finish school at my age. Still, I gotta get that damn diploma if I wanna get ahead. Ain't like it was when you and I was kids an' the farm was more important than school."

Irene placed her hand reassuringly on his shoulder. "You'll do just fine, honey. You're the smartest man I know."

"Yeah, well, there's this colored guy in my class, of all things, and he seems to be gettin' it better than I do. Maybe I ain't as smart as you think."

Irene smiled and patted his hand, then looked away worriedly.

"What is it, Reeny? I know that look."

Irene sighed. "Michael got in a fight at school. There was this colored kid ..."

Eddie interrupted her. "Dammit! I guess Jack Beauford was right after all! Is Michael okay? Did he whip that nigger's ass?"

"No, Eddie, it wasn't like that. Michael said there was a group of white kids—that Billy Harper and his pals—that ganged up on one of Michael's teammates, a Willis somebody."

"Willis Roberts? Best running back they've ever had at that school."

"Yes, that's him, the little boy that played ball with Michael. Anyhow, Michael tried to stop it cause he said it was about five to one, and they turned on him, too. He's got a few scrapes and bruises, but he's ok."

"So, it's the same kid that was in Little League with Michael. Well, I'll be damned. How'd he fare?"

"Okay, too. But you know what they're gonna say about Michael now, don't' you?"

"Yeah, that he's a nigger lover. Why the hell didn't he just leave it alone? I always tell them not to take sides, dammit!"

"Well, it sounds like he was only tryin' to help. I just hope he doesn't have to pay for it. Negroes are gettin' hurt and their churches bein' burned all the time anymore. I sure hope whoever's doin' it don't take Michael for a friend of the coloreds." Irene looked closely at her husband. "Eddie, what happened when you went with Jack Beauford that time?"

"You know I can't tell you that, Reeny. But I'll tell you this much. Things are changin' in ways I never thought I'd see. Coloreds mixin' in with whites everywhere. I don't like it one bit. But there's worse things than that and pure, evil hatred is one of 'em. I seen it, Reeny, and it scared the bejeezus outta me. That's why I never went with Jack again. He seemed a little put out at first, but he finally stopped askin'."

"We almost saw it in Alabama, too, Eddie," Irene replied. "I didn't tell you this before because I didn't want to upset you, but Maggie and I were at the bus station when those Freedom Riders were attacked outside of town. We didn't see the actual riot, but we heard about it, an' Maggie was really upset. Daddy talked her down a little, but she was really unnerved by the whole thing."

"Dammit, I wish we could keep our kids outta this," Eddie said. "But it's gettin' to where it's gonna affect all our lives, I'm afraid." He thought a minute, then asked, "What was you doin' at the bus station that day anyhow?"

"Not important, Eddie, just a favor for Aunt Margaret before she passed."

"Oh, a favor for your abolitionist aunt, huh? Sounds suspect to me."

"Eddie." Irene returned firmly. "Do you think Daddy, or I, would put Maggie in harm's way?" Irene thought to herself that she hoped Eddie never learned how close they came. "Besides," she added, "we haven't been in the Civil War or Reconstruction for a hundred years. Maybe it's time some things do change a little. Nobody deserves to die for bein' born with skin color they have no control over."

"You know I don't hold with killin', Reeny," Eddie answered, "but I don't want our whole way o' life changin' either. It just ain't natural for coloreds and whites to mix, never has been. You know how we were raised."

"Yes, I know how we were raised. An' everybody in our generation was raised like that. But does that make it right?

CHAPTER EIGHT

Churches, Birthdays, and Death Days

"Racism and injustice and violence sweep our world, bringing a tragic harvest of heartache and death."

~ Rev. Billy Graham (1918-2018)
American evangelist, a prominent evangelical Christian figure, and an ordained Southern Baptist minister.

THE OAKWOOD LUTHERAN Church, an imposing stone and red brick structure, sat on the corner of Main Street and Texarkana Avenue, the original stone core facing Main and the brick wing added later stretching down Texarkana. Established in 1890 by a small contingent of German settlers, it underwent many remodels and expansions over the years, and now served the largest constituency in Oakwood, not counting the larger Negro congregation at the Crossroads

Baptist Church on the outskirts of town. The administrative council of Oakwood Lutheran had always been in competition with Crossroads, simply because of the numbers. Thus, it was a source of pride and smugness when Oakwood Lutheran installed the first air-conditioning of any local church. One Oakwood trustee was overheard commenting, "They may have more members, but ours are more comfortable, while those niggers just have to sweat."

On a bright September morning, the sun streamed in through the stain-glassed windows on the east side of the sanctuary, as Maggie and her pals made their way toward the stairs in the rear of the church.

Maggie teased her friends. "You know what NEXT Sunday is, don't you?"

"Oh, let's see...What could it be?" Linda said sarcastically. "No, can't think of a thing that makes NEXT Sunday special."

Rosie chimed in, "Maggie, we've only been hearin' about your birthday ever since school started. You think you've dropped enough hints by now?"

"Well, I just wanna make sure you guys don't forget. Cake and ice cream, my house, 3:00 next Sunday—oh and presents, don't forget!"

Maggie raced on ahead of the other two, up the uncarpeted stairs to the balcony. Linda and Rosie giggled and followed suit. An usher followed them up the stairs and angrily shushed them, then went back down to the vestibule. The girls made stern faces at his back and giggled mischievously.

As the congregation settled into the pews, the sound of the organ filled the sanctuary. Suddenly, the girls heard a disturbance in the rear of the church. When they looked over the balcony, they saw tension on the faces of the worshipers, as heads turned toward the commotion in back. Some scowled, some shook their heads. On widows' row, the older women of the church looked aghast, a few actually clutching their hankies to their throats.

Maggie and her friends looked toward the stairs as the voices came closer. They saw the hats first, as the usher led three fashionably dressed young Negro women into the balcony. He tried to steer them toward the back, but they turned instead for the first row of the upper tier. They smiled nervously at the angry white faces below them, then took their seats and nodded to the minister, who stood open-mouthed in his pulpit. The silence was deafening.

Clearly flustered, Reverend Patterson said, "Pret us lay... uh, let us pray..."

Maggie, Linda and Rosie burst out laughing at the minister's stammering, unable to control themselves. They tried to stop, but each time one looked at the other, they mouthed the minister's stuttered words and started up again. They finally had to leave.

Maggie whispered apologetically to the Negro women, "I'm sorry... It's not you... He just... surely you heard what he said? PRET US LAY!" She couldn't even get the words out without guffawing. The three girls stumbled down the stairs, bent over double in laughter.

As Maggie exited the church and straightened up to catch her breath, she looked into the face of Annalee Roberts, nervously pacing outside the church door.

Annalee spat angry words at Maggie, "I'm glad you're all havin' such a good time at the expense of my people!"

Maggie caught her breath. "No, Annalee—that's not it at all. It's what the preacher said: he said 'pret us lay!', and the three girls snickered again. "Don't you think that's funny? It's got nothin' to do with Negroes or nothin'. It was just funny, so we...that's all." She looked puzzled. "Why are y'all here anyway?"

"Never mind, Maggie," Annalee returned angrily. "I don't think you and your friends could even begin to understand. I'm supposed to be inside, but I just plain chickened out."

Turning more serious now, Maggie said, "Well, I understand that you and your people have every right to be in God's house, Annalee. I just think you're askin' for trouble when you don't go to your own church, that's all."

"Askin' for trouble, huh?" Annalee asked defiantly. "You ever hear of Emmett Till, Maggie? He was a Negro boy some years back that ended up in the bottom of a lake, beat to death, with his eye poked out and a chain round his neck. You know what kind of trouble he asked for? He whistled at a white woman over in Mississippi cause he was from up north and didn't know no better. He was just fourteen years old when YOUR PEOPLE killed him."

"Well, I didn't kill him and this ain't Mississippi. I don't wanna fight about this stuff with you," Maggie said evenly.

"I don't wanna fight neither," Annalee answered softly, "but my fight's done been chose for me by the color of my skin. Now if y'all will excuse me, I'm gonna catch up to my braver friends."

Annalee and Maggie reached for the church door at the same time. There was a moment's hesitation, with each girl wondering what the other's next move would be.

Finally, Maggie said with a sigh, "Aw, come on—I'll take you to them. You'll never find 'em on your own and there's been enough upset in church this mornin' between you and us."

Linda and Rosie slowly walked off a short distance, whispering and glancing back over their shoulders in Maggie's direction. Maggie escorted Annalee inside the church, then returned to catch up with her friends.

She noticed a strange expression on their faces. "What?"

"Nothin', Maggie. Geez!" Linda replied.

Rosie said more bitingly, "Just didn't know you run a colored escort service, that's all."

A week later, Irene Thorpe busily frosted a birthday cake, as a warm breeze blew in through the window. She hummed quietly to herself, as she decorated it, making a "14" in the middle with candles. She covered the cake and set it aside on the counter, then shouted toward the bedrooms.

"Maggie! Michael! Get up, you two. We got lots of things to get done today, ya know. I let you skip church, but you're gonna help me get ready for Maggie's party."

Eddie Thorpe shuffled sleepily into the kitchen and poured himself a cup of coffee. He assessed the cake and gave his wife a thumbs-up. He turned and reached for the knob on the television, which sat just through the arched doorway into the living room. Eddie then sat down at the kitchen table and half-listened to the TV without turning to watch it.

"Good lookin' cake, honey. Now, what's the plan again?"

"Oh, nothin' too fancy. I know you're just comin' off midnights," Irene replied. "After me and Maggie get this house whipped into shape and Michael gets the garbage taken out—and YOU get the grass cut—some of Maggie's little friends are comin' over for cake and ice cream 'bout 3:00."

Eddie feigned his best step-n-fetch-it voice. "Yessum, I guess I gots my marchin' orders. I gonna go cut that grass. Anything else, massa?"

Irene shook her wooden spoon at him. "Now don't get smart with me, mister. And yes, you can go kick those lazy kids of yours outta bed. My word, it's almost eleven!"

Eddie rose from his chair, then stopped mid-stretch and turned his ear toward the television. "D'you hear that? Somethin' 'bout a bomb at a church somewhere?"

Eddie stepped through the living room doorway and stared intently at the television, as Irene came up beside him, wiping her hands on her apron. They both stared solemnly at the screen as a news report was being broadcast. They did not notice a sleepy-eyed Maggie who stopped just behind them and gazed between her parents at the television. The news reported a bomb explosion at the Sixteenth Street Baptist Church in Birmingham, Alabama, killing four young black girls in the blast. Eddie reached out to turn off the TV, then noticed Maggie behind him.

"Well, we got things to do around here today. Best get after it. Oh, hi, Mags. Happy birthday, pumpkin."

Maggie was incredulous, as she reached for the TV knob. "Happy BIRTHDAY? Daddy, did you hear what they said? I wanna watch this!"

Eddie blocked her hand. "No! Ain't no use watchin' this stuff. It ain't our business. Now we got our own things to do today, let's get 'em done."

"But, Daddy—they were my AGE! I wanna know what's goin' on. I NEED to know what's goin' on!"

"You wanna know what's goin' on, Maggie? I'll tell you what's goin' on. Those niggers..."

Irene interrupted her husband. "Oh, let's not get into this, you two. It doesn't have anything to do with us. This is supposed to be a happy occasion. Let's just forget all about this race stuff for one day and make sure Maggie has a happy birthday."

Eddie ignored his wife and continued talking sternly to Maggie. "What's goin' on, is that folks don't know their place anymore, Maggie. There's always been a line that you just don't cross. There's colored and there's white, and they just ain't supposed to mix."

"But, Daddy, those girls at that Alabama church weren't doin' any harm. Just like those bus riders in Aunt Margaret's town weren't doin' any harm when we was there."

"Okay—I don't hold with the hateful kind of thing that happened in Alabama, 'specially those poor girls bein' killed. But if the coloreds would stay in their place and not be causin' all this trouble all the time, there wouldn't be stuff like this happenin. They're bringin' it down on theirselves."

"But, Daddy, tell me where they belong, if not in church? 'Specially their own NEGRO CHURCH?"

Eddie was becoming exasperated with what he saw as his daughter's naïveté. "But that's just it, Maggie, they ain't never satisfied. Remember just last week, when there was some at OUR OWN church? They just keep pushin' it. It all started a few years back with some colored boy from Chicago that had the nerve to whistle down a white woman over in Mississippi. He may not of deserved what he got, neither, but they just gotta know their place, that's all I'm sayin."

Maggie suddenly recalled Annalee's words. "Emmett Till," she said quietly.

"What?"

"Emmett Till. He had a name, you know. The boy from Chicago. Emmett Till. He was fourteen, too."

Irene jumped back into the conversation with another plea. "Oh, let's just forget all about this horrible thing and go on about our day. Maggie, is your brother up? He needs to get that garbage out of the house before your friends get here."

Eddie turned and quickly walked toward the back door, shaking his head. Maggie looked at her mother blankly.

"I don't really feel like celebratin', Mama. I'm gonna call Linda and Rosie and tell them the party's cancelled."

"But, Maggie, the whole thing's planned already. You can't just... Oh, Maggie, you just can't let these things get to you like this. Today's your birthday!"

Maggie sighed. "Yeah, today's my birthday. At least I'm havin' one, right?"

Irene put her arm around her daughter.

Maggie picked up the telephone and started dialing.

Chapter Nine

1963

Evil Descends on Oakwood

"Evil societies always kill their consciences."

~ James L. Farmer, Jr.(1920-1999)
Civil rights activist and leader in the Civil Rights Movement."

The Friday night that started out like any other in Oakwood was fast becoming a nightmare for Maggie Thorpe.

On the industrial outskirts of town, not far from the oil refinery where Eddie Thorpe made his living, his daughter sat on the floor in the back room of a dark, dank warehouse. Bound with her hands behind her back, Maggie was gagged and blindfolded. She had no idea where she was. She could hear noises coming from another room nearby. Beers being opened, and cards shuffled, men talking and laughing.

Billy Harper called out to Maggie. "How ya doin' in there, darlin'? Don't you worry, your Lil' Black Sambo will be here to keep you company soon." That brought hoots and catcalls from the others.

Joey Beauford came to the doorway and peered into the semi-darkness. "Maggie? You okay?" He moved closer and crouched in front of her, lowering her blindfold.

"Don't worry, Maggie. I don't think they're gonna hurt you. It's that nigger kid they're after, the one that kissed you. They just wanna rough him up some and put him in his place, so's he won't be botherin' you white girls no more."

Maggie tilted her head toward Joey and made sounds to indicate she wanted to say something. Joey cautiously looked over his shoulder, then removed Maggie's gag. He leaned in closer, so he could hear her.

Maggie whispered through clenched teeth, "Ain't no colored never treated me as bad as you and your asshole friends!"

Joey shoved the gag back into place and blindfolded her. "Shoulda known no Thorpe was worth worryin' over. That stuck-up jock brother of yours is a nigger lover and you're just like him!"

A commotion outside the room made it apparent that others had arrived. Joey rushed back. A spotlight shined into Maggie's blindfolded face and she flinched. Then Annalee and Willis were shoved into the room with her, each of them bound and gagged just as she was. They made no sound, except for their labored breathing and moaning. Maggie could tell that whoever her new companions were, they had been hurt. She began to shake with fright.

Jack Beauford spoke to the group of men in a lowered, sinister voice. "We got about an hour 'til we gotta be at the meetin'. Wanna have some fun, boys? Personally, I got my eye on a piece of dark meat tonite."

Joey was aghast. "Daddy! You can't mean you'd have your way with a nigger woman? What about Mama?"

Jack backhanded his son. "Shut up, boy! This ain't got nothin' to do with your Mama. Besides, what she don't know won't hurt her!" To the others, he said boastfully, "Now, we can all take turns, boys, but I got the nigger gal first. Y'all can do whatever you want with the other two." Jack grabbed Annalee and drug her off to a corner.

Billy Harper decided to play the big man. "Well, Daddy, we can't let Jack have all the fun, can we? Whatcha wanna do with these two? You wanna go on her first?"

"Be my guest, son, you go first. You other boys might get a turn, after the Harpers break her in," Leland said with a mean grin.

The men moved forward to remove the ropes and gags from their prisoners. Billy Harper ripped off Maggie's blouse and pants, while the others grabbed Willis and began to untie and strip him. Billy proceeded to rape Maggie.

Maggie was terrified. "No, please... please don't... oh, God, please, no..."

Billy slapped her across the face. "Shut up, you white trash!" He removed her blindfold. "Here, I want you to have a good look at your first time—if it IS your first!"

From the floor, Willis moaned in pain, "Oh please don't do this ... please ..."

Leland Harper punched Willis in the mouth. "Shut up, nigger! He removed Willis' blindfold. "Here, watch your girlfriend get it from a real man!"

The thugs laughed and sneered. The Harpers took turns raping Maggie, egged on by the catcalls of the others. They held Willis in a choke-hold and forced him to watch, punching him in the face each time he tried to look away. Finally, the others held Maggie down and forced Willis on top of her. They pushed him, slapped his rear, whooped and hollered.

Willis whispered apologetically into Maggie's ear, "I'm so sorry Maggie... please forgive me... they're animals."

Leland Harper quickly straddled Willis. "I'll show you animal! The only good uppity nigger is a dead uppity nigger!" He angrily grabbed Willis' hair, tilted his head back, and slit his throat.

Paralyzed with fear, Maggie was now terrorized by the sight of Willis' blood gushing from his gaping wound. She screamed a visceral scream and tried to scoot away from his slumping body, but she had no energy left to move.

Jack Beauford made his way over, dragging a limp and whimpering Annalee by the arm. He dropped her bruised and bloody body to the floor beside Willis' corpse and zipped his pants.

Annalee screamed when she saw her brother covered in blood. Maggie reached out her hand toward Annalee. Leland Harper kicked Annalee in the stomach and stomped on Maggie's hand.

Surveying the scene, Jack sneered, "Damn, boys! I used this one up, but I think she's still breathin'. Throw 'em all in the back of Leland's pick-up. He'll drop 'em off at Davis' place on the way. Right now, we gotta haul ass."

Sheriff Jonathan Davis, a stocky, balding man in his mid-forties, was eating supper with his wife in their small house on the outskirts of town. Suddenly a pickup roared into the front yard, horn honking and lights flashing. Davis grabbed his gun from the holster hanging on the back of his chair and cautiously stepped to the window, telling his wife to get to the bedroom and stay there. When he recognized Leland Harper's pickup, he rushed through the front door.

"What the hell's goin' on, Lee?" he yelled at the driver's open window.

"Got no time to explain," came the reply. "Things got outta hand. Just take these three and hide 'em somewhere. We'll finish it later."

"Oh, for hell's sake, you gonna mix me up in some kinda shit?" Davis asked, looking at the three forms in the back of the truck. He shook his head and spat on the ground. "Pull 'round back to the barn for now. Unload 'em in the last stall and cover 'em with hay. Then we better be back to clean up this mess before daylight!"

The pickup sped around the house and three men jumped out to open the barn doors, while Buck Dudley and Roy Johnson unloaded their cargo. Sheriff Davis jumped into the back of the pickup with the others and it sped off.

No one noticed the curtain pulled aside in the back bedroom of the house.

Several hours after the football game, Michael came through the back door, grinning sheepishly at Eddie, who sat at the kitchen table with books and papers spread before him.

"Sorry I'm late," Michael said.

"Could have figured as much, but you'd think you might at least make it home on time when you've got your little sister with you."

Michael looked at his father blankly. Eddie stared into the dark beyond Michael. "Where's Maggie?"

Michael looked puzzled. "I don' know. I thought she came home with you."

Eddie rose from his chair slowly, beginning to panic. "No, we had a ... an argument, and she said she was coming home with you. YOU DON'T HAVE HER?"

"No. I haven't even seen her!"

Eddie ran toward the bedroom, calling Irene, who came stumbling into the hallway, pulling on her robe. "What is it? What's happened?"

"Maggie's missing! Get on the phone and start calling her friends. I'm gonna drive around and see if I can find her. I'll call you soon as I can!"

Michael was now alarmed. "I'm comin' with you, Dad!"

Eddie drove through the night in a cold sweat, looking left and right. In the dark, eerie quiet Michael sensed that his father knew something he wasn't saying.

"You mentioned trouble earlier tonight, Dad. What'd you mean by that? Is it the coloreds?"

“In a way, son. Things just tend to happen on Friday nights. Hell, they’re just tryin’ to get by like the rest of us, I guess. But they gotta know their place, that’s all. What d’you know about this Roberts kid? Has he got the hots for your sister?”

“Willis? Heck no, Dad. He’s a good guy” Michael quietly answered. “Just seems a little too friendly for a colored sometimes,” he added.

“Well, he kissed your sister on the cheek tonight, right there in front of God and everybody!”

“Holy crap! Willis ought to know better’n that. But he’s just that way, Dad. I bet he didn’t mean nothin’ by it. And he’s such a good ballplayer. Shoot, I think we got a shot at state this year with him.”

Eddie turned down a quiet residential street lined with ranch-style houses and tidy front lawns. He suddenly pulled to the curb and stopped.

Michael looked at the house. “This is the Beauford place, ain’t it? Why the heck are we stoppin’ here?”

“You just sit tight,” Eddie replied. “I’ll be right back.”

The grandfather clock in the living room chimed eleven times, as Eddie paced impatiently, waiting for Vivian Beauford to get off the phone. She finally hung up and turned to Eddie.

“He’s not at The Pastime; he’s not at Jerry’s Place. Nobody has seen him tonite, Eddie. Why are you lookin’ for Jack anyhow?”

"Personal matter, Vivian. You sure you don't have any idea where I might find him?"

"Eddie, I don't ask no questions about that man's comin's and goin's, so long as he comes home at night." She stepped into the light where a fading bruise was obvious underneath her right eye. "I don't ask no questions, Eddie, and maybe you shouldn't either."

Eddie turned to leave, then stopped and turned back. "Vivian, my little girl's gone. Maggie's missin' and there was an incident tonight with a colored boy. I think it was innocent enough, but I ain't sure everybody saw it that way, if you know what I mean. Please, Vivian, you gotta help me if you can."

"What d'ya wanna know?"

"Your son, Joey, he's a friend of Billy Harper's, ain't he? What kind of car does Billy drive?"

"A Chevy, I think... dark blue. But surely you don't think those boys are..."

"I don't know what to think, Vivian. But my baby's missin' and I gotta find her. I won't ask you to do it, but will you please call Irene and tell her to call the sheriff if I'm not home by midnight? I know they know where to look, if they just will."

Vivian wrung her hands. "I can't Eddie. I just can't be mixed up in..."

"Mixed up in what, Vivian? Savin' a young girl's life, for God's sake? If Jack and Joey ain't part of it, then you got nothin' to worry about."

"But if they are, he'll kill me for helping you. I know he will."

"I'm sorry to put you on the spot, Vivian, but I got no choice. My baby's out there somewhere, alone and scared, and in the middle of somethin' evil that no grown man can understand, let alone a teenage girl."

Vivian let out a big sigh. "Go! I'll call your wife. God have mercy on us all."

Maggie groaned and tried to move, but her whole body hurt. Through one small slit in her swollen eye, she could see Annalee stirring under a pile of straw next to her. Another form on the other side of her lay motionless, the gunny sack and straw soaked with blood.

"Annalee?" Maggie managed to whisper. "Annalee, can you hear me?"

Annalee's hand went to her face. "Where are we? Where's Willis?"

Suddenly the barn door creaked open. A lantern split the darkness. They could hear someone tiptoeing toward them. The girls reached out their hands to one another underneath the straw and held their breath.

"Oh my God!" gasped a female voice, as the lantern was held above them. When the light panned toward Willis, there was a shriek and the lantern began to shake. "Lord have mercy—no!" whispered the holder of the lantern.

Pansy Davis shook with fright and repulsion. "How could they kill these innocent children?" she wondered aloud.

"What kind of animals are they? I never thought they'd do something like..."

"Help us please," Maggie whispered hoarsely.

Pansy gasped and dropped the lantern as she jumped back. She bent down beside Maggie. "You're alive, thank God!"

"Yes, but hurt bad, both me and Annalee. They killed her brother, Willis."

"Oh, I'm so sorry, so, so sorry. I will get you out of here. Just let me figure it out and I promise I will get you out." She left hurriedly, taking the light with her.

In that moment, Pansy Davis hated her husband all over again, a hatred she thought she'd buried and forgiven him for. She knew he was covering for the Klan. But most of all, she hated him for beating her so badly that she lost their only child three years earlier. Worse yet, he showed no remorse, not about the beating nor about the baby. She was afraid to leave him, heeding his warning that he would kill her if she did. Pansy knew that if she helped those girls, it might cost her life. Her miserable, sorrowful, cowering life.

"How long has it been?" Annabelle whispered, painfully turning toward Maggie.

"I dunno. Maybe she's just as mean as the others. I don't even know who she is, do you?"

Just then, the barn doors opened wide. An old pickup slowly backed in and stopped just outside the last stall. Pansy Davis jumped out and opened the tailgate.

"Can you girls walk at all?"

Maggie spoke tentatively. "We haven't tried; we hurt all over. They beat us up pretty bad."

Pansy sucked in her breath. "Okay, I'm gonna lift you into the back. You gotta help as much as you can. It's gonna hurt, but we got no choice."

Slowly, painfully, the girls were lifted, dragged and carried, sometimes dragging their feet, sometimes unable to do even that. At last, Pansy had them settled in the back of the vehicle. She stopped to catch her breath, then loaded Willis' body, with a whispered, "I'm sorry."

"Where are you takin' us?" Annalee cried.

Pansy looked seriously at the girls. "I'm gonna take you all to a safe place and call an ambulance to come get you. I can't be seen with you or they'll kill me."

"Why're you doin' this?" Maggie asked. "Who are you?"

"It's just time. Don't ask no more questions please."

As the ambulance rushed Annabelle and Maggie to the hospital, Pansy Davis drove the old pickup north on back roads. Jonathan was unaware that the old truck even existed. For more than a decade it had languished under a tarp in the shed next door where her grandparents lived before their deaths. Pansy had secretly been working on it as time and gumption permitted. Her grandfather had taught her a little about auto mechanics when she was a teenager. Enough to get the old truck running. She'd never had the courage to use it before now. But now it mattered; it was more than just for her. She had cleaned out the safe Jonathan thought was a secret. In the next county, she ditched the truck in the river before walking to the depot and boarding a north-bound train. Even if she was caught, she would have at least one good thing to say about her life before it ended.

When Leland Harper's pickup pulled into the woods and the men slipped through the trees, there were signs of struggle and hasty departures all around. Joey Beauford sat on the ground, holding his dying father's head in his lap. Jack had a gunshot wound in his chest, red blood spreading across his white robe.

Joey sobbed. "I'm sorry, Daddy. But you just couldn't go home to Mama that way. You were soiled by that colored woman. My mama deserves better. What am I gonna do now? Oh, Lord, I don't know what to do…"

Jonathan Davis and the others arrived in the clearing just in time to see Joey put the gun in his mouth and pull the trigger. Davis screamed, "God, no! Oh my God Joey **No**!"

Davis rushed to Joey, but he was already dead. He felt for a pulse on Joey and his father, then turned to Leland Harper. "As if this night ain't screwed up enough, now we got another killin' and a suicide on our hands. You guys go on back to my place and wait for me. I'll stay here and try to figure out how to explain this one."

Eddie and Michael drove all over town, searching for the dark blue sedan. Up one street and down another, through the school grounds, out to the juke joints on the outskirts of town. It was a little past midnight when they wearily shuffled through the back door to find Irene sitting at the kitchen table in tears. She jumped up and ran to them.

"Anything?" she cried. "None of her friends know a thing about where she is. None of 'em! I think she's been taken right off the street! Oh, Eddie, we gotta call the sheriff!"

"For all the good that'll do," Eddie replied. "But I guess we got no choice at this point. I don't know what else to do."

There was no answer at the sheriff's home, so they tried the office number. Deputy Jimmy Moore said the sheriff was out on "official business" and he'd relay the message to him. Eddie tried to stress the urgency of finding Maggie, but all the deputy would say was "Yeah, yeah, your teenage girl is missing, Mr. Thorpe, I got it." Moore added with a snicker, "D'ya check with her boyfriend?"

It was all Eddie could do to maintain his composure. He said flatly, "Either the sheriff contacts me on the double, or I'm gonna come down there and find out where he is and go to him. You got that?"

"Roger that," came the deputy's cavalier reply.

Eddie and Irene paced the floor, while Michael made phone calls to his friends to see whether anyone had heard anything. "Nothing," he told them glumly.

Suddenly the phone startled them. Eddie grabbed it from Michael's hand. "Hello? Yes, this is Eddie Thorpe, who's this? Oh my God, we'll be right there!"

"That was a doctor at St. Mary's—she's alive—let's go!"

Jonathan Davis sat in his patrol car, trying to gather his thoughts and words after visiting Vivian Beauford. It unnerved him that the woman had been like a stone when he told her, "Your husband is dead." Then she screamed an inhuman cry and collapsed when he told her about the boy. He got a neighbor woman to stay with her and left as quickly as he could. "How the hell do I get mixed up in this shit?" he wondered aloud, lighting a cigarette with shaky hands.

Just then his radio crackled with the dispatcher's call. Davis listened as the man told him of Eddie Thorpe's call about his missing daughter. Then he went numb all over, realizing what may have happened to her.

"Is that all?"

"Wish it was, boss," the dispatcher said solemnly. "We got us a murder and a couple assaults, too. Nigger boy's dead, he's at the morgue. Nigger gal and a white gal been taken to the hospital, beat up pretty good. They's all found in the ditch out on Twin Lakes Road. You s'pose it's that Thorpe gal?"

"Shit! How'd they... Never mind. Don't mention this to nobody for now. I'm on my way to the hospital. Call Deputy Moore and tell him to get over to the morgue and find out what he can."

Chapter Ten

Maggie

"Trauma creates one of four types of people: victims, rescuers or perps – and if you're really lucky and really strong and very willing and brave, survivors."

~ Allison Anders (1954)
American independent film director.

Maggie lay in the hospital bed, bruised and bandaged, sleeping fitfully. Eddie sat beside the bed with his head in his hands. Irene came up beside him and held out a cup of coffee.

"Here, honey, drink this. You'll need to stay awake on the job tonite, if you insist you gotta go."

"Can't miss my shift, Reeny—who knows how much this hospital bill's gonna be. Least I can be with her 'til time to go."

"Now, the doctor said it'll just take time, honey. She'll be fine—you know she'll be fine." Haltingly, about to lose it, Irene added, "She's just gotta be fine!"

Eddie trembled as he buried his face in his wife's midsection. "I'm almost more concerned about her mind. Her body's gonna heal. But what horrible things did that little girl have to suffer that'll never leave her mind? For God's sake, Reeny, will she ever be the same?"

Irene was strong for her husband now. "You let it out, Edward. You just let all that stuff come on out now. Ain't gonna do you no good all boilin' and churnin' in there."

She knelt beside Eddie and put her arms around his convulsing shoulders, as he finally let go and sobbed. She tenderly stroked his hair and rocked him gently back and forth. After a minute or two, Eddie composed himself, sat up straight, and gave his wife a quick hug.

"I'm okay, I'm okay. Think I'm gonna take a walk and get the kinks out. You okay here?"

"Of course, honey. You go ahead. And ask about Annalee, over in the colored side, will you? That poor girl won't even be able to go to her own brother's funeral." Irene leveled her gaze at her husband before she continued. "They will catch them, you know."

"Yeah, sure, they're gonna catch 'em," he choked out. "It has to be that somebody knows somethin'. Hell, one of these girls'll be strong enough to talk one of these days and we'll find out who was in on it and track 'em down."

Maggie slowly healed during her six-week stay in the hospital. A month after her discharge, she was rushed to the emergency room. Irene sat on the edge of her daughter's bed, patting her arm.

Irene asked worriedly, "Are you feelin' better, honey? You 'bout scared us to death, faintin' at breakfast this mornin'."

"I ain't feelin' great," Maggie replied. "You don't think there's nothin' wrong that we can't see, do ya, like internal injuries, with them takin' blood and runnin tests?"

Eddie walked over and patted his daughter's hand. "No, honey, I'm sure everything's fine. You've come so far and healed up so good. Ol' doc probably just wants to check you out good again. Probably gonna tell ya to drink more water or eat better or somethin'."

Irene chimed in brightly. "Mags, I bet that's it, honey. I told you to eat more, young lady. Dr. Hammond wants to tell us all together so's we can keep a better eye on you."

Roland Hammond, M.D., entered the room wearing a white medical coat and a stethoscope around his neck. He nodded to the Thorpes, then turned to close the door.

"Eddie. Irene. I've run some blood tests on Maggie. Well, there's no easy way to say it." He took a deep breath, then dryly announced, "Maggie is gonna have a baby."

Irene shrieked, then covered her mouth with her hand. Maggie stared disbelievingly at the doctor, then began to shake. Eddie squinted at the doctor as though he hadn't quite heard him.

Trying to keep his voice steady, Eddie spoke quietly, "No, Doc. You made a mistake. Somebody's made a terrible mistake. This can't be true. You mixed up somebody's records. You go check again."

Doctor Hammond answered, his voice apologetic but clinical. "I wish it was a mistake, Eddie. But it isn't. I reviewed the tests myself. There's no doubt." To Maggie, the doctor offered sympathy. "I'm sorry, young lady. I know this is awful news, considering everything you've been through."

Irene could barely speak. "What... what are we gonna do? What's gonna happen? Eddie, what are we gonna do?"

Doctor Hammond put his hand on Irene's shoulder. "There are, uh, procedures you might want to consider."

Maggie whimpered loudly now. She looked from her mother to her father, with tears streaming down her face, but she was unable to speak.

The doctor continued. "Of course, if you want to give it up for adoption, that can certainly be arranged, too. There's a place over in Memphis she can go, arrangements can be made, so that she's as comfortable and, uh, as discreet as possible while she waits to deliver."

Maggie blurted out, almost screeching, "No! No! I won't throw it away! NO, I CAN'T! oh, God, why this? Why THIS"

Eddie shouted, "Maggie! You're only fourteen years old! There ain't no way you can keep it! An' besides, we don't even know whose..."

Irene flashed her husband a horrified look, and Maggie stared at her father with wounded eyes.

"Oh, God, honey, I didn't mean nothin'. I'm sorry, baby, I know it ain't your fault. We'll figure somethin' out..."

Dr. Hammond reached for the door handle. "Well, you folks have things to talk about. You don't have to make any decisions right now, but if you decide upon termination, then the sooner the better, of course. Otherwise, my nurse can provide some information for you on places, people to contact, and all that. I'm sorry, folks."

Irene, still sitting on the side of the bed, turned to look at Maggie, then fell across her, holding Maggie tight and sobbing. "Oh, my sweet child! Oh, Mags, you're just a baby yourself!" She willed herself to pull it together for Maggie's sake, then continued steadier, as she straightened up and wiped the tears from her eyes. "It's okay, sweetheart. We will manage. We will handle this. God doesn't give us nothin' we can't handle."

Maggie fell against Irene, who wrapped her arms around her. The room was ghostly silent as Mother and daughter tearfully rocked together. Eddie stepped to the window and looked wearily out at the sky.

Wanting to comfort the two, but feeling awkward, Eddie said into the window glass, "It'll be okay. We'll make it okay. We'll fix this, somehow, some way."

Chapter Eleven

Adult Education

"Self-education is, I firmly believe, the only kind of education there is."

~ Isaac Asimov (1920-1992)
American writer .and professor of biochemistry.

Six weeks later, Eddie and Irene took their seats in the Oakwood High School gymnasium, awaiting the GED graduation ceremony.

Eddie whispered to Irene, "I wish you'd have let me skip this whole thing. I passed the course, why do I hafta be here for this?"

"Because you earned this, honey. You worked hard for this diploma, and you deserve to graduate. Besides, Maggie's in good hands, and she didn't want you to miss this."

"Yeah, well, after all that's happened, I don't know... this just doesn't seem important, somehow."

"Edward Thorpe, you bite your tongue! This is an accomplishment, and I will not have you makin' it anything less than that. Your wife and children are proud of you. Michael woulda been here if he wasn't in the playoffs. Now, you just shut up and feel proud."

Eddie's class instructor stepped to the podium and started to speak, but the microphone crackled as it fed back. He winced, then leaned closer to the mic. "Ladies and Gentlemen, uh, may I have your attention please? Thank you, thank you. I must say I am very proud of all my students. They've done a wonderful job, sometimes under extraordinary circumstances. It's now time for the awarding of the diplomas. As I call your name, will you please step forward to receive your certificate."

The instructor called out names, in alphabetical order. Eddie and Irene politely applauded as each name was called. After a while, they were stunned by the name that was read, Winston P. Roberts. Eddie and Irene looked at one another in utter surprise and disbelief.

Eddie whispered in Irene's ear. "All this time, I never knew his name. I never knew it was him. He missed some classes. My God, now I know why."

A tall black man rose from his seat and slowly made his way forward. His shoulders were slumped, giving the appearance he carried a heavy burden. He took his certificate, shook the instructor's hand, and returned to his seat.

The class instructor continued, "Edward D. Thorpe."

Still reeling from the revelation about Winston Roberts, Eddie stood and mechanically made his way up front. He shook the instructor's hand and returned to his seat with his certificate. Irene clapped loudly and excitedly for him. Eddie looked at who he now knew to be Winston Roberts, who returned the stare with a smile and a nod.

Following the ceremony, Eddie was compelled to hurry after Winston Roberts, who had already turned to leave. He gingerly grabbed Winston's arm. "Mr. Roberts? Mr. Roberts, may I have a word with you?"

Winston stopped and slowly turned to face Eddie. "Of course, Mr. Thorpe."

"You knew. All along, you knew who I was in that class. Why didn't you tell me who you were?"

Winston sighed and collected himself. "Mr. Thorpe, first of all, I am most grateful to you for checkin' on my daughter at the hospital, and the card and flowers you and your wife sent for Willis' funeral. But, with all due respect, I was just some Negro in your class, competing with you for more education. Had I told you who I was, you might have pitied me, but I don't want your pity."

"But, if I'd have known who you were, I would never have..." Eddie couldn't complete his sentence.

Winston replied, "What, never have considered me just another nigger out to get what you've got?"

Eddie got a little defensive. "Oh, I don't hold it against you gettin' your education. I ain't like that."

"Oh, we've met before, Mr. Thorpe," Winston said. "Before the class and long before that terrible night our children were together. I was lyin' in the street, bloody and bruised. Then I pulled myself up and leaned on the car of whoever had stopped before they ran me over. Don't you remember when our eyes met, Mr. Thorpe? I certainly do. And I knew right then to keep on runnin.' Not that I blame you for not gettin' involved. Not safe for a white man to help a black man, wasn't then and ain't now. Probably never will be."

Eddie shook his head. "That was you? Well, I... I thought about helpin' you, but then you disappeared. You said yourself, it ain't safe to help sometimes. What happened that night, anyway, did ya get in a fight or what?"

Roberts emitted an ironic chuckle. "A fight? No, Mr. Thorpe. I was on my way to an interview for a night janitor job at Socony cause I heard they were hirin' without regard to color. I was runnin' late and took a short-cut through the white part of town. Then, as luck would have it, my old car broke down. I had no choice but to try to hitch a ride. Obviously, the wrong car stopped, and you know the rest."

"But I'd never wish any of this on you or us or anybody for that matter. I'm sorry you got hurt, I'm sorry 'bout your son and your daughter. I'm sorry about my Maggie. Hell, I'm just plain sorry."

"I'm sorry, too, Mr. Thorpe."

"We'll get 'em, ya know," Eddie stated. "The ones that did it. They'll be brought to justice, one way or another."

Winston replied wearily, "I doubt that very much. But you keep believin' it if you need to. Good night, Mr. Thorpe. Oh, and uh, congratulations on your diploma."

Eddie looked blankly at the certificate still in his hands. "Yeah... you, too, I guess.

Chapter Twelve

Truth Seekers

"The truth will set you free, but first it will make you miserable."

~ James A. Garfield (1831-1881)
20th President of the United States.

The Garland County Sheriff's Office occupied a separate annex behind the courthouse in town square. The dingy anteroom held one desk and a few chairs out front, with cells in the back. Winston Roberts was already seated when Eddie and Irene arrived. He and the Thorpes nodded to one another.

Sheriff Jonathan Davis fidgeted behind his desk. He was itching to find Pansy before somebody else did. He still couldn't believe that she not only left him, but she also betrayed him by turning those kids loose. Now the only thing standing between him and a midnight visit by the Klan boys was the fact that Pansy apparently didn't say anything to the kids about who she was or where they were. At least, it hadn't been mentioned yet by the one gal talking, that Roberts girl. Surely, she'd name a witness if she thought she had one. *Better get my mind back where it belongs,* Davis thought to himself.

Another man, who was a stranger to the Thorpes and Winston Roberts, stood against the wall in the back of the room.

"Before we get started, Sheriff Davis began, "that there's Agent Langford. He's gonna be investigatin' this kidnappin' or somethin', I guess, cause the FBI seems to think they need to send somebody down here cause we can't handle..."

Agent Langford, tall and broad-bodied with close-cropped brown hair, interrupted the sheriff. "Nice to meet you folks. I'm sorry for what you've been through, and I'll try to be as respectful as I can."

The sheriff continued, "Okay then. As I told y'all on the phone, Mr. Roberts' girl has made some serious allegations against Mr. Leland Harper and his son, one Billy Harper. I called y'all together here, so we could talk about if a case can be made outta this, you know, what we might be up against."

Winston Roberts leaned forward in his chair. "With all due respect, Sheriff Davis, IF a case could be made outta this? Seems to me it's pretty cut and dried. My Annalee done named the men she knows for a fact violated her and killed my son. You got yourself an eye witness—a victim who's willin' to testify. Against my better judgment, I might add. What more do you need to make yourself a case?"

Eddie joined in, "You have to charge them, Davis! Now you got your witness, like Win... Mr. Roberts says. You gotta file charges."

Agent Langford replied. "I'm afraid it's not that simple, folks. With all due respect to all of you, we must be realistic. If Sheriff Davis files charges now, with only Annalee's word to go on, no jury within 500 miles would convict them. Now, I want to dig deeper on this and, hopefully come up with enough to substantiate Annalee's allegations."

"Why don't you just go ahead, Mr. Langford?" Winston asked wearily. "Why do you even need our agreement on this?"

"I don't need it, Mr. Roberts. But before I go any further, stirring up emotions and sentiments all over this county, I want you folks to know what you're up against. There's more to this that all of you ought to know. Leland Harper and his son both say that Annalee is lying."

Winston was furious. "You can't possibly believe THEM!"

"What—what exactly are they sayin'?" Eddie asked tentatively.

Agent Langford paused a moment, and as the room grew quiet, he replied, "That Willis and Maggie were, well... involved. That they know Negroes who have witnessed the relationship first hand. And that some 'unknown Negro persons' must have taken offense and tried to teach them a lesson. They say that Annalee was probably included because she was friends with Maggie and knew firsthand about Maggie's relationship with her brother."

"They're LYING!" Winston shouted. "My boy knew BETTER than to mess with a white girl! They're just tryin' to throw blame off their own selves!"

Eddie and Irene were dumfounded. Eddie put his head in his hands and stared at the floor.

Langford hated what he had to say, but continued. "Well, as I told you before, Mr. Roberts, it's probably going to take more than your daughter's word on this—things being what they are around here."

Eddie looked questioningly at Langford, although he already knew the answer. "I think what Mr. Langford is trying to say is that another eye witness, a WHITE witness, might be the only thing that will convict those bastards, if he can't dig up any hard evidence. Do I understand you correctly, Mr. Langford?"

Langford looked grimly at Irene, then nodded to Eddie.

Irene finally understood. "Oh no—oh no, not Maggie! No, there's no way I'm gonna let her get mixed up in this! Absolutely not!"

Langford spoke gently to Irene. "Mrs. Thorpe, your daughter was mixed up in this the minute somebody laid a hand on her. Now I understand she can't recall anything that happened that night, but I still need to question her."

"But, she's not well. She's... she's gone to stay with my parents until... until she feels strong enough to come back home. We can't just yank her outta there now and make her come home to face this. No, I won't hear of it!" Irene looked at Winston Roberts. "Oh, I'm so sorry, Mr. Roberts. I wasn't thinkin' when I said that. Of course, your little girl has had to try and forget everything—right here where it all happened."

"But, you see, Mrs. Thorpe," Winston began, "once she started feelin' a little better, a fire took hold of my Annalee. She's thought of nothin' but rememberin' that terrible night. She's worked at it, struggled with it, rolled it over in her mind 'til she's almost gone mad, tryin' to put the pieces together. Now that she's finally started to remember how it was, if I'm gonna have to tell her that her word ain't good enough, well I just don't know what that'll do to her. I just don't know."

"We'll talk to Maggie," Irene said to Agent Langford. "We will see if she has started to remember anything. It's the least we can do, for Annalee's sake. Meanwhile, maybe you will turn up somethin' and neither of those girls will have to relive that horrible night."

Eddie was unsure what to believe at that point. "Irene, we better just let Mr. Langford do his job. Then if we need to talk to Maggie, we will. Ain't no use gettin' her all upset if we don't have to. I say we wait and see." Eddie Thorpe and Winston Roberts exchanged uneasy glances.

Langford addressed the three parents. "Mr. and Mrs. Thorpe, Mr. Roberts, I promise you this much. I will do everything I can to turn over every rock and find every snake that had anything to do with harming your children. Word of warning, though: whether your daughters have to testify or not, things may get pretty ugly for you during the investigation and the trial, if it comes to that."

Sheriff Davis sneered at Langford. "Y'all bring me an iron-clad case against anybody in this county, and I'll lock 'em up."

Eddie, Irene and Winston stood up, shook hands all around, saying thanks and good-bye. Then they went through the door and wordlessly headed in opposite directions.

Langford sat down on the corner of the sheriff's desk. "I don't want any turf wars with you on this, Davis. I hope you meant what you just said to those folks, but I have a feeling that you only said it because you don't think there's a chance in hell we can turn up any evidence against the good ol' boys down here. Just remember this: federal trumps state, and state trumps county. You wanna stay in this job, you'd best cooperate on this case."

Davis slammed his desk drawer shut. "An' I got news for you, Langford. I got my resignation all typed and ready to sign in this drawer. Things get too messy around here, and I'll just quit. What'd that do to your case halfway through, huh? Don't make no threats to me, Mr. FBI. You do your job, I'll do mine."

"Well, I guess that's how I'll know whether somebody is pulling your strings or not. Surely the Klan, or whoever is behind all this, will want to keep someone they can trust in charge of this case. I hear they don't take kindly to someone that quits them. So, any way you look at it, Sheriff, it appears that you're in this for the duration, just like I am."

Langford put on his hat, nodded at Davis, and went out the door, leaving Davis staring after him with a worried look on his face.

As Eddie and Irene slowly drove home after the meeting at the sheriff's office, both stared silently through the windshield. Irene looked over at Eddie, then back. He glanced sideways at her. They continued on without communicating.

Finally, Eddie broke the silence. "What if it's true, Irene?"

"What if what's true?"

"He kissed her at the football game without battin' an eye, ya know. What if there WAS somethin' goin' on?"

"Eddie! You can't be serious! You know that Maggie knows her pla... Maggie knows better. She wouldn't cause that kind of trouble."

"But what if there was somethin' to it? Or what if that boy tried to get friendly, and she rejected him, and somebody seen it and drew their own conclusions?"

"Would that make it okay, Eddie? Could you abide what happened then, if Maggie was just in the wrong place at the wrong time, and those coloreds were gettin' what they deserved? Would that make it all right, for God's sake?"

"Nothin's gonna make it all right and you know it! I'm just tryin' to understand it. I'm just tryin' to figure it all out."

"Even if it means that Maggie was carryin' on with a colored boy, or if she just got caught in the middle, you'd rather take the word of white over colored, no matter what, wouldn't you?"

"This ain't my fault, ya know, Irene! Don't go tryin' to blame me for any of this."

"Well, it ain't Maggie's fault, either! It sure as HELL ain't Maggie's!"

Suddenly, an egg smashed on the windshield and they both instinctively ducked. Eddie pulled over to the side of the road and jumped out to see where it came from.

A figure ran down the alley in the shadows. Eddie followed until he lost his breath. He stopped, bent over, with hands on knees, gasping for air.

Irene ran up behind her husband. "Eddie! Eddie! Are you all right?"

"Yeah... (gasping) Yeah, I'm okay."

"Did you see who that was?"

"No, I didn't see who it was. I just saw what."

"What do you mean?"

"It was a white boy, Irene. A white boy egged our car. Oh, it was probably just some kid out to cause mischief."

"My God, Eddie, hasn't it sunk into your head yet that whites have done much more to you than egg your damned car?"

Eddie straightened up, looked quickly around, and pulled Irene by the arm back to the car. He pushed her into the passenger seat and got in behind the wheel, then peeled out into traffic.

"Irene, don't you never stand in the street talkin' like that again! Whatever is goin' on here, don't make it worse, for God's sake!"

Irene was in tears now. "How's it gonna get worse, Eddie? Maggie was almost killed. The Roberts boy WAS killed. The Roberts' girl was almost killed. And Maggie was... was violated and's gonna have a baby when she's just a baby herself. You just tell me—how's talkin' about it make it worse?"

"I don't know, Irene! I don't have all the answers! It's just that—well, if we got enemies, I wanna know who they are. I wanna know who we can trust and who we can't."

"Sometimes, I think we've been changed by this as much as anybody, Eddie. I don't seem to know us anymore."

Eddie sighed deeply. "Things used to be so much clearer, Irene. Everybody knew their place and stayed in it. Things were just easier to understand, just somehow..."

"What, Eddie? Things were black and white?"

"That's not funny, Irene."

"It wasn't meant to be, Eddie, it wasn't meant to be."

They rode on in silence, both staring pensively at the edifice of the Oakwood Lutheran Church as they went by. There on the reader board were the words, SUNDAY'S SERMON: A LITTLE CHILD SHALL LEAD THEM.

Chapter Thirteen

Dead Men Tell No Tales

"Death is not the greatest loss in life.
The greatest loss is what dies inside
us while we live."

~ Norman Cousins (1915-1990)
American political journalist, author, professor, and world peace advocate.

The Oakwood Cemetery covered several hillsides on the south edge of town, just outside the city limits. It contained the graves of generations of white Oakwood citizens, dating back to the 1800s. While the older part had fallen into weedy disrepair, the modern area, closer to the road and gates, was carefully mowed and maintained.

On a gray, overcast afternoon, Vivian Beauford kneeled at her son's gravesite and laid fresh flowers against the headstone. "They say things are gonna get worse 'round here, Joey. Maybe it's just as well you're not alive to be drug through the mud." She wiped her eyes and continued, "I still miss ya, son. Always will, I guess."

Vivian Beauford had lived a hard life. Born and raised in a shack in the woods of the Missouri bootheel, she was the oldest of eight children. She had a drunk for a father, and a mother who lost her mind after the seventh child. Vivian practically raised her siblings, the five besides her that survived birth, that is. She buried two that died in childbirth, along with their afterbirth, in the backyard. They had been her own, fathered by their grandfather. Vivian had always stoically accepted whatever happened to her. She never tried to tell her uncomprehending mother about the babies she buried. When she was seventeen, she left them all behind, fleeing with a gandy dancer that knocked on their door for a meal.

Left alone and penniless in Little Rock some time later, Vivian found a job as a cashier in a small café. She roomed with the owner's daughter, Trixie, in a one-bedroom apartment above the restaurant. The girls worked together and became fast friends. Trixie, much more experienced and adventurous than Vivian, introduced her new friend to roadhouses along the highway. Eventually, both girls left the small family café for more exciting work, serving drinks at the Mainline Roadhouse Inn, despite being under-age themselves.

One night, two handsome men in their thirties came in for beers. They began to flirt with the girls, who were flattered by the older men's attention. After several nights of flirting and a whirlwind romance, Jack Beauford and Leland Harper took the girls on a road trip. They ended up in Las Vegas, where they held an impromptu double wedding. Little did Vivian know she was whisked off her feet by a man very much like her father. At first, they enjoyed married life in Oakwood, where both men worked at the oil refinery. The Beaufords had fun times with their pals, the Harpers. But Trixie Harper soon became pregnant, which didn't sit well with her. As far as Trixie was concerned, her partying days weren't over. She ran off one night with a traveling salesman, leaving Leland to raise their baby boy, Billy.

It was around that time that Jack became angry and violent with Vivian, blaming her for all the rotten women in the world. He wanted a child, but was afraid Vivian would react much the same way as her friend, Trixie. He began to beat her and threaten her with death if she even looked at another man or thought about leaving. Vivian was amazed that she had ended up with a man so like her father, but figured it was simply her lot in life.

Jack began chasing other women, but Vivian didn't mind, as that kept him away from her longer. He still beat her, belittled her, and bullied her. He forced her to have sex when no one else was available. She grew to hate him, but never had the nerve to leave him.

When Joey was born about a year after Trixie took off, Vivian was enthralled with the new life she had helped create. With Jack gone so much, she began to think of the baby as hers alone, and she made him her whole life. She coddled him, protected him, doted on him, and gave him her whole heart. Her son was all she lived for; he gave her a reason to live. Vivian knew Jack was up to no good a lot of the time, but she never questioned him. As long as she had Joey to dote upon, her husband was an inconvenient shadow in their lives.

Now, Vivian grimaced at the painful irony that in finally gaining her freedom from Jack Beauford, she had lost her only reason for living. After a while, she stood and started to leave the cemetery. She turned briefly to the adjacent grave of her late husband and spat. Hatefully, through clenched teeth, she snarled, "Burn in hell, you rotten sonovabitch!" As Vivian slowly walked away from the graves she was approached by James Langford, who tipped his hat.

"Mrs. Beauford?"

Vivian eyed him suspiciously. "What do YOU want?"

Langford showed his badge. "Mrs. Beauford, I'm agent James Langford, FBI. I'd just like to ask you a couple of questions, if I may."

"I know who you are. Got nothin' to say to ya." Vivian tried to step around him, but he wouldn't be brushed off so easily.

"Mrs. Beauford, please. Just a few questions. We can go somewhere more private if you like."

Vivian looked around and noted that the graveyard appeared empty except for the two of them. "Guess the dead don't hear. Make it quick."

Langford motioned to a nearby bench. "Please have a seat. First of all, Mrs. Beauford, I'm sorry that you lost your husband and your son."

"I only had one real loss. Jack bein' killed was probably a gain."

"Excuse me?"

Vivian continued with a sneer. "Jack Beauford was a dirty, rotten sonovabitch, Mr. Langford. He was mean, and he was ornery. He cheated on me and knocked me around. But that's all I'm gonna say about him. He was what he was, but my Joey... my Joey was a good boy."

"Mrs. Beauford, wouldn't you like to get to the bottom of this? Wouldn't you like to know exactly what happened the night your boy died?"

"No sir, it really don't matter to me. I lost the only thing I care about that night. Unless you can bring my Joey back, then you can't do nothin' for me"

Langford decided to try another way. "You know, another parent lost a child that night. His only son, too."

Vivian stiffened. "Yes, I know that colored boy got killed that night. Maybe he wouldn't have, if he had stayed where he belonged. I hear he was chasin' after a white girl, that Maggie Thorpe. Too bad about her, though."

Langford sensed an opening. "Do you know Maggie well?"

"No, just know who she is, and heard she got beat up pretty bad that night. My Joey didn't have a thing to do with that. He wouldn't hurt a girl that way, I know he wouldn't. Now, his daddy, well that's another matter, no tellin' what he'd do if he had enough liquor in him. But I've already said enough."

"Please, Mrs. Beauford. Please indulge me just a little longer."

"Like I said before, unless you can somehow bring Joey back ..."

"You know I can't do that, Mrs. Beauford. But maybe I can bring back the last few hours of his life for you, if I can get to the bottom of what happened that night. Maybe somebody who was there could give you that much. I think, deep down, you'd really like to know, wouldn't you?"

Vivian looked at him with cold, dead eyes. "Of course I want to know about Joey's final hours, Mr. Langford. The problem is, I probably can't get that without bein' covered by his daddy's dirt in the process."

"Do you know who Joey was with that night?"

"No.

"And what time did Mr. Thorpe come by?"

Vivian thought for a moment. "He come by around 11:00 that night, I think, lookin' for Jack. He said his girl was missin' and there might have been an incident with a colored boy."

"Why would Mr. Thorpe come looking for Jack?"

Vivian looked down at her hands in her lap. "Oh, hell, it just don't matter anymore. They ripped my heart out that night, and they can't hurt me any more than losin' my boy hurts." She sighed deeply, then continued. "Eddie Thorpe come lookin' for Jack because he knew what everybody else around here knows. Whenever somethin' happens to coloreds, folks expect that Jack will know about it. As I told Mr. Thorpe that night, I didn't ask Jack questions. I just didn't ask. Maybe if I had, my Joey would still be alive."

Gently, he prodded her for more, "Is there anything else you can tell me, Mrs. Beauford? Anything at all?"

Vivian had a wide, wild look in her eyes that unnerved Langford when she spoke. "I can tell you that where Jack

Beauford went, Leland Harper wasn't usually far behind. I didn't like Joey bein' friends with that hoodlum son of his, either, but I couldn't stop it. A woman just can't make much difference when she's married to a man with a mean streak, Mr. Langford."

"Thank you, Mrs. Beauford. I appreciate your time. Can I walk you to your car?" Sounding far away, Vivian replied, "No, I like walkin' through the cemetery. I feel like I died the night my Joey died, and this is where I belong. Besides, no offense, but I'd just as soon not be seen with you."

Langford said with a nod, "I understand. No offense taken. Thanks again."

CHAPTER FOURTEEN

1964

The Long, Long Road

*"Change does not roll in on the
wheels of inevitability, but comes through
continuous struggle."*

~ Martin Luther King, Jr. (1929-1968)
American Baptist minister and activist who
became the most visible spokesperson and
leader in the civil rights movement.

WINSTON AND ANNALEE Roberts sat at the lace-covered dining room table in their small, tidy row house in the Negro part of town, "across the beltline," as the neighborhood was known in Oakwood. Father and daughter silently pushed the food around on their plates. Annalee gazed across the room to the china hutch, where a photo of her mother and father on their wedding day sat beside a photo of Willis in his football uniform.

"Daddy, you ever notice how much Willis looked like Mama?"

Winston followed his daughter's gaze. "Lord, I guess he looked like your mama, child. Wasn't a day I didn't look in his eyes that I didn't miss her and see her all at the same time."

"You think they're together?"

Winston replied with a chuckle, "Oh, sure they are. Ain't no doubt in my mind that those two are stirrin' up things in heaven, just the way they did right here."

"Daddy, I gotta do somethin'," Annalee said somberly. "I got Mama and Willis ridin' on my shoulder, tellin' me I gotta do somethin' about this."

"What you gonna do, baby? Those white men don't wanna hear what some colored gal got to say. The ones in charge don't, anyhow. And the ones that ain't in charge, well, they'd as soon kill you as listen to you. So, what's one skinny little colored gal gonna do?"

"Maybe I can't do nothin' by myself, but I'm not the only one's got a stake in this. If I could talk to Maggie Thorpe, if I could tell her what I remember, maybe it would cause her to remember, too. And maybe if the two of us stood up together, those bastards wouldn't get away with it."

"Now, honey, don't you go stirrin' up no trouble. It's best to leave well enough alone. Soon's we got enough money together, we'll be leavin' this place behind for good, so just leave it alone, like I told you before."

Annalee was exasperated. "Leave it alone! Let it go! Don't make trouble! Run away from it! How long we gonna just take it like that, Daddy? They killed your son and beat your daughter almost to death." She began to choke up. "What d'ya think Mama would say about all that? You think she'd say just leave it alone? You think she's proud o' the way we step and fetch and shuffle around those white folks that caused us so much pain?"

Winston was fearful and forceful at the same time. "Annalee, you listen to me! You ain't got no IDEA how much better it is than it used to be." He calmed down a little and said more soothingly, "Things are gettin' better, little by little, honey. But it ain't safe to push things." Choking up, he added, "I don't wanna lose you too. Please, baby, please don't do nothin' that might take away the last thing I got to love on this earth."

"Okay, Daddy, don't worry, you'll have me around a long, long time," Annalee said over her shoulder, as she left the room.

Winston Roberts continued to sit at the table, lost in his own thoughts. He knew things could be a lot worse. He remembered his favorite uncle, Reggie, even though he had been only six when Reggie died. Winston remembered hiding behind the bedroom door as his father broke the news to his mother, his uncle's sister. She screamed a heart-wrenching sound, and his father covered her mouth so no one outside the thin walls of their shack in colored town could hear.

Win, as they called him back then, went to his mother and crawled into her lap. "I'm sorry you're sad, Mama," said the boy. "Is Uncle Reggie comin' back?"

He remembered how his mother held him close and rocked back and forth, saying "Win, Win, my innocent little boy."

Then his father took him out of her arms and carried him to his bed. "You need to go back to sleep, Win."

"But, Daddy, what about Uncle Reggie?" the small boy asked.

"Uncle Reggie died tonight, boy. Cause he asked too many questions. Now don't you be like him. You go on to sleep."

"Ain't he ever comin' back?" the boy pleaded with tears in his eyes.

"Naw, he ain't never comin' back. An' you better stop askin' questions, like I said."

Winston cried himself to sleep that night after he overheard his father telling his mother the story of how her brother died.

Uncle Reggie's friend Jonah, who had gone with Reggie to the Collier place but walked on, overheard an argument between Reggie and Mrs. Collier. He heard the rest of the story later in town. On the night of his death, Jonah said, Reggie was hanging around the Collier place, hoping to have a word with their maid, Leonora, a woman he'd been courting. As he sat on the back-porch steps, waiting for her to leave for home, Mrs. Collier happened to see him.

"What you doin' here, boy?" Mrs. Collier shouted at Reggie, her hands on her ample hips.

"Why, I's just waitin' to walk Miss Leonora home, Mrs. Collier."

"Well, she ain't done with her work yet, and she's gonna be a while. You go on now and git outta here."

"Beggin' your pardon, ma'am, but I'm content to just sit here and wait for her," Reggie said.

"Well, I ain't content with you lurkin' out there, boy. Now go on and git!"

Reggie stood up silently and walked to the alleyway beside the Collier home. There, he leaned against the fence post of the neighboring property and stared at Mrs. Collier.

"I told you to git!" Mrs. Collier yelled. "I'm gonna tell my husband you're trespassin' if you don't git on outta here!"

Defiantly, Reggie replied, "I ain't on yo property, Mrs. Collier. You can't run me offa city property, that's what this here alley is."

"Why, you uppity nigger! I'm gonna run you off, all right, and you're gonna cost Leonora her job to boot!" And with that, Mrs. Collier stomped off into the house in search of her husband, Willard.

Ethyl Collier could be heard a mile away when she found her husband sleeping off a bender on the sofa. "Willard, you git your lazy, drunk ass up off that couch! There's a nigger out back waitin' for Leonora and he sassed me! Now you go chase him off while I call the sheriff. I'm gonna fire that girl, too, cause she's the one that brung him here."

Willard Collier stumbled out the back door, pulling his suspenders up over his dingy undershirt, yelling at his wife over his shoulder. "Aw, don't fire Leonora, Ethyl, ain't her fault he come, and 'sides, you ain't never gonna clean up this place the way she does. I'm gonna chase off that nigger, but you leave Leonora outta this."

When Willard Collier stepped off the back porch and headed toward him, Reggie stiffened. He could tell by the man's walk that he was drunk. He tried to reason.

"Now, Mr. Collier, I ain't got no fight with you or your missus, I just come to walk Miss Leonora home, thas all."

"Oh yeah, you black sonovabich?" Willard slurred, weaving and stumbling. "Well my woman told me you sassed her, and I ain't gonna stand for that!" He lunged for Reggie and swung at him, missed by a mile and fell on the ground in a heap.

Reggie knew he'd better run. The sheriff's siren could be heard down the street, just as Reggie hopped the fence and ran through the neighbor's back yard. It just so happened that the neighbor was John F. Beauford, one of the town's most vocal bigots. Beauford chased Reggie with a shotgun, while his little boy, Jackie, stood at the edge of the yard, yelling, "Git that nigger, Daddy, git him!"

Reggie ran for his life, all the way to the edge of the woods, where he dove into a creek and hid behind some bulrushes. When John Beauford tried to jump the creek, Reggie raised up and grabbed at his gun for protection. The gun discharged, shooting the sheriff as he pursued them. Reggie was able to get away, but it did him little good.

He came upon a white man at a campfire in the trees, not far from the railroad track where hobos hopped the trains. The man took one look at Reggie and offered him a drink of water from his canteen.

The mob caught up with Reggie at the campsite in the hills of the Ouachita Mountains. The hobo couldn't stall them, and ultimately wished he hadn't even tried. The group had conveniently brought along a rope and lynched both men on the spot, unaccompanied by the sheriff, who was headed to the local hospital to get a bullet removed from his foot. So, there would be no official record of how or why Uncle Reggie met his death, nor the vagrant who made the mistake of offering him a drink of water.

"No, girl, you ain't got no IDEA," Winston said aloud from his reverie, though his daughter had left the room.

Chapter Fifteen

Memphis

*"Every single time you help somebody stand up,
you are helping humanity rise."*

~ Steve Maraboli (1975)
Renowned world-wide consultant.

On a warm June day, Annalee stood on a residential street in Memphis, looking at a white, two-story frame house with the number "204". She looked again at an address written on a piece of paper, then walked onto the porch and rang the doorbell. A young black girl holding a feather duster answered the door, spoke briefly with Annalee, then stepped away and closed the door. After a few minutes, Maggie stepped out onto the porch.

Annalee was astonished to see Maggie pregnant. "Oh, Maggie… I didn't know…" Slowly, Annalee started to comprehend the situation. "Oh my God, Maggie! I had no idea! I'm sorry. I probably shouldn't have come."

Equally surprised to see Annalee, of all people, Maggie asked, "How'd you find me? How'd you get here? What?"

"I asked your friend Linda for an address where I could write to you and tell you I hoped you were doin' okay. I think she felt sorry for me. And, of course, she'd never in a million years think I planned to come all this way."

"But what are you doin' here? How'd you get here?"

"Never mind how I got here. Maggie, I just had to talk to you."

"Annalee. I've thought about you, wonderin' how you're doin'. I'm really sorry 'bout Willis."

"I've been told you can't remember stuff, Maggie. I couldn't either, at first. But then I started rememberin'. Maggie, it was pretty awful. It's not somethin' you want to remember, but sometimes you got to do things whether you want to or not."

Maggie looked around. "Annalee, come sit in the back yard with me. We can talk in the swing back there and nobody will bother us."

"But ain't this your grandparents' place? Won't they wanna know what's goin' on?" Annalee asked.

"Is that the story my folks are tellin'? No, Annalee, this is a home for unwed mothers. Mama wouldn't dare send me to her parents and bring shame on our family. C'mon, let's go to the back yard."

Annalee held the big swing steady for Maggie, who slowly, clumsily lowered herself into it. When Annalee sat beside her, they started to rock the swing with their feet.

Annalee reached out to touch Maggie's belly. "May I?" Maggie nodded. "I just can't believe it, Maggie. How're you feelin'? Is it terrible? Oh God, of course it's terrible. Look how it happened. Oh shit, I'm so sorry!"

Maggie smiled at Annalee's awkwardness. "Don't worry about it. You know, at first, it WAS terrible. I mean, you know, thinkin' about how it happened and everything, even though I ain't clear on just exactly how it happened. And I was so sick at first, couldn't keep anything down. But then, after a while, I don't know, a calm just come over me, and this 'thing' started to feel like a part of me." She rubbed her belly tenderly.

"Do you remember anything from that night, Maggie?" Annalee asked.

"Yes," Maggie replied softly.

"Can you tell me what you remember?"

Maggie looked at her shoes, then at Annalee. "All of it."

Annalee was incredulous. "What! You remember it? You remember everything? But your parents said..."

"Well, my parents just don't want the shame of the whole town knowin' their teenage daughter is expectin', no matter how it happened. They don't want no trouble and just want it all to go away."

"THAT message sounds familiar. So, are you gonna keep it?"

Tears began to escape Maggie's eyes. "I want to, so bad. But they're gonna make me give it up for adoption. They just want me out of sight 'til the baby's born, then to hand my baby off to some stranger and go home like nothin' ever happened."

"Maggie... then why haven't you told them what happened? Why haven't you told anybody what you remember?"

"Oh, I have Annalee. I told my mama just as soon as I started rememberin'. But she told me to keep quiet and not to tell a soul, not even Daddy. She said it would only cause more trouble and more pain, and that they might even go to finish you off and come after me, too. When I first saw you on the porch, I thought maybe you were here to warn me or somethin'."

"Maggie, I came here to tell you that you gotta say what happened. They won't take my word for it. When I started rememberin', I almost went wild with grief and anger, and I made my daddy take me to the sheriff. But they don't wanna take a colored gal's word for it, not against white men."

"Surely you see why I can't go back now. I just can't shame my parents like that. But what about that white woman that helped us and called the ambulance?"

"Oh my God, I forgot about her 'til you just now mentioned it! But who was she? And why ain't she gone to the sheriff? Oh, Maggie, I came here thinkin' that if I told you everything I remember, maybe you'd start rememberin' too. But I see you're all too clear on what happened, livin' with a reminder that's gettin' bigger every day. Now I just don't know. I thought I knew what to do, but now I just don't know. Maybe I should go back and try to find that woman..."

Maggie got an idea. "Maybe there IS a way, Annalee. If you'll help me, maybe we can both get what we want."

"What do you mean?"

"Annalee, I want you to help me keep my baby."

"Oh, lord. You don't know what you're sayin'. You can't keep a baby. You know that. And besides, you don't even know who..."

Maggie cut her off. "You're right, I don't know who fathered this child. But I know one thing for certain. This pure, innocent child growin' inside me didn't have nothin' to do with the evil thing that happened to us. Annalee, I gotta hold onto the ONLY right thing that happened that night, don't you see?"

Annalee took a deep breath. "How in the world could we..."

"Annalee, help me. Please? Help me keep this baby and we'll go back and get those bastards together."

Annalee sighed in resignation. "Okay, I'll help you. But you and I ain't had a good past together, and if we start this, we gotta stick together. Do you think you can trust me?"

"I guess I could ask you the same thing. We gotta trust EACH OTHER now."

Annalee smiled mischievously. "How hard would it be for you to pack a few things and sneak outta this place after dark?"

"Hester, the guardian, is asleep by 10:00. I can meet you in the alley. I'll be the one with a big round tummy, slidin' down the drain pipe."

"Once we start this, you gotta go through with it, ya know. There can't be no backin' out when the goin' gets rough."

"Annalee, if you help me save my baby, I'll stand by your side, no matter what. Mostly, I want to keep my baby, but I want justice, too, for what they done to us and to Willis. It just ain't right."

Later that night, Annalee paced nervously in the alley, looking all around and waiting for Maggie. She heard a window opening and quickly ran to help Maggie, who slid awkwardly down the downspout with a small bag in her hand. The girls tumbled together on the ground.

"Maggie, you okay? At least I broke your fall a little," Annalee giggled.

"Yeah, I'm okay. Thanks! You broke my fall, alright. Did I break anything of yours?"

"Nah, I'm fine. Now, let's get the hell outta here!"

"I'm all for that, but I can't run very fast or very far, ya know."

"Won't have to. I got transportation waitin' for us round the corner."

The girls quickly ran down the alley and around the next corner, where Michael Thorpe's pick-up sat idling beside the curb.

Maggie squealed. "Holy shit, Annalee, that looks like Michael's truck! Don't tell me you brung Michael's truck over here?"

"SHHHH! What you wanna do, stir up the whole neighborhood? Just you hop in and don't stop to ask no questions!"

The girls jumped in through the passenger side and the pick-up roared off down the street. Michael was at the wheel, and Maggie, recognizing the driver, screamed with delight. She hugged her brother as he tried to steer.

"Maggie! Geez, Sis, don't make me have a wreck," Michael teased. "God, it's great to see you, Mags. They must be feedin' you good at that place; looks like you gained some weight."

"Very funny. Annalee musta told you, cause I know Mama and Daddy ain't braggin me up back home."

Michael turned more serious. "Yeah. Annalee told me. Oh, God, I'm so sorry, Sis. Ain't bad enough what happened, but now you gotta go through this, too. All the more reason to get those bastards."

Annalee sat quietly for a few minutes, watching their reunion, but was eager to share her plan. "Maggie, Michael and I been talkin' and he's willin' to help us hang those sonsovbitches any way he can."

Michael nodded his head. "Nail their balls to a cross in their own front yard, and set THAT afire!"

Maggie asked, "I take it by this surprise visit that Mama and Daddy don't know nothin' about any of this, right?"

"No, course not," Michael answered. "Sis, you didn't deserve what happened to you. And, you sure as hell didn't deserve to be treated like somethin' to be ashamed of. If they can't see that, well, we just don't have to toe the line the way they'd want us to. Annalee told me what you want to do. You got a right to keep that child."

Maggie turned to Annalee and said proudly, "This is my big brother. Since you lost a brave big brother, we can share this one."

"Well, he's a little pale, but I guess he'll have to do," Annalee teased.

Chapter Sixteen

Secret Revealed

"I do not care so much what I am to others as I care what I am to myself.

~ Michel de Montaigne (1533-1592)
A significant philosopher of the French Renaissance.

Eddie paced his kitchen floor while Irene talked on the telephone. Agent James Langford was seated at the kitchen table, drinking coffee and watching Irene.

Irene said worriedly into the phone, "Well, I don't understand how she could just disappear like that. Are you sure she isn't in another girl's room, or gone out for ice cream with somebody or somethin'?"

Eddie yelled to Irene, "Ask 'em if they checked all the bathrooms? That place has three bathrooms, for Christ sake!"

"Yes, and my husband wants to know if all the bathrooms were checked? Are you sure? Well, yes, of course, we want you to wake up the other girls and ask them if they know anything—for goodness sake, why didn't you do that already? Okay, okay. Just call us back just as soon as you've talked to everyone." She hung up the phone and started another pot of coffee.

Agent Langford shook his head wearily. "I wish you folks would have told me where Maggie was from the start. I could have had somebody in Memphis watching out for her. Can't undo what's done, so let's think this thing through carefully. Now, either Maggie has left this place on her own, or somebody has taken her out of there. So, who else knows where she is?"

Eddie seemed distracted as he angrily snapped, "Nobody, not even our Michael. We just didn't want anybody to know about what kinda condition she's in."

"Well, you say that Maggie wants to keep the baby. Is there anyone else, maybe a minister or a friend, that she might contact to help her run away?"

Irene suddenly shouted, "LINDA! Remember, I gave Linda Franklin the address and told her it was my parents' place. She kept hounding me that she missed Maggie so much and wanted to at least write to her."

"Okay, I'll go over and talk to Linda," Langford replied. "Meanwhile, wake up your son and see if he knows anything."

"Michael ain't here. He went huntin' with some buddies and won't be back 'til Sunday," Eddie said sharply.

Langford began to get a little suspicious. "Are you sure he went hunting? Is there anyone we could check with to verify that?"

Irene said defensively, "But we already told you, Michael doesn't even know where Maggie is. There's no way he could get her out of there."

"Unless he got the address from Linda," Langford replied, standing to leave. "Well, let's hope someone less friendly didn't get it. Okay, Mrs. Thorpe, you stay here to answer the phone. Eddie, you go check with one of Michael's friends. I'll go talk to the Franklins. We'll meet back here in an hour, and if we don't have anything else to go on, then I'll call for some men to go after the Harpers."

Eddie seemed about to blow a gasket. "Aw, hell, why don't you just TELL him, Irene? Go ahead and tell the man what you think you know!"

Irene shot Eddie an angry look. "You still won't believe it, will you? You just can't accept that colored gal's story is the true one, can you?"

Langford sat back down, feeling a bit bewildered. "Excuse me? Will somebody please enlighten me here?"

"I'll let my wife tell you the same story she told me just before you got here," Eddie replied heatedly.

Irene began evenly, staring at Eddie, not Langford. "It's true, Eddie, if you wanna believe it or not." To Langford, she said, "What Annalee told you is the same thing that Maggie told me."

"Whoa, wait just a dog-goned MINUTE," Langford said. "I thought you said that Maggie couldn't remember what happened?"

"She remembers it all. She told me not long afterward, the same thing that Annalee's sayin'. It was the Beaufords and the Harpers and some of their cronies."

Langford couldn't believe his ears. "Mrs. Thorpe, if what you're telling me is true, then why didn't you say something before?"

Irene spoke haltingly, on the verge of tears. "Don't you think it's been eatin' me up, Mr. Langford? Specially, seein' those Harpers struttin' all over town like nothin' happened? It's made me sick to my stomach just to see 'em drive by. But I did it for Maggie. Don't you see that I was protectin' my little girl? What do you think this kind of thing would stir up? And, 'course she'd have to come back and face 'em. How could I ask her to do that?"

"With all due respect, Mrs. Thorpe, how could you NOT? Brutal, awful crimes were committed against your daughter and the Roberts family. How can you not want the animals that did it punished?"

Irene held her head down, then looked Langford squarely in the eye. "I ain't proud of this, Mr. Langford, but I didn't want the shame on us, either. Or on Maggie. Surely you can understand that? And besides, I knew Eddie wouldn't accept it. He just can't believe that it was white men that did this, no matter how that reflects on Maggie."

Eddie piped up, "I don't know WHAT to believe. Seems to me folks been lyin' left and right about this whole thing. Now it's come to this and we gotta fight our neighbors. But it's by God OUR fight now. Why didn't Maggie say anything to me in all this time, anyhow?"

"Because I told her not to, Eddie," Irene replied. "I knew you'd have trouble accepting it, and I didn't want her to think we didn't believe her. She was banged up so bad, then sick for so long. I thought we'd get through this somehow, she'd give the baby up and come back home, and we could all just get on with our lives."

Langford stood again. "Well, this puts a whole different light on things, folks. We've got to file charges against the Harpers and, now that Maggie's missing, it's even more urgent that we track them down."

"That's why it's time I brought it out now," Irene said tearfully. "If Maggie's in any kind of danger, I'll never forgive myself for tryin' to sweep everything under the rug."

As he approached the back door, Langford said reassuringly, "We'll find her, Ma'am. Meanwhile, I'm going to call in some help and pay the Harpers a little visit. I'll be in touch as soon as I can. You folks just sit tight and... well, just help each other through this the best you can."

"Agent Langford?" Irene said. "There's one more thing. Maggie said a white woman helped them after they'd been dumped in a barn. She doesn't know who it was or where they were, but that woman took them somewhere along the road and said she'd call an ambulance. Maggie said if it hadn't been for her..."

"Well, that's another lead to follow, isn't it? Wonder why the Roberts girl didn't mention that? You folks hang tough and I'll get back to you as soon as I can."

Chapter Seventeen

It Don't Take Brave

"Freedom is never given; it is won."

~ A. Philip Randolph (1889-1979)
Leader in the Civil Rights Movement, the American labor movement, and socialist political parties.

Michael's old pick-up drove slowly through a seedy part of Memphis. Up ahead, a dingy motel's neon sign flashed "vacancy." Michael turned in the motel's parking lot. Maggie was asleep with her head on Michael's shoulder. Annalee, barely awake herself, opened her eyes fully when Michael stopped.

Michael gently shook Maggie, then said to both girls, "Okay, now just let me do the talkin'. Anybody asks you anything, Maggie and I are a young couple travelin' to her folks' place with her colored maid. Sorry, Annalee, but we gotta make them believe us."

"Then you better tell 'em that I'm a midwife, cause you sure as hell can't afford no maid, drivin' this piece o' junk."

Michael smirked at Annalee. "Do you ALWAYS have to be right, Annalee Roberts? Okay, whatever you say. Hopefully nobody'll even see you two."

Maggie yawned. "All right, now, stop arguin'. I just wanna lay down and sleep for days."

Michael got out of the truck and walked to the motel office. In a few minutes, he returned to the truck. "So far, so good, no questions asked," he reported.

The girls gathered their belongings and followed Michael. He opened the motel room door and flipped the switch just inside. A dim light came on, provided by the lamp on a small table between two rumpled double beds covered with threadbare chenille bedspreads. There was no other furniture in the small room. Maggie entered the room and collapsed on the bed farthest from the door. Annalee moved into the room slowly, a little unsure of herself. Michael closed and latched the door, then stepped around Annalee to put Maggie's bag at the foot of her bed.

"Sit down, Annalee, on the bed there, if you want," Michael said. "Or if you need to use the bathroom... well, I guess we only got one of those... that's okay, you go ahead and use it if you want to, and I'll go on out back"

Obviously feeling quite nervous and uncomfortable, Annalee whispered, "Maggie, do you need to go to the bathroom? Maggie, you wanna use the bathroom?"

Michael looked at his sister on the bed. "I think she's out cold, Annalee. You go ahead and she'll use it later on when she wakes up."

Annalee hesitated. "No… I'll be alright."

Michael finally understood why she hesitated. "Annalee, it's okay, you're with friends."

Embarrassed, Annalee replied, "No, it ain't okay. I ain't never been in a motel before, and I've never used a toilet that white folks use, 'cept at school. I can't use that room before Maggie does." She looked down at the floor, then continued, "I just can't do it."

Michael awkwardly tried to make a joke to ease Annalee's discomfort. "Well, I guess it ain't true what I heard about you. I heard you was one of those 'uppity' coloreds."

By now, Annalee was almost in tears. "If you're tryin' to be funny, there ain't a thing funny 'bout the way I feel right now."

"Oh, I'm sorry," Michael replied. "I was just tryin' to make you feel better, and it was a stupid joke, and now I've made you feel worse. I'm truly sorry."

"It's okay," Annalee said. "Maggie told me one time that I got my feelin's stuck out all over me, and I guess that may be true. Sometimes, I just don't know how to feel or who to hate."

"Well, don't hate me," Michael said. "I don't hate you, never have. As a matter of fact, I have an awful lot of regard for you, seein' what you been through and how strong you been. Truth be told, I liked you from the first minute I saw you, Annalee." Michael blushed before continuing, "An' as long as I'm bein' honest, I even had a small crush on you when I was little."

Annalee chuckled. "Willis always liked you, Michael. I remember that. He used to say that you was one of the good ones. I had my doubts when you come barrellin' into our neighborhood on your bike when you were little, but I've since changed my opinion."

"I liked Willis, too. Fact is, I'd almost say we coulda been friends, except I ain't sure how, things bein' what they are. I guess that just proves it takes somebody braver than me to stand up against it."

"No, it don't take brave. It just takes doin'. Most of the colored folks I know that got their heads bashed in or their houses burned, they weren't brave. They just wanted a close-by drink of water or a nearby seat in a café."

"I wish it WAS that simple, Annalee. But it's a lot more complicated for us white…"

Annalee interrupted him. "You're NOT gonna tell me how hard it is bein' white, now are you?"

"No, no, that's not what I meant. It's second-nature for most whites, drilled into 'em since birth. It's just, well, it's just hard to buck hundreds of years of people thinkin' a certain way."

"Yeah? Well, you oughtta try it from this side."

"I know, I know. But ain't it changin' some, though? Ain't there a little progress, with Dr. King and Bobby Kennedy and all?"

"Some folks say it was the KKK that killed the president, ya know. But it ain't white folks that's gonna make a difference, anyhow. It's us, ourselves—my own people—standin', and standin' again, over and over, and comin' back no matter how many bashed heads or lynchin's it takes. We gotta be willin' to die for it. That's somethin' you can't be white and understand."

Maggie raised up on her elbow from the bed. "She's right, Michael. I never understood it 'til they almost killed me, like I was no more important than a bug under their shoe. It's gonna take coloreds standin' up, all right, but it's gonna take whites, too, cause right now, coloreds got no voice."

Annalee smiled at Maggie. "How you feelin? We thought you would sleep the night through. You need to use the bathroom?"

"Yes, but I ain't movin' from this bed 'til after you've used it. So, you'd best get in there cause I don't know how long this bladder's gonna hold out."

Annalee stepped cautiously, making her way to the bathroom, shaking her head at Maggie as she passed her. Maggie and Michael exchanged a look, then Michael headed out the door.

Chapter Eighteen

Just Desserts

"Hell is empty, and all the devils are here."

~ William Shakespeare (1564-1616)
English poet, playwright and actor.

In a clearing in the woods near the Ouachita foothills, an informal meeting of some local Klan members was taking place around a fire pit. No robes or hoods this time, just a bunch of good old boys, drinking, laughing, spitting and swearing.

Leland Harper belched loudly, cleared his throat, and then began to pontificate. "Tell ya what I think, fellas. I think that little white trash gal's too damned scared to show up in these parts again." He took a long pull on his beer. "Tell ya what else. She does come back, it's either me or my boy she's wantin' more of!" He slapped his knee and laughed along with his buddies.

Deputy Jimmy Moore spoke up. "Too bad ol' Joey Beauford didn't kill them gals while he was shootin' that night. Then you wouldn't have nothin' to worry about."

Roy Johnson added, "Musta thought they WAS dead, or he'd of killed that nigger gal for sure, if he killed his old man just for screwin' her."

Leland laughed. The sound was sinister. "Lordy, I'll never forget the look on ol' Jack's face when he realized he was chokin' on his own blood, all for havin' a little poontang like he'd done a hundred times before."

Moore spat into the fire. "Ol' Jack's mistake that night was bringin' his snot-nosed kid along."

Leland sneered disdainfully, "Aw, that kid always was a sissy, ya ask me. Killed his own daddy for his mama's honor, of all the damned things. If Jack'd broke him in on poontang like I did my Billy, his mama's honor woulda been the farthest thing from his mind." He laughed, then added more seriously, "Course my Billy never had no mama. Even if she HAD stuck around, there wouldn'ta been no HONOR to need protectin'."

"Well, I don't think you got nothin' to worry 'bout, Leland," Moore said. "Davis told me ain't a chance in hell they'd force him to file charges on just that nigger gal's story. An' if she keeps flapping her yap, then we'll just hafta give her a second smile like we did that brother o' hers."

"Speakin' o' Davis," Leland began, "how 'bout his old lady? Musta been her that put those kids out to be found. But Davis said that nigger gal didn't mention her, so she musta done it all sly like. Or else Davis did somethin' to her and is just coverin' his own ass. Either way, don't think she's a problem."

Buck Dudley didn't share his optimism and asked worriedly, "What about that Thorpe gal? Supposin' she does show up talkin'?"

Leland's dark side showed in his response, "Takes a tongue to talk. That gal comes back, she's apt to lose hers."

The men started to stretch and yawn. One of them pissed on the fire.

"Damn, I wish that was all beer did to me," Leland joked. "I gotta go out to the crapper, boys. Go on ahead an' I'll put out the fire when I get back. See ya in town tomorrow."

The others mumbled good-byes and headed for their cars, as Leland stumbled through the trees toward the outhouse. He didn't realize he had been watched for hours. Just as he stepped back out, zipping up and buckling his belt, a hooded figure in a robe stepped silently in front of him.

Leland stumbled back, startled, and caught his breath. "Shit, brother, you damn near give me a heart attack! Uh, there wasn't no official meetin' tonite. Just a few of us talkin' over some stuff. Jackson, that you?"

Suddenly the robed figure raised its arm and plunged a blade into Leland's chest, twisting the knife before pushing him backward off the weapon. As Leland lay gasping his last breaths in the dirt, the hood was lifted, and spittle shot into his face.

The knife rose again, only this time, it was aimed lower. Leland emitted a visceral, high-pitched squeal as he felt the first excruciating tugs of castration before losing consciousness.

Chapter Nineteen

Miss Salina and New Life

"When everything is lost, and all seems darkness, then comes the new life and all that is needed."

~ Joseph Campbell (1904-1987)
American Professor of Literature at Sarah Lawrence College in comparative mythology and comparative religion.

Michael's pick-up traveled south along Highway 78 heading into Mississippi, carrying three frightened but determined teenagers.

Maggie said to Annalee, "I ain't so sure about this. Mississippi ain't the safest place for two whites and a colored to be travelin' together, is it?"

"Well, it ain't far and it's the only way I know to get you help for that baby," Annalee replied. "My mama told me when she lay dyin' from TB that if I ever needed any kinda female help, I was to head to Miss Salina, who practically raised Mama. I only been there once or twice a long time ago. I just hope she ain't near no sundown town."

"What's a sundown town?" Maggie asked.

"Lordy, I keep forgettin' just how dang white you two are," Annalee smiled. There's places got signs posted that say, 'whites only' after dark."

Michael remarked, "Holy shit, you serious? Let me get this straight. We're two whites and a colored teenager, travelin' in Mississippi to see an old Choctaw medicine woman who's practicin' her voodoo in the north of the state cause she got kicked off the reservation down south? Naw, guess that don't sound too dangerous at all."

Maggie and Annalee exchanged bemused looks.

Annalee chuckled. "Any time you wanna pull over and let us go on without you, white boy, you just say the word."

"Oh, I'm sure he'd rather face whatever's up ahead than go home and face Mama and Daddy right about now," Maggie answered.

"Now that's for damned sure!" Michael chimed in.

Not too much later the trio passed a roadside sign proclaiming, "WELCOME TO HERNANDO: COUNTY SEAT OF DESOTO COUNTY."

Annalee said excitedly, "There sure ain't much marked around here, but it ain't far, cause I know it's near that town. Turn down this dirt road here, Michael. I got a feelin'."

"Oh great, now we're goin' on female intuition?" Michael replied.

They drove slowly, as they moved under low-hanging willow branches, getting farther away from town on the rough dirt road as they went.

Suddenly, Annalee shouted, "THERE IT IS! That's Miss Salina's house all right. It's older and more run down, but I know that's it."

Michael rolled the truck to a stop in the dirt beside the house. Seated on the sagging front porch was an old Choctaw woman doing handwork. She raised her head when the truck stopped. She looked blankly into the distance, reaching for a cane propped against her chair.

"Who comes to see an old woman on this fine evening?"

Annalee slowly approached. "Miss Salina, it's me, Annalee—Ruby's daughter."

Salina dropped her yarn and clapped her hands together. "Annalee! My goodness, child, I haven't seen you since you were small. Come closer, my dear. These old eyes can no longer see very well. You must come close and let me feel your face." She reached out her hands.

Annalee slowly kneeled before the old woman, then gently placed Salina's hands on her face.

"But you are crying, little one," Salina said. "Surely they are tears of joy for this reunion and not pity for an old woman going blind. Oh my. Yes, yes, you have your mother's fine beauty, may the Great Spirit rest her precious soul. And how is it with YOUR soul, dear one?"

"Miss Salina, I'm here with two—uh, two friends of mine—Maggie Thorpe and her brother, Michael, from over in Arkansas. We come to ask for your help. Mama said if I ever needed female help of any kind, that I should come to you."

"This sounds serious," Salina said thoughtfully. "You are in the right place. Shall we go inside and have a little 'pow-wow'?" She chuckled at her own little joke, then added, "Young man, why don't you pull your vehicle around back."

Inside the small, low-ceilinged house, Salina walked over to a potbellied stove where a kettle simmered. Going by touch, she pulled cups from a shelf, opened a jar and scooped loose tea, then added water to each cup. Annalee sat on the edge of a cane rocker, while Michael and Maggie looked around the room in wonder. There were stacks of books everywhere, as well as rocks, bones, and other various artifacts strewn throughout the small room. Feathers, beads and stones hung on leather strands and in clumps from various places on the ceiling. One wall held a medicine wheel above a bookshelf holding bottles and jars filled with unknown substances.

Turning from the stove, Salina said, "So you find my artifacts of interest, do you?"

Michael and Maggie looked over at Annalee in amazement. She smiled knowingly.

"You'll have to excuse my friends' curiosity, Miss Salina. They're just plain old white folks that ain't never been around spiritual people."

Salina settled on the small sofa. "Annalee, while our tea is steeping, you must tell me how it is with your father and Willis before we begin."

Annalee said softly, "Daddy's doin' just fine, went to night school and got his high school diploma an' he's real proud of that."

Salina smiled. "And your brother?" she asked.

Annalee sighed and collected herself. "Willis was... was killed by some mean whites, Miss Salina. Same ones beat me and Maggie to an inch of our lives." She added more quietly, "Took advantage of us, too."

"Oh, my dear child," Salina said sadly as she took in the news. "And my beloved Willis. When will this evil end?" She placed her hands in a prayerful posture in front of her face, then continued. "Oh, Great Spirit who has reunited Ruby and her boy, Willis, give them peace forevermore. And bring peace also to the warring tribes of men on earth."

Salina spoke directly to Annalee. "Why have you come to old Salina, dear one?"

"It's Maggie, Miss Salina. She's goin' to have a baby any day now, and her people don't want her to keep it."

"When was this child conceived?" Salina asked.

Maggie spoke hesitatingly, "On the night of... When we was..."

Michael jumped in. "My sister was raped by evil men, Miss Salina. The ones that killed Willis and beat these two girls half to death."

"I see." Salina remained quiet for a while, then continued. "We must bring this child into the world as the single light that shines from that dark night."

"Oh, thank you!" Maggie said joyfully. "That's how I feel about this baby. That's what I told Annalee. This innocent child I'm carryin' is the only thing right about so much wrong."

Salina continued solemnly. "But then, you must take the child home to your people, so that they, too, will have reason to rejoice and put the pain behind them. You must promise me this, if I am to help you."

"But my folks don't want the child, ma'am," Maggie explained. "They want me to give it up for adoption. It won't make them happy, only mad and ashamed if I take it back home."

"Ah, but new life has a way of easing old pains, my child. You must allow your mother and father to see and hold their grandchild. It is a sacred blessing that you cannot deny them."

Salina stood and reached for some of the feathers and beads, then moved around the room and gathered some leather strips. She walked to Maggie and gently stroked her face, then pulled a couple strands of her hair and placed them with the other items on the low table in front of the sofa. She picked up the feathers, Maggie's hair, and some of the beads and leather, and began to weave it all together into a talisman.

"Maggie—is your given name Margaret?"

"Yes, ma'am."

"Then I will call you Margaret. Take this talisman and hold it close to your heart. When the pains begin, hold it against your stomach."

Salina stood and shuffled around the little stove, eyes closed, chanting something in her native tongue.

Michael whispered to Annalee, "How can she tell where she's goin'?"

"She just feels it, I guess," Annalee replied.

Suddenly Salina stopped her dance. Maggie let out a scream, then reached for the sofa.

Salina called out instructions. "The spirits have heard; it is time. Margaret, close your eyes and thank your God for this child. Hold the talisman close. Annalee, bring some towels and a pail of water from the kitchen. Michael, carry your sister to my bed." She pointed to a doorway in the corner, "That way."

The bedroom housed only a bed and a small table beside it with a hurricane lantern atop. Salina struck a match and lit the lamp. Maggie lay on the bed, moaning, groaning and sweating, as the contractions came closer and closer. Annalee sat on the side of the bed and placed a wet cloth on Maggie's forehead. Michael paced the small space at the foot of the bed.

Salina said to Michael, "Young man, you must go in the other room and make sure the fire doesn't die. If you need more wood than what's in the box, it is stacked on the back porch. Please go now—this is surely women's business. And remember—the fire must not die."

Michael nodded his head and left the room. Salina moved to the foot of the bed and began to remove the quilt. Michael moved closer to the fire, hoping to find comfort as Maggie's screams became louder and more frequent.

Salina spoke to Maggie in a calm, reassuring voice. "Now Margaret, it is time for me to check on this little papoose. To do that, I must examine you, which you may find unpleasant. But you have already proven that you are a strong, brave girl." She began to chant softly as she continued the examination.

"Aw, God, here comes another one!" Maggie yelled. "Please, Miss Salina," she pleaded through clenched teeth, "can't you do somethin' to make the pain stop?"

"No. You must endure the pain, Margaret. But soon, it will be replaced by joy, I promise you."

After another piercing scream, Annalee asked, "Is she alright, Miss Salina? Is it supposed to be like this?"

"Oh, in fact it can often be much worse. But the spirits are helping, and all shall be well."

Maggie grunted, panted, and screamed as Salina peered between her legs. "It is crowning! Margaret, I am touching your little one's head! Just a few more pushes now!"

Maggie pushed and squealed in agony.

Salina shouted, "Here it comes, Margaret. Your baby is almost out!" Then, with sudden alarm, she added "No, NO!"

Maggie gasped, "What is it? What's wrong?"

"The cord is around the neck," Salina replied. She shouted into the other room, "MICHAEL, DO NOT LET THE FIRE GO OUT!"

Michael had been looking around the room at Salina's mysterious belongings, and had forgotten her caution about stoking the fire. He rushed over to the stove, quickly stirred the fire and added more wood. At first it smoked and appeared to be dying out. Then the flame caught, and the logs began to burn brightly.

"It's OKAY! I'm sorry, it almost went out, but it's OKAY now."

Annalee was beside herself with worry. "The fire's goin' again—is it all right? Is everything all right?"

Salina had at last freed the baby from the cord. "Yes. All is well. Miss Margaret, you have yourself a fine baby boy!" She slapped the baby's bottom and he let out a newborn's indignant cry. Salina smiled and swaddled the infant.

"Annalee, come take this baby to his mama while I clean up the mess he made coming into this world," Salina said with obvious relief.

Annalee carried the tightly wound bundle to the head of the bed, then laid the baby beside Maggie, next to the light. Maggie pulled the blanket back for her first look at her son. She stared wide-eyed and looked up at Annalee in shock. Annalee bent down to look at the baby and her eyes widened in disbelief.

Salina remarked, "I've always felt the birth of a child is a miraculous thing, but I've never heard such quiet before at such a time as this. This young boy must be especially blessed."

Annalee stepped to the doorway. "Michael, I think you better come see our new nephew!"

Michael rushed into the room with a chuckle. "Annalee, you got so excited, you said come see OUR new nephew!" Then Michael looked at the baby. "Holy moly!"

Salina moved to the bedside. "And now it is my turn to greet this special child." She laid him on the bed, unwrapped the blanket, and began to move her hands over him, from head to toe.

Maggie asked tentatively, a little fearfully, "What do you 'see', Miss Salina?"

Salina responded admiringly, "I see a fine warrior, who is perfect from head to toe. But this little warrior has come from chaos to bring peace to the hearts of men."

Michael took Annalee's arm, "Let's you and me go in the other room so's Maggie can have a minute with Salina and the baby."

Once outside the bedroom, Michael stopped and turned a quizzical look on Annalee. "How can this be? Who? What really happened that night?"

Annalee was shaking. "Michael, the last thing those bastards did was put Willis on Maggie, while they stood by a hootin; and a hollerin'." Her voice quivered, as she added, "Then they slit his throat." She broke down in tears. Michael put his arm around Annalee's shoulder to comfort her.

"It's okay, Annalee. It's gonna be okay." He thought for a minute, then added, "Hey, you know what? You were right in there, we got ourselves a nephew." He slowly exhaled, "Willis' child. We've got Willis' child, Annalee."

"Yes, Willis' child," Annalee sighed. "But, how can we ever go home this way? How can Maggie take a little colored baby home to your mama and daddy?"

"I'll tell ya how. With her head held high and her brother by her side. Will the baby's aunt be joining us?"

"Of all the crazy white folks in the world, I've gone and got mixed up with two of the craziest! I don't see how you think this will work out, Michael, I surely don't."

Salina came to the doorway. "Michael, Annalee, come and say goodnight to Margaret and her child."

Michael and Annalee sat on either side of Maggie, as Salina stood at the foot of the bed. Maggie was propped up by pillows and the baby slept peacefully, wrapped in a blanket on her tummy.

Maggie stroked the baby's face. "Ain't he about the most beautiful baby boy since Jesus himself?"

Annalee smiled and said tearfully, "He looks like his daddy's baby pictures, Maggie."

Maggie reached out to take Annalee's hand. Michael put his hand on top of theirs.

"Whatcha gonna name our perfect little nephew, Sis?"

"I don't know. I hadn't thought of that. What should I name him? I never named anything before, not even pets. Salina, what should I do?"

Salina answered wisely, "It will be a while before he needs to be called. Let your inner spirits guide you. For now, you must rest."

Salina gently pulled the curtain that separated the two rooms of her tiny house. Michael lit a hurricane lamp on the table, casting eerie shadows of feathers and beads, rocks and humans that danced upon the walls. Annalee sat on the edge of the sofa, staring into the fire in the opened stove.

"Miss Salina, you heard us talkin' earlier, didn't you?" she asked.

Salina sat down in the cane rocker. "These old ears have grown stronger to make up for what I cannot see. I heard you."

"So, you know then that's Willis' child in there, even though he was conceived in the most awful of ways?"

"Annalee, we are blessed to have Willis' child among us, no matter the path he chose to get here."

"But don't you understand the terrible situation we're in?" Annalee asked. "We can't possibly take a little colored boy home to Maggie's folks. They're already shamed by what happened to her. And they're WHITE, Miss Salina! They'll NEVER accept a colored grandchild."

Michael sat beside Annalee on the sofa, staring at the hurricane lamp on the table, saying nothing.

Salina questioned Michael. "What have you to say about this, young man?"

"I don't know, ma'am. At first, I guess I was carried away by the moment. But maybe Annalee's right. I'd like to think I've got the courage to take that baby back home, but I realize there's more than Mama and Daddy to be afraid of."

Salina nodded her head, then said softly, "It has been said that courage is not being unafraid, but acting in spite of your fear."

Annalee spoke up. "You both know how things are. Ain't a chance in hell that baby could be raised by a white girl, no matter what her folks say about it. I think it would be best if I took the child home with me. Then me and my daddy could raise him, without too much trouble being stirred up. After all, he's got Willis' blood in him."

Salina said sharply, "So, you would rip the newborn babe from his mother's arms?"

"But he's Willis' child, too."

"And is Willis here to speak for him? No. The only parent that child has on this earth is Margaret. She must decide, and she alone."

"Annalee has a point, though," Michael said. "Folks of the same kind gotta stay with their kind, or all sorts'a trouble happens. Hell, in a way, that's what started all this."

"So, what would you do then, Michael? Split the baby down the middle? He is not colored, and he is not white; he is of mixed blood. How do you separate that into his 'kind'?"

"I don't know. I just don't know."

Annalee addressed Salina softly, "You have lived away from your own people for most of your life, Miss Salina. Why? And how is it with YOUR soul?"

Salina packed a pipe, lit it and took a deep draw, then exhaled before she spoke. "There is a town near here named after a man that slaughtered my ancestors. He killed Choctaw and Chickasaw and many others, and confiscated their lands. There was much bloodshed and sorrow. For many generations, my people carried that wound. Sadly, they were eventually forced to live on a reservation down south, herded together like cattle. I chose to leave there and live here among others of mixed blood."

Salina paused, considered, puffed on her pipe, and continued. "In my lifetime, I have learned other ways, but I have also kept my Choctaw ways. And I have learned forgiveness. If we all live where everyone is like us, we will learn nothing. But if we stop and listen to one another's stories, one day we will all be as blind as this old woman to the color of skin."

Michael looked appreciatively at Salina. "I wish we had days on end to listen to YOUR stories, Miss Salina. But after Maggie gets some sleep, I guess we'd best be heading home."

Annalee stood up, "Meanwhile, I'll make some tea, if you're of a mind to tell us just a few of those stories, Miss Salina?"

Salina thought for a moment. Feeling her way, she picked a flower from the miniature white rose plant in a pot on her table. She handed the bloom to Annalee.

"This was a gift from my German neighbor. I will tell you the story of the White Rose Society. You will see why it has become a symbol of nonviolent resistance to tyranny. The same kind of non-violent resistance preached now by your Dr. King."

"It began with a group of students and a professor at the University of Munich, during the second World War. They printed leaflets defying Hitler's regime and distributed them throughout Munich and beyond. They were but one of many resistance groups working underground throughout Europe. Brothers and sisters, husbands and wives, and students full of youthful idealism gave their lives. All in the hope of ending the Nazi stranglehold on Europe and the mass murder of the Jewish people."

Michael and Annalee were enthralled. "Did any of them survive?" Annalee asked.

"Some did, but not those who began the movement. They sacrificed all."

"I'm beginning to think that's the kind of sacrifice it will take before my people are free and equal," Annalee said solemnly.

"Yours is a different struggle," Salina replied. "But any kind of oppression is a form of shackles. May your struggle not consume your life, my dear."

Chapter Twenty

Fire, Fear and Hospitality

"Nothing is black or white."

~ Nelson Mandela (1918-2013)
South African anti-apartheid revolutionary, political leader, and philanthropist.

James Langford stood in the middle of a residential street, hands on hips, watching a raging fire consume Leland Harper's house. Firemen worked to put out the fire, without much success. A few yards away from Langford, Sheriff Davis stood talking with firemen. He turned when he spied Langford.

"Couldn't serve any warrants for you tonight, even if I wanted to," Davis said to Langford.

"And you wouldn't have any idea how this fire got started either, would you, sheriff?"

"There you go again, Mister FBI," Davis replied, "just assumin' everybody down here is a good ol' boy and we're all in cahoots. Tell you the truth, I never had much use for those Harpers anyhow. Shame about that boy, though. Whoever tied him to that chair must have intended to roast him alive, but the smoke got him first."

Langford turned to see Eddie and Irene Thorpe running up the street toward him. He blocked their way to keep them from getting too close to the conflagration.

Eddie said breathlessly, "We came because we heard all the commotion. That's Harper's house, ain't it?"

Langford replied rather matter-of-factly, "Yeah, it's Harper's alright. By the time we got over here with warrants, this is what we found."

Irene was visibly distraught. She drew a breath and asked, "Did anyone… Was there anyone inside?"

"Yes, Mrs. Thorpe. One of Maggie's tormenters won't bother her anymore. Billy Harper's body was found in the fire."

"Somehow, I can't feel good about that, Mr. Langford. He was just a boy."

Eddie asked, "What about his old man?"

"Nobody knows. Here comes the sheriff, maybe he knows somethin' else."

Sheriff Davis walked up to the group.

"So what d'ya think happened here?" Eddie asked shakily

"Can't say that I know, Mr. Thorpe," the sheriff replied. "Won't know nothin' until the fire's completely out and we can search for some kinda clues, I guess. Or if we find the boy's old man, if he knows somethin'. Meantime, y'all oughtta just go on home. Ain't nothin' else gonna happen tonite." Davis walked back toward the deputy and firemen.

Irene frantically grabbed Langford's lapel. "Where is our Maggie?"

"Now just calm down, Mrs. Thorpe. We don't know if one's got anything to do with the other or not. Didn't you say nobody but Linda Franklin knew where Maggie was?"

"Yes, as far as I know." A light bulb suddenly went on. "Oh no, Linda's back in Virginia right now. She goes to her aunt and uncle's place every summer. It's gotta be the wee hours back there."

"I think it's time we call up that girl," Eddie said, "the hour of the night be damned."

Langford agreed. "I think you're right. Come with me. We can take my car over to the Franklin place."

No one noticed the lone figure standing apart from the crowd of onlookers, staring transfixed at the fire and mumbling, hissing, "Spawn of evil, burn in hell! Spawn of evil, burn in hell!"

Langford knocked on the Franklins' door, as Eddie and Irene waited at the bottom step of the front porch. After a few minutes, the porch light came on. They heard muttering, along with the door latch being unlocked. Joe Franklin angrily opened the door then softened a little and smiled, as he noticed Eddie and Irene behind Langford.

Langford showed his badge. "Sorry to bother you, Mr. Franklin. But I'm afraid it's urgent that we call your daughter, Linda, right away. Can you give me the number?"

Franklin was obviously confused. "What d'ya need Linda for?" Fighting the fear rising in his heart, he looked at the anguished faces of the Thorpes. "Oh, it's somethin' bout Maggie, ain't it? Well, come inside and use our phone. All of you, come inside."

Eddie and Irene sat tensely on the sofa while Joe Franklin picked up the receiver on the phone and began to dial. Langford stood anxiously beside the table, waiting to be handed the phone.

Franklin said into the phone, "Wilma, it's Joe. YES, I KNOW what time it is! D'ya think I'd call if it wasn't pretty damned important?" Trying to cover his frustration, he said, "Now please wake up Linda. We need to talk to her right now. No, no, everybody's okay. Just get Linda to the phone please?"

Covering the mouthpiece, Franklin whispered to the others, "Damned sister-in-law can't think straight in the middle of the day, let alone middle of the night."

Back on the phone, Franklin spoke to his daughter. "Linda? Hi, honey. "I'm sorry to wake you up. I'm gonna hand the phone to Agent Langford of the FBI; he needs to ask you about somethin'. Just tell him what you know. It might help Maggie. Don't ask questions, we'll fill you in later."

Langford took the phone. "Linda, hi, I'm Agent Langford with the FBI. Okay, here's what I need to know: Has anyone, and I mean anyone at all, asked you for Maggie's address?

When? Did she say why? Okay, anybody else at all? Okay, then, for now that's all we need to know. Thanks, young lady, you can go back to sleep now." He hung up the phone and turned to the others.

"Let's go. Mr. Franklin, thank you. Oh, and please keep this on the QT for now."

Franklin assured them of his discretion. "Yessir, I will. Eddie, Irene...well, I just want to say I hope for the best for Maggie. We all do."

Eddie and Irene shook hands with Franklin and followed Langford out the door.

"Annalee Roberts got Maggie's address from Linda so she could write to her," Langford said, as he started the car.

Across town, Langford pulled to a stop in front of the Roberts house and turned to his passengers. "I'd ask you to come with me, but if there is anything going on here, Mr. Roberts might not be too hospitable. Better let me go by myself from here. If I want you, I'll come back for you."

Eddie was alarmed. "You mean, you want us to stay here in the car, in THIS neighborhood?"

"Just lock the doors, Mr. Thorpe," Langford sighed as he considered why he was even making this call. "I'm sure you'll be perfectly safe, and I won't be long."

"Well then, how 'bout leaving me your gun?" Eddie loudly whispered, as Langford left the car.

Langford turned and proceeded up to the Roberts house, pretending he didn't hear Eddie's last plea.

Winston Roberts peeked through the curtained window at the sound of Langford's knock. He looked alarmed when he saw the FBI agent and quickly opened the door.

"Come in, Agent Langford, come in. What is it? Oh, lord, don't tell me somethin' s happened to my baby?"

"Sorry to disturb you at this hour, Mr. Roberts, but we have a situation that I need your help with. I take it from what you just said that Annalee is not at home?"

"No, sir, I put her on the bus two days ago for N'Orleans. She's visitin' some old family friends."

"Are you SURE that's where she went? Did she say a word of anything about Memphis?"

"MEMPHIS? Why on earth would she go to Memphis? No, sir, I bought her a ticket for N'Orleans."

"And did you see her leave on that bus, sir?"

"What do you mean, 'did I see her leave'? I bought her a ticket, I kissed her goodbye, and I watched her get in line for that bus."

"But is it possible that she could have waited for you to leave and then gone back to the ticket counter and cashed in the ticket, or traded it in for Memphis?"

"Memphis again! Now, just what the hell is going on here, Agent?"

Langford sighed. "Mr. Roberts, Maggie Thorpe is in Memphis, or was, and Annalee got her address from Linda Franklin. Now Maggie is missing."

Winston suddenly remembered his conversation with Annalee when she wanted to contact Maggie. "Aw, no! That child done gone around behind my back and done what I told her not to do. And used my money to do it!"

"What do you mean, Mr. Roberts?"

"Annalee was awful upset when they wouldn't take her word for what happened to her and Miss Maggie. She kept sayin' if that Thorpe girl would just remember and back her up, they could get those bastards that wronged 'em. But I told her not to stir things up. I just tried to tell her to leave it alone and let it settle, cause she almost got killed before. I didn't want to lose the only child I got left, Mr. Langford."

"I understand, Mr. Roberts. Can you please give me the name and address of the friends in New Orleans? If we can't find the girls, we'll need to check there."

"I'll call 'em right now."

Winston Roberts quickly stepped to the telephone in the hallway and dialed a long-distance number. He spoke into the phone out of earshot of Langford, then returned. "Appears Annalee ain't there. She called an' told 'em she was sick and couldn't come."

"Okay, Mr. Roberts, I need you to think carefully. Is there anyone that Annalee might go to for help over that way?"

"But why would she need help? If she did go after Maggie, why wouldn't they just come back?" He added worriedly, "Unless somethin' happened to 'em on the road?"

"There's another complication, I'm afraid," Langford said. "Maggie is pregnant—from the attack. Her parents sent her to a place for unwed mothers in Memphis. She was supposed to give the baby over for adoption, but she wanted to keep the baby, and they're afraid that may be why she left the home. Would Annalee help her? Can you think of anywhere they might go?"

"Oh, Lordy, ain't that poor little gal done been through enough already, now this. Mm, mm, mm, don't hardly seem fair." Thinking for a moment, Winston said, "There's an old Choctaw woman over in Mississippi, not too far south from Memphis, that practically raised my wife. She's a crazy ol' medicine woman that practices some kinda voodoo or somethin', but my Ruby loved her dearly, and she took the kids over to see her when they was little, and kept in touch with her. Let me see if I can find her in Ruby's old address book."

Roberts left the room and returned with a small, worn spiral notebook. He flipped through it, looking up and down pages, then stopped with a puzzled look on his face.

"All I ever knew her by was Salina. Don't even know a last name. Looked all through here, but don't see her anywhere."

"Do you know a town, or even a street, anything at all?" Langford asked in desperation.

"All I remember is Ruby makin' some comment one time that Salina left the reservation. Said she went up to northern Mississippi somewheres and started over there, and I remember it ain't too far south of Memphis."

"If we looked at a map of Mississippi, would you know the town name if you saw it?"

"She don't live in a town, but near one. I heard it spoken once or twice. Seems like maybe she's near a little town named after somebody. I got an atlas on the bookshelf, let me get it."

Roberts opened the atlas to Mississippi and laid it flat on the coffee table. He and Langford started poring over it as the clock on the wall slowly ticked away.

"I don't know, Mr. Langford," Roberts said, "it's been so long... HERNANDO! That's it!" he said as he excitedly pointed to the map. "She's just a few miles from there."

Langford stood up. "Of course. It was named after Hernando DeSoto, the explorer. Thank you, Mr. Roberts. "I'll be in touch just as soon as I know anything."

"But can't I go with you? That's my little girl out there. Please, I want to be there when you find her."

"It's against the bureau's policy to have civilians along on out-of-town investigations, Mr. Roberts. I can't take you with me. But I do need to ask something of you."

"And what would that be?"

"Mr. and Mrs. Thorpe came over here with me from across town. They're outside in the car and it would sure save me time if I didn't have to take them home before I head out. I figure you're all parents of missing children and, well, you know what they say... 'misery loves company'."

Winston Roberts reached for his keys from a hook on the wall. "I will take them home Mr. Langford."

Langford held up his hand. "With all due respect, it might not be the time of night you want to be driving through a white neighborhood. I was wondering if maybe they could stay here for a while, and I'll call you just as soon as I know something. Come daylight, you could give them a ride home, if I'm not back."

Winston chuckled. "I doubt those folks wanna wait with me here, Mr. Langford. Why this is probably the first time they've been east of the beltline."

"That may be, but if I can actually convince them to stay here, would you be good enough to open your home to them?"

"Yessir, they are surely welcome, if they choose to wait here with me."

"Thank you. I'll go talk to the Thorpes."

Winston said solemnly, "Mr. Langford? What does it say when it ain't safe for me to drive through a white neighborhood at this hour, and yet you ain't the least bit worried about a white couple stayin' in colored town?"

Langford shook his head, thought for a moment, and then said, "I guess maybe it says that graciousness doesn't have a color, any more than meanness does, Mr. Roberts."

Langford stepped to the passenger door of his car and Eddie rolled down the window to talk to him.

"Folks, I have a good lead that the girls may be in Mississippi, and I'm pretty sure they're not in any harm. But it's official FBI business at this point, and I need to go on from here alone. It'll save me a lot of time if I don't have to take you back across town first."

Eddie looked puzzled. "So, what are you sayin'?

"I want you to stay here with Mr. Roberts until I contact you, or until daylight, when it'll be safe for him to drive you home. He's fine with it. I'll call you just as soon as I know something."

Eddie was incredulous. "You want US to stay HERE? In a COLORED MAN'S house? Are you CRAZY...or just plain ol' STUPID?"

"What I AM, Mr. Thorpe, is pressed for time. Now, Mr. Roberts is willing to let you stay here until daylight and then drive you home. Think about it. He's missing a child right now, too. And you'll be safe in his house, but would HE be the least bit safe driving you home in YOUR neighborhood this time of night?"

"Why, I never heard of such a thing! It ain't MY fault things are like that! And you can't expect..."

Irene calmly interrupted her husband. "Eddie, shut up. Just shut up and get out of the car. You're wasting precious time when Mr. Langford could be looking for Maggie. Besides, that man in there needs our support right now. We're not gonna insult him by turnin' down his hospitality."

Langford opened the car door. "Thanks, I appreciate your cooperation. I'll be in touch just as soon as I can."

Langford pulled quickly away, as Eddie and Irene watched his taillights disappear. They stood in the yard, looking around nervously, while dogs barked nearby.

"Shit, you can't even see your hand in front of your face," Eddie said indignantly. "Would it kill them to have some street lights round here?"

Irene put her arm through Eddie's. "Why don't you bring that up at the next city council meeting, Eddie? Right after you suggest pavin' the streets an' installin' sidewalks in this part of town?"

Eddie replied, only half-jokingly, "Ya know, Irene, you're gettin' to be kind of a smart-ass lately."

Winston Roberts met them at the front door. "Mr. and Mrs. Thorpe, I'm sure sorry that we meet again under bad circumstances. Please come in. I started a pot of coffee. The living room is just around this way. Y'all go in and have a seat and I'll bring the coffee."

"Thank you for your kindness, Mr. Roberts," Irene said sincerely, as she entered the house.

Eddie reluctantly followed Irene and acknowledged Winston. "Roberts. Uh, yeah, thanks."

Irene sat stiffly on the edge of the sofa. Eddie stood beside her, and looked nervously around the room. Winston entered with a tray of coffee and cups.

"I didn't know how y'all took it, but I'll get milk and sugar if ya want it."

Irene answered, "Black is fine, Mr. Roberts."

"Yeah, black for me, too," Eddie echoed.

Winston grinned at Eddie. "You can sit right down, Mr. Thorpe. Why, I had the whole place disinfected just yesterday."

Eddie looked at Winston with a frown and then at Irene, who was smiling into her coffee cup.

"Oh, you're jokin', ain't ya? Okay, okay, I get it. Poke fun at the white guy, huh? Alright, I may have asked for that." He seated himself on the sofa beside Irene.

Winston said apologetically, "Mr. Thorpe, I didn't mean no offense. Guess this is kinda awkward for us all."

They sat in uncomfortable silence, sipping their coffee, occasionally clearing their throats, as the night wore on.

Suddenly, the sound of the phone startled them. Winston jumped up to answer, while Eddie and Irene looked on anxiously.

Winston said into the phone. "Hello? Yessir. But why? You mean you ain't even... okay, okay. See ya shortly."

Eddie felt nervous as he stood beside Winston, almost afraid to ask, "Was that Langford? Does he know anything?"

"It was Langford all right. Said he got pulled over by the sheriff's deputy just outsida town cause of somethin' that happened. Said he's been with the sheriff the last couple hours and he's comin' over here to get you and fill us all in."

Irene came up beside them. "But what about the girls? Did he say anything about the girls?"

"No ma'am. Didn't say nothin' 'cept what I just told ya. He'll be here soon."

Langford replaced the receiver on the desk phone. He looked at Sheriff Davis, who sat in a nearby chair, looking a little rattled.

"You okay, Davis? You look a little pale."

"Yeah... Yeah, I'm okay. It's just that—well, I seen a lotta things done to coloreds and a few dead white bodies in this job, too. I just never seen a white man with his manhood stuffed in his mouth before."

"Well, we've got bigger problems than that, you know. Here we thought Leland Harper probably killed his kid. Would've been a little hard to do in his condition, don't you think?"

"That's the other thing. D'ya suppose whoever set that fire at the Harpers' house set the one in the woods too? Did they mean to burn Leland up and somebody just happened to see the smoke? Or have we got ourselves some kinda homicidal maniac on the loose or somethin'?"

"Or something, I think, is more like it. Tell me, Davis, you a married man?"

"Yeah, why?" Davis didn't like where this was going, and he racked his brain for a satisfactory story.

"Just wondered, didn't see a wedding band on your finger. You and the missus separated, or maybe you don't like jewelry?"

"Ain't really none of your business, and what's it got to do with anything anyhow?"

"Just curious. Wonderin' if you'll be free to chase this thing down with me if it runs into the wee hours. You live here in town?"

"Naw, I got a little farm outside o' town, but I can stay in one o' the cells if need be."

"Yeah, that might just be necessary, Sheriff. The Harpers were obviously targeted. We just need to figure out who would want them dead. Got any ideas?"

"Hell, Leland Harper rubbed everybody the wrong way, 'cept for Jack Beauford, and he's already dead. Now, the kid, I dunno 'bout him. And don't forget, FBI, there's two gals out there somewhere claimin' the Harpers messed 'em up."

"Don't suppose you'd know of anyone else that would want to keep the Harpers quiet for any reason, would you?"

"There you go again, FBI. What about you, you're the fed with all the *ex-per-tease*—you got any ideas on this?"

"None that I'm prepared to share just yet. Right now, I've got something I need to do. I'll be in touch with you tomorrow. Stay close here in case I need you before that."

Langford left the office and Davis stared after him. *How'm I ever gonna find Pansy before somebody else if I'm stuck here? Damn that woman, she'll be the death o' me yet!* He felt anger at his wife, but also an unexpected deep yearning. Despite their up and down marriage, Jonathan Davis knew he needed Pansy more now than ever. If only he could find her, talk to her, protect her.

Back at the Roberts home, Winston quickly opened the door to let Langford in. Eddie and Irene stood anxiously behind Winston in the hallway.

Langford held up his hands before he was hit with a barrage of questions. "I don't know anything new about the girls, but you might want to sit down for what I do have to tell you."

"You folks wanna go back to the livin' room and be more comfortable?" Winston asked.

"Just tell us what's goin' on," Eddie said angrily.

"Please, Mr. Langford," Irene added.

Langford took a deep breath and exhaled. "Leland Harper's body was found tonight in the woods. Another Klan meeting place, I figure. Anyhow, there was a fire; we're not sure whether it was set to cover up or if an earlier campfire just got out of hand."

"Was it the fire, or suicide, or did somebody kill him, or what?" Eddie said with a puzzled look on his face.

"He was definitely killed. Brutally so, as he was somewhat, uh, mutilated, too."

Winston asked, "Now just what d'ya mean by that, Mr. Langford?"

Langford looked at Irene. "Begging your pardon, ma'am, but this may be a little indelicate for you to hear."

"Mr. Langford, after the past several months, I think I can handle just about anything. Go ahead."

Langford nodded. "Leland Harper had been stabbed to death and castrated. We don't know in what order."

Winston and Eddie winced. Winston looked at the floor, shaking his head. Eddie glanced at Irene and was stunned to see a slight grin at the corners of her mouth.

Irene, half not wanting to know the answer, looked squarely at Langford. "Under the circumstances, Mr. Langford, do you suspect that Maggie and Annalee had anything to do with this?"

"Under the circumstances, Mrs. Thorpe, it certainly can't be ruled out. They may not be in any further danger from the Harpers, but it's just as urgent as before that we find your daughters. Maybe more so."

"So, what is your plan, sir?" Winston asked.

"Right now, I'm going to take Mr. and Mrs. Thorpe on home. Then I'm going to pick up another agent in Little Rock and head on over to Memphis and see what I can learn. Then on to Mississippi if need be."

"And I s'pose you can't take anybody along, just like before, right?"

"I'm afraid that's right, Mr. Roberts. But I promise to call you the minute I know anything. Mr. and Mrs. Thorpe, you ready to go home?"

"Damn right I am," Eddie said without thinking. "Uh, no offense, Roberts. Just anxious to get home."

"None taken, Mr. Thorpe. Know what you mean."

Irene shook Winston's hand. "Mr. Roberts, thank you for your kindness. Maybe we can repay... well, hopefully we can pay you ba..."

Winston interrupted to ease her discomfort. "Of course, Mrs. Thorpe, of course. Goodnight, now."

Chapter Twenty-One

First Homecoming

"Home is the place where, when you have to go there, they have to take you in."

~ Robert Frost (1874-1963)
American poet.

On the street, Langford, Eddie and Irene got into Langford's car and drove away. Just as they turned the corner, Michael's pick-up rolled slowly to a stop in front of the Roberts house.

Michael asked aloud, "Now what the hell d'ya think that was all about?" To Annalee, he said, "Who d'ya s'pose that was leavin' your house with our parents?"

"I'm guessin' that's the FBI man my daddy told me about. They probably been tryin' to figure out where we are. And they musta figured out that we're together, or least me and Maggie. They may not know your part in this yet."

Well, it won't be long 'til all the shit's gonna hit all the fans," Maggie said. "You sure your daddy's gonna want us here, Annalee?"

"Oh, he may growl at first, but my daddy's just a big ol' teddy bear. Besides, it's just for tonight. Tomorrow you two—excuse me, THREE—get to go face your own folks."

"We got here none too soon," Maggie said. "This baby's startin' to smell a little funny."

Michael laughed. "Oh great, I can just hear it now, 'Here's your new grandson, Mr. Roberts, and by the way, he just shit his diaper. Wanna hold him?'"

They exited the pick-up laughing. The laughter waned, the closer they got to the door. Annalee put her key in the lock, then took a deep breath and turned it. Winston Roberts came charging into the hallway with a gun, then stopped in his tracks when he saw Annalee.

Startled, Annalee flinched and yelled, "DADDY, DON'T SHOOT! IT'S ME! IT'S ANNALEE!"

"GOOD LORD, GIRL! You damned near got your head blowed off! Get on in here, child! Who's that you got with you?"

"It's Maggie Thorpe and her brother Michael. They need a place to stay tonight, Daddy."

"Annalee! Are you crazy? You know their folks and even the FBI's out lookin' for them? What you mean, bringin' those white kids here, girl?"

"Please, Daddy, we need your help. It's just for tonight and then they'll go on home. Please, Daddy, we're so tired."

Winston sighed. "Sure, sure, y'all come on in." He muttered to himself, "Don't have no white folks cross my threshold in all my life, damned if tonite somebody ain't opened the flood gates."

"We appreciate your kindness, sir," Michael said sheepishly as he entered the house.

"Yeah, yeah, your mama and daddy was just here, and they appreciated it, too. Looked like they was sittin' on a damn pin cushion almost the whole time." Spotting Maggie's baby, Winston said to Annalee, "What is THAT?"

Sit down, Daddy. Take a breath... I gotta tell you about your grandson."

"My WHAT?"

Later, Maggie lay in Annalee's bed, snuggled under a quilt, with the baby sleeping on a pillow between her and Annalee.

"Well, that went pretty well, all things considered," Annalee said. She chuckled softly. "I swear I thought Daddy turned pale there for a minute, if that's possible."

"Yeah, but did you see his face when he took the baby in his arms?" Maggie asked. "It was like all the mad just drained right outta him. He damn near melted and run down into his shoes."

"Ain't that SOMETHIN' 'bout the Harpers? I guess they got what they deserved, ya ask me. You feelin' scared about tomorrow, Maggie?"

"Yeah, but like Salina said, a child needs his people."

"Ya know, Maggie, me and my daddy are his people, too. I hope you'll let us be part of his life."

"Annalee, how can I look at this boy, and not see his colored people? Not just his skin, but the way he looks like his daddy did when he was a baby. Long as I got a say in it, you and your daddy will always be a part of my baby's life."

"D'ya think your mama and daddy will agree?"

"Don't matter. If they can't accept my baby or his colored people, then I'll leave again. That's how strong I feel about it."

"May not have no choice, Maggie," Annalee replied. "We may be kiddin' ourselves to think things can go that easy. After all, a colored bastard is considered about the lowest kinda human round these parts."

"Then doncha think it's 'bout time we changed that? This little baby can't stand up for hisself, Annalee. We gotta do the standin' for him."

Winston slipped over to their room and peeked in through the door, knocking gently.

"Come on in here, Daddy," Annalee said. "We ain't sleepin' yet, and I know you want one more look at your grandson before you go to bed."

Winston was apologetic, but tickled. "Don't mean to disturb you gals, but I just can't get over how much he looks like my Willis did when he was a baby. Yessir, I gotta have one more look before I close my eyes tonight." He turned to Maggie, "By the way, you never told me this child's name."

Maggie looked proudly at the baby, then at Winston. "His name is Willis, Mr. Roberts. Willis Emmett Thorpe."

Clearly touched, Winston let the words slip softly over his tongue as he slowly repeated the name. "Willis. Emmett. Thorpe. Yessir, that's a real fine name. For a fine boy, with a fine mama. Thank you, Miss Maggie. Thank you from the bottom of this ol' achin' heart."

CHAPTER TWENTY-TWO

Pansy

"It is never too late to be who you might have been."

~ George Elliot (1890-1919)
English novelist, poet, journalist, translator.

PANSY DAVIS STRUGGLED to sleep. She tossed the blanket off, then felt a chill. Finally, she got up and pulled on the robe that hung on the back of the bathroom door. Her sister Violet's robe. The two of them had been sharing the home and Violet's bed since Pansy arrived in Memphis. She was intruding, but she had no other option at the moment, and Violet had welcomed her with open arms.

Violet had never cared for her brother-in-law, but she kept her opinions to herself. Even when Jonathan forced

Pansy to have that abortion. What kind of small, selfish man would force his wife to abort their child? Just so he didn't have to share her attention, was Violet's opinion. She thought there was more to it than that, but her sister would never say so.

They had only been in touch through occasional phone calls and monthly letters, until Pansy showed up on her doorstep in the middle of the night a week before. Though her home wasn't roomy, and she had two small children, Violet welcomed her sister. She waited for Pansy to talk. She knew the time would finally come when her big sister would have to share her story. That time came on the morning of Pansy's birthday.

"So how we gonna celebrate your big day, Sis?" Violet asked over coffee. "I can get a sitter for the girls if you wanna go out somewhere and kick up your heels."

"Thanks, Vi, but I don't really feel like celebratin'. Here I am in my forties and I'm not sure what the future holds. And I'm livin' off my little sister, to boot."

"What happened, Sis? You've got the weight of the world on your shoulders and you're as skittish as a little bird. I'm thinkin' somethin' bad happened. Or you're afraid somethin' bad's GONNA happen."

Pansy smiled ruefully. Just how did she tell her sister what had happened? She thought, *I guess there is no time like the present!"* Actually, Vi, somethin' good happened. I mean I did somthin' good. But now I'm afraid I might get killed for it. That's why I'm leavin' today. Jonathan don't know your new address and he's got his hands full right now. But it won't take him too long to track me down, one way or another. I gotta get away from here so you and the girls ain't in harm's way."

"Oh, Sis, you're talkin' nonsense. Jonathan may be a scoundrel, but I'm sure he wouldn't actually KILL you. Specially if you did somethin' good. And I don't want you to take off not even knowin' where you're goin'. I guess you better tell me what this is all about—right now."

Pansy related the whole story to her sister, leaving nothing out, including the horrible way she had really lost her baby. "I've been figuring on how I could get away ever since, but it just didn't seem possible or even worthwhile. Guess I was just survivin', not really havin' much of a life, but not knowin' what else to do. Kinda funny, strange-funny, that those kids give me a reason to leave."

"That S.O.B. hadn't better come 'round here, cause I'd just as soon shoot him as look at him right now. I just knew there was more about that baby you weren't tellin' me." Violet considered for a moment, then continued. "D'ya think maybe those girls was a way of makin' up for losin' your own little one?"

Pansy nodded her head. "I thought of that, too, Sis. I don't know, maybe. All I know is, I had to help 'em, just had to. Couldn't leave 'em there to die, even if it meant I might die for doin' it."

Violet looked worried. "Is it somebody else besides Jonathan that might come lookin' for you?"

"Maybe. I can't be sure." Pansy looked down into her coffee cup and became very silent. Violet knew her sister well enough to know the subject was closed. She tried a different subject instead to lighten the mood.

"Grampy's old pickup! I just can't believe you actually got that thing started. Oh, I remember you and him with your heads in that ol' engine all the time, but I never dreamed you actually knew enough to get it goin'. Almost like you had some kinda inklin' or somethin', ain't it?"

"Well, I always had runnin' in the back of my mind, just never had the courage 'til those poor, beat-up little girls were dumped there. But understand, Vi, it wasn't Jonathan that done it; those Klansmen just always want him to clean up their messes. And he usually does, but down deep, he's better than that. What he done to me, well, it was the last time he ever took a drop, I swear."

"Well, good for him, he stopped drinkin.' It's just too bad it took 'til after he killed your baby. Don't expect me to ever see a good thing about that man, Pansy. And if you're thinkin' of goin' back to him, I got no sympathy for you. But I'll always take you in if he hurts you again. Just prayin' you'll be alive to need a bed."

"Well, I can't stay here, that's for sure. And I don't know where else to go, but I gotta go somewhere. Been thinkin' of goin' down and talkin' to Salina bout things."

"Now, that's 'bout the smartest thing you said since you been here. You can hide out there for a while, and maybe that ol' Indian can put some of her wisdom into ya. She was just about the best thing that ever happened to us after Mama and Daddy died. Truth be told, I'da much rather been raised by Salina than Gram and Grampy, but they did alright, I guess."

"Yeah, Salina woulda just been more fun," Pansy said. Gram and Grampy was so grim and sour all the time. Guess they was hurtin' that their only child died so young and maybe we reminded 'em of Mama."

"I think they blamed Salina, all because that wreck happened on the way to her place. Course, they shoulda known Daddy well enough to know he never took a trip like that without plenty of moonshine for the road. I still remember that curve, do you?"

Pansy closed her eyes. "Yeah, I can still see it in my head. Mama screamin' at Daddy, the whole car rollin' over and over, us bein' tossed round like rag dolls. It's a wonder we didn't die along with 'em."

"Well," Violet began, "if you ask me, Salina saved our lives. Whatever medicine she used on us, and all that chantin' she did, I think that's what kept us alive. If Gram and Grampy hadn't yanked us outta there so soon after, I'd surely have liked to live with Miss Salina."

"Yeah, I've always felt a kinship with her, too, ever since those summers with Ruby over there. Wonder whatever happened to Ruby? She was such a sweet kid. I hope she had a nice life. S'pose it's time I spent a little time with Salina again."

As Pansy rode the bus into Mississippi, she drifted through childhood memories. Playing hide-and-seek with Violet and Ruby on long summer days. Working with Salina in her garden. Snapping peas on the tiny front porch in the cool evenings. Canning vegetables in the small kitchen during the waning days of summer. The old Choctaw stories that Salina used to tell them at bedtime. She and Violet never wanted to leave for home when the time came. Ruby's parents were divorced, and she spent every summer with Salina. Pansy and Violet came each summer for a month or so. After their parents died, their grandparents refused to let the girls go back to Salina's. Their reasoning, as explained by their grandmother, stunned the girls. "Bad enough your Daddy took your pregnant Mama to that old Indian woman for medicine, but then they let you girls go over there every summer for years, and that little colored gal there all the time, too. No good can come of mixin' the races, specially three at once, for goodness sake."

The bus let Pansy off in Hernando and she walked out to Salina's road. *Not much has changed in all these years,* she thought to herself as she walked along under low-hanging willow branches. Suddenly she saw the house. A little more weathered, a little more frayed around the edges, but there was no doubt that it was Salina's warm, cozy home. The smell of freshly-baked bread greeted her as she walked onto the porch and tapped gently on the screen door.

"Miss Salina?" she called out. "Miss Salina, it's a voice from your past, Pansy Davis. Uh, I mean Pansy Hawkins. Do you remember me?"

A small form with a cane moved slowly toward the door.

"Oh, my goodness! What a wonderful surprise! This is my lucky week, without a doubt." Salina pushed the screen door open and reached out her thin arms to embrace her visitor. She touched Pansy's face, adding, "These old eyes are failing me, but I can tell you have grown into a beautiful woman. Come have some tea, my dear."

Over a serving of fresh bread and tea, the two women reminisced. Pansy was enthralled with some of Salina's memories that she had all but lost.

"Such good times for us little girls, Miss Salina. You have no idea how much impact you had on our lives."

"And you mine, my dear. You three were the lights of my life and I anxiously awaited your return each year. Your mothers had been like my own children and you my grandchildren. Such wonderful memories of you and Violet and Ruby."

"Whatever happened to Ruby, anyway? That was a double blow when grandma forbid us from coming to see you, since we lost all touch with Ruby at the same time."

Salina lit her pipe and took a long drag, blowing the smoke into feathers and beads overhead before answering. "Ruby had a good life. She married a good man and had two beautiful children before succumbing to that awful TB."

"Oh, I'm sorry to know she's passed. I would have loved to look her up again. Where is her family?"

"Somewhere in Arkansas," Salina quickly answered before she changed the subject. "Now, tell me about your sister Violet and her family. You said you just came from her home in Memphis. How is it with her these days?"

"Oh, Vi's doin' pretty well. Not easy raisin' younguns on her own, but she seems to take it all in stride. Sometimes, it seems like she's the older one instead o' me."

"How so?"

"Well, here I am in my forties, and I just had to hide out at my little sister's place. Seems a little childish, doncha think?"

"I suppose that would depend on the circumstances. Do you care to tell me a little of just how it is with you?"

Pansy sighed deeply before she began. "I had to leave my husband, Miss Salina. I still love him, and we been through a lot together, but those 'circumstances' you mentioned can be mighty powerful and frightful sometimes. Jonathan's been doin' the Klan's biddin' and he can't seem to get out of it. I went against them, and now either him or them are on my trail. 'Cept I don't think they'd ever find me now, cause he don't even know about you."

"You are welcome here just as long as you like, my dear. Why don't we get some rest and talk more in the morning?"

"Oh, I am bone-tired, Miss Salina." She yawned as she said, "Sleep sounds wonderful."

Chapter Twenty-Three

Second Homecoming

"No man ever steps in the same river twice,
for it's not the same river and
he's not the same man."

~ Heraclitus
Pre-Socratic Greek philosopher.

Maggie sat at the Roberts' kitchen table, the telephone receiver in her hand, its cord stretched around the doorway from the hall. The baby nursed at his mother's breast under a blanket. Michael pushed eggs around his plate while listening to Maggie's end of the phone conversation. Annalee and Winston stood against the kitchen sink listening to Maggie, while pretending to wash dishes.

Maggie said into the phone, "No, Mama, I ain't gonna tell you where I am until you calm down. No, the FBI ain't lookin' for me cause I talked to that Agent Langford on the telephone a while ago. I wanna come see you and daddy but you gotta promise me you won't take my baby away. Mama, I mean it. I'm keepin' this child and if you can't accept that, I'll go away and never come back. You sure? No matter what? Okay, then, I'll be seein' ya sometime later today. Bye-bye."

"Well, that didn't sound TOO bad," said Michael. "Ya think it's safe to go on over there?"

"We both know it ain't gonna be better or worse now or later Michael, so might as well pick our time. When you're ready I'm ready."

Michael pursed his lips. "Ya know, I could just go on home and tell 'em the huntin' was lousy and then let you come later. They ain't never gonna know I been in on this."

"Yessir, you surely could do that an' my lips'd be sealed for the rest of my life. I owe you that much for comin' to get me and stickin' by me and little Willis."

"Yeah, Little Willis. Aw, now what kinda example'd I be settin' as an uncle if I took the chickenshit way outta this? No, ma'am. I'm gonna face the music right there with ya Sis."

Winston spoke to Michael. "Son, I don't think you'll be sorry for tellin' the truth on this. Takes a brave man to take his medicine sometimes."

Well sir," Michael said, "a wise old woman once told me that bein' brave don't mean you're not afraid. It just means do the right thing even though you're scared."

Maggie looked at Winston. "Mr. Roberts, I'd be honored if you'd carry little Willis out to the truck for me."

Winston beamed. "No ma'am. That'd be MY honor entirely."

Just as Michael started up the truck, Agent Langford pulled behind Michael's pickup. He walked over to the truck where Winston and Annalee stood outside the passenger door talking to Maggie and Michael through the open window.

Langford nodded then looked into the truck. "You must be Maggie and let me guess, you're Michael. I'm Agent Langford of the FBI. That's a precious baby you got there Miss Maggie. What's his or her name?"

Still a little suspicious, Maggie replied, "His name is Willis Emmett Thorpe. You come to arrest him, too?"

"No, ma'am, I'm not here to arrest anyone. But I do need to take you and Miss Roberts in for questioning just as soon as you leave your baby with your mama and daddy."

"What's this about Agent?" Winston asked, pulling Langford aside. "You can't possibly think these girls had anything to do with Harper's killin'."

"Mr. Roberts, I don't have all the answers but the sooner I get to the truth, the sooner we can all rest easy. Would you and your daughter like to come with me, or do you prefer to drive to the sheriff's office yourself?"

"We'll drive ourselves, Winston replied. "Come on Annalee," he said to his daughter. "I'll fill you in on the way."

"Michael," Agent Langford said, "I'll follow you to your parents' house then I'll wait to take you and Maggie to the sheriff's office. I've already spoken with your folks."

The bright sun was high in the sky as Michael's pick-up turned the corner on Maple Street. It rolled to a stop under the shade of a large tree about three houses away from the Thorpe home. Nursing her baby in the passenger seat, Maggie looked slightly terrified.

Michael turned to his sister. "Mags it's only mama and daddy, two people that love ya. You been through worse than this. Let me go in first and fill 'em in so they don't pass out from the shock or somethin'."

"Okay. But Michael?"

"Yeah?"

"If I do have to go away I just wanna tell you that you're 'bout the best big brother around and I'll never forget what you done for me and for us."

"Can't say it ain't been an adventure Mags. Well, best get on with it."

Michael slid out of the pick-up and headed slowly up the sidewalk. Maggie watched anxiously as her brother approached the front door of their home, turned the knob, then disappeared inside. He seemed to be gone forever and Maggie became more and more nervous. She noticed that Michael left the keys in the pick-up. Considering whether to just drive off she tightly squeezed the talisman in her hand, saw Langford's car in the rear-view mirror, and sighed deeply, holding her baby closer.

Suddenly, Michael exited the front door followed first by Irene and then Eddie. They approached the pickup, but Maggie didn't get out. She was frozen in place.

Michael came to the passenger window. "It's now or never Mags." He opened the door for her.

Maggie slid down from the seat and clutched the baby to her, not sure what to do next. She looked shyly at her mother. In tears, Irene ran over to Maggie and hugged her tightly. Maggie had to pull away to let the baby breathe.

"Oh, my goodness!" Irene exclaimed. "The baby, I almost forgot, I was so happy and relieved to see my own baby!"

Maggie turned the baby around and pulled back the blanket. "Mama, Daddy, this here is your grandson Willis Emmett Thorpe."

Irene took the baby in her arms. "Oh Mags," she said haltingly. "Oh honey... Maggie, he's beautiful!"

Maggie looked at her father. Eddie stood next to Irene looking at the ground, the pick-up, anywhere but at the baby.

"Daddy he's your grandson, too. You gonna let me keep him?"

Eddie stalled. He looked at Maggie but not the baby. "Aw lordy, this ain't easy Mags. D'ya know what you're askin' me?"

Michael spoke up. "I believe she's askin' you to be a part of your grandson's life Dad."

Eddie was obviously struggling. "Yeah, but he's... he's... Maggie, he's half-colored."

Irene was furious. "Eddie can't you get past that? For God's sake, not only was Maggie's life spared but we've been blessed with this precious child too."

"Daddy you told me one time that nothin' worth havin' comes easy," Maggie said. "Well this here is your grandson. Your own flesh and blood, half mine and, yes, half part of a fine colored boy named Willis that died tryin' to protect me." She choked up. "Good lord, Daddy, I'm only askin' ya to let us come home."

Irene calmly held out the baby. "Edward Thorpe you take this child into your arms and look at his sweet innocent face."

Eddie awkwardly took the baby from Irene and held him out stiffly, looking away.

Irene scolded him. "LOOK at him Eddie!"

Eddie reluctantly looked at the baby. He stared into the baby's face for a long time, saying nothing. He adjusted the blanket around the baby's body, awkwardly stroked its forehead, then handed the baby back to Irene.

"Well y'all go on into the house. Me and Michael'll get the things outta the truck."

Irene took the baby and put her free arm around Maggie's shoulder, gently leading her to the house. Michael busied himself unloading his bag while Eddie grabbed Maggie's. Father and son looked awkwardly at each other across the bed of the pickup but didn't speak.

A carload of young boys drove by honking. Several of the occupants leaned out the windows yelling obscenities. Eddie and Michael both shook their fists and chased the car for a few yards, cursing.

Michael leveled his gaze at his father. "Ya know Dad, there's others that were there that night. It ain't over."

"No, it ain't over. Hell, they don't even know we got a half-breed baby yet. Wait'll that gets out. S' only gonna make it harder… 'specially on Mags."

"Remember how you always told us not to take sides Dad? We gotta stick up for Maggie."

Eddie exhaled deeply. "Yeah well, we got our own side now, and I reckon it comes right through the middle with that boy bein' half and half."

"Ya know I don't think Maggie'd like you callin' him 'that boy' or 'half-breed.' Mr. Roberts is proud to call him Willis even though he's half Maggie's.

"Then I guess I'm gonna hafta be proud to call him a Thorpe even though he's half Roberts," Eddie replied.

Michael put his arm around his father's shoulder as they went up the sidewalk toward their front porch. "I'm proud of you Dad."

"Well I guess it's a little easier when it's your own flesh and blood." He stopped and looked at Michael then added, "He is a cute little rascal ain't he?"

"That's the spirit Dad," Michael replied, slapping Eddie on the back. "And besides, once you get used to the idea, there's a girl I want you to meet."

Eddie groaned, "Oh, lord Michael, I ain't used to nothin' yet but I'm tryin'. Don't throw nothin' else at me, okay? "

Chapter Twenty-Four

Questioned and Sequestered

"Wherever a man commits a crime, God finds a witness. Every secret crime has its reporter."

~ Ralph Waldo Emerson (1802-1883)
American essayist, lecturer, philosopher, and poet.

At the sheriff's office, Agent Langford and Sheriff Jonathan Davis questioned Maggie and Annalee about their whereabouts and actions the past several days. The girls told the truth leaving nothing out and Michael corroborated their story.

"You can understand that all we have is your word on this and you're all either related or friends. Might be hard to prove you weren't involved in Harper's killin'," Sheriff Davis said.

"Easy, Davis," Langford replied. "We've got no reason not to believe these kids and the Indian woman can provide an alibi, so we'll check with her."

Jonathan Davis was uneasy. He was already under the microscope with the Klan because of his wife's betrayal. He had to plead for his life when they showed up at his place after Pansy betrayed him. He now knew she released the kids and escaped. He had to convince the Klan that he was just as mad about it as they were, but he wasn't. Jonathan was tired. He had been looking for an out from all this Klan business. If only Pansy would have told him she wanted to go away they could have run together. But now the only woman he'd ever loved was gone and he had to clean up the mess.

"So, pardon any offense kids, but Langford here thinks the word of three teenagers, one black and two related, plus an old Indian woman's word will be enough to keep you from bein' charged for Harper's murder. But I don't think so. I think we need more proof before some angry crowd comes in here lookin' for justice. You got anything else that'd prove your case?"

Annalee had a thought. "We were at my daddy's house that night, what time was Mr. Harper killed?"

"Before you got there," Langford replied, "because I had gone there to tell him and Mr. and Mrs. Thorpe about it before you arrived."

Maggie asked solemnly, "Mr. Langford, if we don't have any other way to defend ourselves, what's gonna happen?"

Langford took a deep breath before answering. "Well, I doubt you have to worry about that 'angry crowd lookin' for justice' that Davis mentioned. The way I hear it, Harper didn't have many friends around here. Regardless, we will trace your path, talk to Miss Salina, and figure out the timing between there and here, which might tell us all we need to know."

"Do I lock 'em up in the meantime?" Davis asked.

"No such luck Davis. But I do think they need to be held in protective custody until we sort this all out. Got any ideas about a safe place? What about that farm of yours?"

Davis sat up quickly and came to his feet. "No, no, that won't work, agent. I got the wife's relatives stayin' out there and there's chaos enough. Plus, everybody knows where I live and there's folks comin' and goin' all the time."

Langford studied Davis for a moment. "Okay then, we'll just have to place guards at both of your homes. I'll set that up and then drive all of you home. Davis, I trust this information will stay confidential?"

"Yessir, I got no reason to tell nobody nothin'. The sooner we get this sorted out, the better for me."

As Langford drove toward the Thorpe home, he pulled over on a side street to talk to his passengers. "Kids, I'm afraid we have a situation here. I'm not taking you to your parents' homes. Eddie and Winston will stay home with undercover agents positioned inside the houses and nearby. Your dads will continue to go to work as usual, for appearances 'cause if anyone's gonna try something, it'd be after they leave for their jobs. Just in case the Klan wants to find you and silence you, I'm takin' you to a safe house the FBI has outside of town.

"What about my baby?" Maggie cried.

"Your momma's bringing him to us Maggie and she'll stay with you kids. Don't worry."

Michael was curious. "So, I guess you don't really trust Sheriff Davis then?"

"Don't know what to think about Davis, Michael. But I can't take any chances that he wouldn't expose you. This way, you're safe and I can still keep an eye on him."

Langford turned to Maggie and Annalee. "Girls, do you remember anything about that farm where you were held? Anything about the woman that helped you? Any little detail might be of help in our investigation."

Wanting to do whatever she could to get back to Little Willis, Maggie spoke first. "She took us away in an old truck. She said somethin' kinda to herself bout puttin' us in 'Grampy's truck' before she loaded us in the bed."

"The barn was behind the house," Annalee added. "There was moonlight and I remember we drove under an umbrella of big ol' trees when we left there."

"Okay, that might help. Keep thinkin' about it, girls."

"As if we could think of anything else," Annalee said.

Chapter Twenty-Five

Wrong and Right

"What's right is what's left
when everything is wrong."

~ Robin Williams (1951-2014)
American actor and comedian.

Pansy Awoke to the long, low whistle of the morning freight train rumbling through the countryside outside Hernando. She stretched and threw off her blanket then got up to make some tea. Through the kitchen window she saw Salina gathering vegetables from her garden. The old woman seemed to have shrunk a foot since Pansy's childhood. She was bent and slow beneath her wide straw hat, but she met the day and her tasks with the same enthusiasm she always had.

"Good morning my dear!" Salina warmly greeted Pansy when she stepped through the back door. "Isn't this a glorious morning? I hope you slept well on that old sofa."

Pansy took the full basket from Salina. "The sofa was just fine, and I slept like a baby. Nothing like the country to put you to sleep but in a good way."

"Let's have an omelet and a good long talk," Salina offered.

After breakfast, they took their tea to the small front porch and sat in the matching cane rockers. "I remember these chairs from my childhood," Pansy said with a smile. "We always wanted to rock in them, and you said they were only for adults."

"And do you think I'd still have them if you girls would have played in them?" Salina asked with a chuckle. "These chairs are all I have left of my dear mother, God rest her soul. And so, how is it with your soul, my child?"

"Oh, it would be an understatement to say there's a little turmoil and uncertainty at the moment, I'm afraid."

"Why don't you begin at the beginning? We have all the time you want."

Pansy sighed and slowly collected her thoughts. "The reason I'm hidin' is because I know some things that the Klan doesn't want me to know. And I done some things that they probably see as betrayal, 'cept I haven't been caught yet. I don't know whether to go back and tell what I know or to just keep hidin' out for a while until I'm more sure of what to do and where to go."

"As I said before, you are more than welcome to stay here as long as you like. But I gather from what you've said that you may have unfinished business to see to."

"Miss Salina," Pansy started, resting her head against the back of the chair, "what do you do when you don't know what to do?"

"You listen my dear. To the still, small voice inside you that does know what to do. It's there. You just have to quiet yourself and your thoughts enough to hear it."

"Well, I made what was wrong as right as I could and if I go back and tell what I know, the only folks that'd be hurt are bad people. And probably me of course."

"And is your husband one of those bad people?"

"Yes and no. He's helped them do bad things in the past, but he's a good man and I really think he'll do the right thing if I go back. And I don't think he would hurt me, but he might not be able to stop others."

"Would anyone else be hurt by your return? Or by your failure to return and tell what you know?"

"I guess in a way. If I don't go back, some kids that have been hurt won't have the justice of seein' those who done it locked up. And a young boy was killed, and his killers are walkin' around free as birds."

Salina's eyes narrowed as she began to get a sense of Pansy's story. "Why don't you tell me the whole truth now Pansy?"

Pansy proceeded to tell Salina about the night the kids were brought to her farm, how she helped them escape and left Willis' body for authorities to find after her call.

"It can't be and yet it must be!" Salina exclaimed.

"What? What do you mean?"

"Pansy, the Negro girl you helped was Ruby's daughter Annalee. She and her friends came here for help just days before you arrived. Her friend Maggie was with child from the attack and they needed help with the birth."

"Oh my God! I can't believe it! That was Ruby's little girl... so beat up and traumatized like that? And her brother, killed by the same men, that was Ruby's son? And that other little girl pregnant from rape? Lord have mercy." She thought for a moment, then added, "But that must mean they lived in Oakwood right under my nose?"

"Yes exactly, Oakwood. You didn't mention the name of your town but that is where Ruby's family lives. As I told you, Ruby died years ago from TB, but her family was still in Oakwood. Anyway, I helped with the birth of Maggie's child and they were headed home to their parents when they left here."

Pansy shook her head and buried her face in her hands for a moment. "Miss Salina, I guess I've got my answer. I gotta go back and help those kids and their families. No matter the risk I gotta go back. I'm the only one that CAN help them."

The women were suddenly distracted by a car slowly turning on the dusty road that ran in front of Salina's house.

"Oh, dear God," Pansy said flatly.

Deputy Jimmy Moore stepped from his patrol car and stretched. He folded his sunglasses and stuffed them into his shirt pocket then strode toward the porch.

"Well, well, well, look who we got here. Hello, Pansy. Folks been missin' you back home ya know, 'specially Sheriff Jon."

Pansy quickly noted that Moore seemed to have come alone. "You're a bit out of your jurisdiction ain't ya, Jimmy?"

"Oh, I ain't here for you. No, just tracin' down a tip. Sheriff got wind of some Indian woman over this way that might be a material witness in a murder case. Guess that must be your friend here, huh?"

"I don't know what you're talkin' bout Jimmy, but Miss Salina here's got nothin' to do with nothin' that happened to those poor kids in Oakwood. She's an old friend of mine from childhood."

"Oh no ma'am, I ain't talkin' bout that. Not directly, anyhow. I'm talkin' bout whoever killed Leland Harper. I mean after all, if those kids been blamin' him for what happened to 'em makes 'em likely suspects in Harper's murder, doncha think? An' then there's the fact that he was castrated, too. Well that only adds fuel to that fire."

Pansy laughed and slapped her knee. "So, somebody finally took care o' that ol' bastard Leland Harper huh? And they castrated him too? Well, sounds like he got what was comin' to him but ain't no way those kids was involved."

Moore lost some of his bravado in the face of Pansy's comebacks. "Now, that ain't for you nor me to say Pansy. Sheriff Davis told me to find this here Indian woman and check out the distance from here to Oakwood and that's why I'm here. Bringin' you back's only gonna be a bonus."

"Ha!" Pansy spat. "If you think I'm goin' anywhere with you Jimmy, you got another think comin'. You ain't got no charges on me and no jurisdiction here even if ya did."

Salina spoke up for the first time. "Pansy, where are our manners? This man is our guest and we must treat him accordingly. Deputy Moore, is it? Can we offer you some nice cool sweet tea?"

Moore looked from Salina to Pansy and back again. "Why that'd be right kind of you, ma'am."

"Alright, then young man, we have some in the fridge. You sit down here and talk to Pansy while I get the refreshments." Salina shooed away Pansy's offer to help as she went through the door.

Once the old woman was gone, Moore learned over to Pansy and whispered, "Okay now Mrs. Davis, why'd you help those kids? You know you got a death warrant hangin' over your head doncha?"

"Don't threaten me Jimmy. I ain't goin' back with you. You just stumbled onto me by accident and nobody else needs to know where I am. By the time you get back to Oakwood, I can be long gone anyhow."

"Oh, I'm takin' you back alright. It'd be a big feather in my cap with the boys. I just don't wanna get that old woman in the middle of the fight, so I'm bidin' my time. But first I wanna know why you done it, you just lose your mind or somethin'? Get fed up with ol' Jonny's ways or what?"

"Here we are at last," Salina said cheerfully, as she brought a tray through the door and sat it on the small table between the rockers. She poured a glass for Moore and one for Pansy then herself. Moore quickly rose to give her his seat.

"Why, thank you, young man, and here's to friendships new and old."

They drank in silence, until Moore put his empty glass down on the porch rail. "Ah that was mighty fine tea, ma'am. Now if you ladies will excuse me for just a minute, I gotta go to my car for a few things."

As Deputy Moore stepped off the porch, he began to stumble. Then he started spinning in circles, his eyes rolling back in his head as he tried to regain his balance. He landed on the ground with a loud thud—out cold.

"Salina!" Pansy exclaimed. "But we all drank from the same tea! What did you... how could you...?"

Salina sat rocking gently and sipping her tea for a moment. "You know, a wise old friend once told me that people waste a lot of time stirring. She said that if you place the additive in the bottom of the glass first, the pouring will do your stirring for you."

"And just what did you put in his glass?"

"I think they call them 'mickeys,' but I'm not sure why. Seems to me that sleeping powders more accurately describe them."

Pansy grinned and shook her head. "So how long will he be out?"

"Hard to say. Man of his size? At least a few hours, I would think."

"And what do we do with him in the meantime?"

"Well, I know of an old cave not too far from here, but far enough that he'd not find his way back in his fuzzy condition.

His car could be driven right into it and then they'd both be out of view."

"Why Miss Salina. Were you this crafty way back when we was kids?"

"Oh, more so, I'm sure. You know it's much harder to deceive children than adults!"

Salina enlisted the help of her German neighbor and his son to deal with Deputy Moore. "Don't worry about their discretion," she reassured Pansy. "I trust them implicitly."

Chapter Twenty-Six

Law and Disorder

"There is no refuge from memory and remorse in this world. The spirits of our foolish deeds haunt us, with or without repentance."

~ Gilbert Parker (1862-1932)
Canadian novelist and British politician.

Agent Langford decided that Sheriff Davis' deputy could be trusted to track the distance from Oakwood to Hernando. He didn't see any problem with the deputy checking out the old Indian woman's location and gauging the mileage. Meanwhile he wanted to do some snooping of his own, having obtained the sheriff's address from a call to his headquarters.

The day was warm and sunny, and he drove around in a rambling way just in case anyone followed him. He made several stops, throwing stones in the river, feeding ducks, and appearing to be enjoying a day off. He slowed at forks in the road as though deciding upon his next move when he knew his destination all along. After about an hour with no one on the road behind him, he turned down a dirt road almost obscured by brush and trees. As he drove farther off the beaten path, it became clear that he was on a long driveway. Overhead a row of large elm trees on either side formed a canopy.

He stopped at a clearing, looking straight ahead to a scene that told him all he needed to know. The house sat in front of a barn. The number matched the one he had been given. The sheriff's house. He slowly drove forward and stopped outside the house. He intended to knock on the door and feign being lost if anyone answered.

Just as Langford approached the house a car drove up. Sheriff Jonathan Davis in his patrol car. Langford thought quickly. "Hello, sheriff, is this your place? I'm afraid I've been out exploring the countryside and gotten myself totally lost."

Sheriff Davis looked at him skeptically. "Let's cut the crap Langford. You think you figured somethin' out, but it ain't what you think and I wanna set the record straight."

"Okay, I'm listening."

"Come in the house. I don't wanna talk out here."

"You sure we won't be disturbing your wife?" Langford asked, as they went through the front door.

Davis glared at him. "No, she ain't here."

Langford looked around at the small cabin-like house, a little unkempt but comfortable enough. "Will she be back soon?"

"She run off. Now will you let me tell my story?"

"Sorry, go ahead," Langford answered, wondering whether he would get the truth or something to distract him from the truth.

Davis placed a bottle of whiskey on the kitchen table and sat down facing Langford.

"I'm afraid I'm on duty and can't drink," Langford said.

"Ain't meant for you anyway. For my nerves. I quit when... well, let's just say I been sober for years. Might have to have a little sip o' courage now though." Davis took a quick gulp from the bottle and began.

"I'm ashamed to say I've been cleanin' up after the Klan down here for a while now, keepin' their secrets and keepin' 'em outta jail. I got no love for the coloreds and figured it was all just part o' things 'round here. Go along to get along, know what I mean?"

"To a point," Langford replied.

"Yeah well, I reached that point when they started killin' kids and rapin' white girls."

"Hadn't occurred to you to object to burning out families or raping colored women?"

"Okay, okay, I ain't innocent and never said I was. I know there'll be consequences for tellin' you all this. But your consequences ain't fatal like some o' my former cronies."

"Former? Since when?"

"Since I ain't gone after my wife for turnin' those kids loose."

"Whoa! That was YOUR WIFE who helped the Thorpe and Roberts girls escape and then left the boy's body for discovery?"

"Looks that way. I ain't talked to her since all hell broke loose, but I can put two and two together. Only reason I ain't gone after her is 'cause I don't know exactly where she is, and I don't wanna lead the boys to any places I think she might be. No use draggin' her kin into this."

"Then what have you told 'the boys'?"

"That I'll go after her on my own when the time comes 'cause I want to wring her pretty little neck myself. Folks 'round here let folks take care o' their own messes."

"And is that your true intent? To wring her neck?"

"D'ya think I'd be tellin' you any o' this if it was?" Davis took another big sip of his whiskey before continuing. "I miss her, Langford. She's the only thing I ever loved in this world and I know she thought she was doin' the right thing. Hell, she probably was."

Hmmm, Langford thought to himself, *I think this guy may be on the level after all.*

"So, what now?" Davis asked.

Langford rose and took the bottle to the sink where he poured out its contents. "Just so you don't go off the deep end, Sheriff. I'm gonna need you sober and alert. What you've just told me is between us for the time being and we'll deal with those consequences later. Right now I need to find your wife.

I'm sorry to say that she just became another suspect in Harper's killing."

"Couldn't help but wonder 'bout that myself. But surely she wouldn't be careless enough to come back here."

"Probably not but all the more reason to find her and clear things up. Got any ideas?"

"She's got a sister over in Memphis, I'll get you the address. And Langford?"

"Yeah?"

"If you find Pansy, will you tell her... well, just tell her I miss her?"

Langford headed for the door. "I'll tell you what. Pansy will have to be brought back under guard. Once your deputy returns, let's you and me go find her together."

CHAPTER TWENTY-SEVEN

Wrong Place, Wrong Time

"A nuisance may be merely a right thing in the wrong place—like a pig in the parlor instead of the barnyard."

~ George Sutherland (1862-1942)
English-born U.S. jurist and politician.

DEPUTY JIMMY MOORE woke up with a pounding headache in near-total darkness. At first, he thought he'd tied one on and slept in his patrol car again. But then through the rearview mirror he saw flashes of light outside the car like patches of daylight visible through trees or brush. He shook his head to dislodge the cobwebs. Wherever he was there was only blackness up ahead with bits of light behind him.

Moore didn't know where he was or how he got there. He couldn't remember anything since leaving Oakwood. But wherever he was he needed to get back and report to the sheriff. About what though? His memory ebbed and flowed with the merciless pounding in his head.

He started the engine, put the car in reverse, and gunned it. The wheels churned up mud and dust and rocks as he shot backward. Branches scratched the sides of his car like nails on a blackboard. Once free of the darkness, he braked to a stop in a rocky clearing. He saw before him a huge cave that he'd never seen before. This wasn't anywhere near Oakwood. *Where the hell am I?* he wondered.

The deputy put his patrol car in gear and slowly drove toward what appeared to be a dirt road that forked at the end of his vision. When he got to the Y, he looked both directions. To the left, nothing but more dirt road. To the right, some kind of structure off in the distance. He drove toward the building.

The deserted house had been abandoned long ago. Moore stumbled through the dust and debris of the former tenants, searching for any kind of headache relief. To his amazement, he found a small tin of aspirin mixed in with dirty broken plates and utensils on the floor of what used to serve as a kitchen. He quickly pressed the corner and headed for the sink. There were two dusty pills inside the tin but no water at the sink. He grimaced, chewed the pills and swallowed the bitter powder as best he could.

As he turned to leave, Moore stopped as he noticed a faded calendar on the wall. The photo of a baseball team was captioned "Hernando, Mississippi, Home of the Rebels." A pocket of fuzziness popped in his brain with the realization that he was apparently in Mississippi. The dominoes barring his memory began to topple. *Hernando. Indian woman. Pansy*! Moore's mind became clearer as the headache began to recede. He sped off in the direction that seemed most likely to yield results.

Deputy Moore was still fuzzy, but he thought he was on the right track to find the Indian woman's place again. As he approached the town of Hernando, his pulse quickened, and his foot pressed the accelerator. Suddenly he saw the road that led to Salina's house and made a last-minute turn, spreading a rooster tail of dust in his wake. He cursed to himself as he saw red lights flashing behind him, but he continued on, figuring he could talk his way out of any trouble with the local law.

Moore pulled to a stop in Salina's front yard, the flashing lights just behind him. He exited his car and stood with his hands on his hips awaiting the officer who followed him. A very tall, burly, dark-haired man in a gray uniform opened the door, stepped from the other car, and approached.

"Afternoon officer," Moore began, as he flashed his badge. "I'm Deputy James Moore from over in Oakwood, Arkansas. Here on official business."

"Yeah," the other man said, "I seen your patrol car flyin' through town. I'm Chief Dan Bridges and this here's my jurisdiction. Now tell me why you're after an old Indian woman that'd never hurt a soul."

Shit! thought Moore. *He's a damned injun too!*

"No sir. Definitely not after her. She had a visitor from Oakwood the other day when I was here, and that woman needs to go back to Oakwood with me."

"When were you here, deputy?"

Moore fumbled through his hazy memory, trying to determine a timeline, but he didn't even know the day today.

"Uh, well sir, this is gonna sound kinda strange, but I'm not sure. When I was here they gave me some tea that knocked me out. And I woke up a while ago in some cave way back yonder somewheres. My memory's been comin' back in bits and pieces and I'm not even sure what today is."

"Just gave ya some tea huh? Sweet tea?" Bridges grinned. "Don't rightly see how that could knock a man out. Why would they wanna do that anyhow?"

"Like I said chief, I need to take that other woman back to Oakwood with me cause she may be a suspect in a murder."

"I see. Got yourself a warrant, do ya?"

"No, I ain't got no warrant cause when I come here, we didn't know she'd be here."

"So, you WAS after Miss Salina then when you come here?"

"No dammit!" Moore was losing his patience but figured he'd best play it cool. "No sir, I wasn't after nobody when I come here. I was followin' up on a lead in that same murder case. We got us some suspects that claim they was here when the murder took place and I was sent over to see what the mileage is between here and there."

"Suspects was here? Why didn't ya contact the authorities, namely me?"

"No, no, they were in Oakwood and told us they was visiting the Indian woman when the murder took place. I was sent over to check the distance and see if the Indian woman could back up their story."

"So, you were after Salina when you first come?"

"No, no, no! I wasn't after nobody. I wanted to ask the old woman some questions. The other gal that was here was hidin' out and I stumbled on her by accident."

Chief Bridges pushed his hat back on his head and turned to spit on the ground. "Well deputy, I'll tell ya what. Ain't nobody here now. Miss Salina left town to visit some family down on the rez, and she asked me to keep an eye on her place while she was gone."

"Now that seems mighty convenient, doncha think, chief?"

"You questionin' what I said deputy?"

"No, no o' course not. I just need to verify for myself that nobody's in that house. You care if I take a look?"

"Yeah I do. Miss Salina asked me to keep her place secure while she's gone, and I don't think lettin' a stranger comb thru her house would be upholdin' my responsibility."

"Aw now look, I've about had it with this game. One injun protectin' another injun, tribe loyalty, is that it? Well I'm goin' in that house to look for Pansy and you better not try to stop me 'less you want a whole heap o' trouble from the Oakwood sheriff, not to mention the FBI that's workin' with us too!"

As Moore marched defiantly toward the porch, he was knocked down from behind. He tasted dirt as he felt his hands clasped behind his back and cuffed together.

"Have to let you know trespassin' is a misdemeanor 'round here deputy," drawled Chief Bridges. "I'm gonna have to run you in."

CHAPTER TWENTY-EIGHT

Hernando

"Anyway, it doesn't matter how much, how often, or how closely you keep an eye on things, because you can't control it. Sometimes things and people just go. Just like that."

~ Cecelia Ahern (1981)
Irish novelist.

LANGFORD CHECKED IN with his agents to make sure the Thorpes and Roberts families were doing alright. He was relieved to hear there had been no attempts on either house and the kids were still tucked away in the safe house. Maybe the Klan was waiting to see what the sheriff would do about his wife. Maybe they were waiting for the feds to leave town.

Maybe they didn't trust each other and were lying low wondering who might turn up dead next.

In any event, Langford and Sheriff Davis decided it was time to head for Memphis to talk to Pansy's sister. Also, to bring the sheriff's wife back home, at the very least to tell her story and possibly to face charges in the killing of Leland Harper. Langford secretly obtained a warrant for Pansy Davis' arrest just in case he needed it.

When Langford told Violet that he wanted only to take her sister into protective custody, Violet gave them vague directions to Salina's place in Mississippi, but her childhood memories were slightly hazy. Agent Langford sensed the tension between Sheriff Davis and his sister-in-law, and he left Memphis as soon as he could. Since Langford didn't know the exact location of the Indian woman's house, he thought it best to stop and ask the Hernando police.

As they stepped into the dimly lit reception area, they were greeted half-heartedly by a middle-aged female clerk who was typing and didn't look up. "Take a seat, I'll be with ya in a minute," she said in between curses under her breath at her typewriter.

"Wonder if we might have a word with the man in charge?" Langford asked.

The woman looked over her glasses and gave Langford the once-over then turned her attention to Davis. "You here on official business?" she asked Davis, ignoring the plain-clothed Langford.

"Uh, yes ma'am I am," Davis began, standing and reaching out his hand to her. "I'm Sheriff Jonathan Davis, this here's Agent Langford of the FBI." Both men showed their badges.

The clerk sighed and turned in her chair. “I guess that dang form can wait a little while longer. What can I do for you gents?”

“We’d like to speak to the head man if you don’t mind, ma’am,” Langford said. “Confidentiality and all that, I’m afraid.”

“Hmmph! I know everything Chief Bridges knows and then some,” she shot back. “But if you wanna talk to the chief, then you can just sit back down and wait for him. He’s out on a call, should be back ‘round 2:00 or so.”

“Lunch call?” Davis smiled at the clerk.

The woman just glared at him and turned back to her typewriter.

“Ma’am!” called a voice from back in the cell area. “Ma’am, I’m starvin’! Where’s lunch?”

Davis looked strangely at Langford. “Does that voice sound familiar to you?”

Meanwhile, the clerk turned and yelled, “Shut up! They ain’t brung it over from the café yet so there ain’t nothin’ I can do ‘bout it. Now leave me alone.”

Davis approached the clerk’s desk. “Excuse me, ma’am, but who’s that you got in the back there if you don’t mind my askin’.”

“Just a trespasser. Chief caught him red-handed trespassin’ Miss Salina’s property.”

“Uh, ma’am, is that Jimmy Moore from Oakwood, Arkansas, by any chance? Cause if it is, he’s my deputy and I sent him over here on official business.”

"Ha! Now, if that don't just take the cake. Wait'll the chief hears 'bout this!"

"Can you release him to us?" Davis asked, already knowing the answer.

"No siree, I ain't gonna release nobody 'til the chief gets back and maybe not even then cause there's trespassin' charges pendin' on your boy Jimmy."

"Trespassing?" Langford asked, incredulously. "But Sheriff Davis just told you that he was sent over here on official business so that charge is probably a stretch."

"Ain't for you or me to question what the chief says. Chief Bridges will deal with it when he gets back and that's all I'm gonna say on the matter."

Langford knew better than to press his luck with the officious clerk. He gave Davis a *"let it go"* look, and settled back in his chair with a *Field & Stream* magazine from the table beside him.

Ten minutes later, the door swung open and Chief Bridges casually strode into the office. He looked briefly at Langford and Davis then asked his clerk "What's up?"

"These two wanna talk to you 'bout the guy in the back, and somethin' else that I'm not privy to know," she said indignantly.

After introductions, Bridges led Langford and Davis to his office in the corner and shut the door behind them. "Coffee?" he asked, then looking at the near-empty pot on the burner, added, "Oh never mind, don't look like we got coffee and I ain't askin' Broom Hilda to make us some. So, what can I do for you?"

Langford explained their search for Pansy as well as their interest in talking to Salina if possible. Davis piped up that he discovered his deputy was locked up for trespassing, when he had sent him here on official business.

"Oh, that's YOUR deputy, huh? Kinda cocky little shit ain't he? I'da sent him on his way 'cept for that attitude o' his. And his disrespectin' me and my people."

"Look Chief," Langford began in a conciliatory tone. "We don't mean any disrespect to you or your people nor to anyone who lives around here. But it is important that we find Pansy Davis because she may be a suspect in a murder investigation, and she may need to be in protective custody. Deputy Moore may be a dipshit but he's OUR dipshit and we'll take him off your hands and save you some paperwork if that's okay with you."

"Davis you say? Now ain't that your name, too, Sheriff? Ya wouldn't be usin' OFFICIAL BUSINESS to track down your own old lady, would ya?"

"No sir, I ain't and I resent what you're implyin'."

Langford interceded again. "Chief, the woman we're looking for does happen to be Sheriff Davis' estranged wife but that's got nothing to do with this case. We really do need to put her into protective custody, but she may also turn out to be a suspect. Either way, the FBI wouldn't be wasting its time on a simple domestic dispute, believe me."

Chief Bridges considered for a second, looking from one to the other. "Well boys, I'm afraid you won't be talkin' to Miss Salina cause she's down visitin' some family on the rez. Asked me to keep an eye on her place. That's when I run into your deputy snoopin' 'round. Miss Salina told me she'd had some company and she needed to go away and rest for a while. I went out there and helped her pack and secure the house. Ain't nobody else there and that's a fact."

"Okay Chief guess we'll take your word for that," Langford replied. "So, if you'll kindly release Moore to us we'll be on our way back home. Sorry to have bothered you."

Davis didn't like the way they had treated his deputy, but he knew Moore could be a pain in the ass sometimes, so he begrudgingly let it go. Moore drove back to Oakwood in the muddy scratched up deputy's car, while Langford and Davis returned together.

"So, where's Pansy?" Davis asked after they were on the road a while.

"That appears to be the million-dollar question," Langford replied.

Chapter Twenty-Nine

Third Homecoming

"In any moment of decision, the best thing you can do is the right thing. The worst thing you can do is nothing."

~ Theodore Roosevelt (1858-1919)
American statesman, writer, and 26th President of the United States.

Pansy wasn't sure whether she could trust Vivian Beauford, but she had nowhere else to turn. The two women had commiserated several times in the past about their husbands' involvement in the Klan and how dangerous it could be. Plus, Vivian was the only person Pansy had ever told about her lost baby. The two had been closer ever since.

She had last spoken to Vivian after Jack and Joey died. Took her a pie; tried to comfort her. She knew then that Vivian would never be the same again, but she didn't know how to reach her or to help her in her grief. Now she dialed the pay phone at the bus stop in Little Rock hoping that Vivian would accept the charges.

"Pansy? What on earth? Where are you?" Vivian asked in a shocked voice.

"Vivian I can't explain everything right now, but I will. I need your help, Viv. More than I've ever needed anybody's help in my life. Can you please come get me?"

"Right now? In the dead of night?"

"Please Vivian. It's important that no one see me or know that I'm around but I've gotta get back to Oakwood."

Vivian capped the bottle of Jim Beam she'd just opened and put it back in the liquor cabinet. She looked around at her house, so messy and unkempt. She just didn't have the wherewithal to do any housekeeping since losing Joey. She picked up some trash and tidied up a little before grabbing her purse and keys. She couldn't imagine what kind of trouble Pansy had gotten herself into, but she felt a certain loyalty to the only other Klan wife she'd ever had a friendship with.

On the way back to Vivian's house Pansy filled her in on what had transpired.

"My God, Pansy," Vivian exclaimed. "I had no idea you were mixed up in any of that. I knew about those kids o' course but other than that, I ain't exactly on the good ol' boys' party line these days. You must have been petrified. I doubt I'd have the courage to do what you did."

"I ain't sure it takes courage, Viv. Just doin' without thinkin' mostly. 'Cept I couldn't leave those girls to die. They'd already killed that little negro boy and no doubt they were comin' back to finish the girls off, too."

"Was Jonathan in on it?"

"Yes and no. He didn't know about it 'til they showed up at our place with the kids, wantin' him to hide 'em and do their dirty work like usual. He went off with 'em after they stashed the kids in our barn. Who's to say he'd of come back and killed the girls for 'em, but I like to think not. He was gettin' real tired of cleanin' up after the boys and I don't think he's really evil."

"Not even after your baby?"

"I dunno. I've thought about that a lot, but I don't think he meant to make me lose the baby. He was drunk, Vivian, and you know what that does to 'em. I really don't think Jonathan's got the same kinda mean as the rest of 'em."

"Wish I could say the same for Jack, but I know he was evil. Evil incarnate if you ask me. Weren't for him, I'm sure my Joey would be alive today."

"I'm so sorry Viv. I know you're still grievin' Joey. I hated to put this on you but I've gotta help them kids and I didn't have anybody else to turn to."

"S'ok honey. But I dunno who you think you're gonna take down cause the head's already been cut off the snake. Somebody killed Leland Harper and then his boy died in a suspicious house fire at their place. Lots'a rumors flyin' around but I dunno if they arrested anybody yet."

"Yeah, I heard 'bout Leland. Couldn't happen to a nicer guy. Too bad about his kid, though. But that makes me wonder—with me disappearin' and then Leland bein' killed, do you suppose they'll think I did it?"

"Did you?" Vivian's face was stone cold serious, but there was a strange gleam in her eye at the same time.

"No! I told you just where I been and exactly what's been happenin'. Now I guess you can believe me or not, it really don't matter at this point."

Vivian got a far-away look in her eyes. She spoke softly, her eyes glazed over as she stared straight ahead. "Yeah nothin' much matters anymore, least that's the conclusion I come to."

"Well I still gotta set the record straight with the authorities. I think that much does matter despite any consequences."

"You can stay here long as you like. I ain't afraid o' nobody anymore. They come after you, I'll shoot 'em on sight."

"Thanks, Vivian. It's good to know somebody's got my back. I might end up in jail anyhow if they think I killed Harper."

"Oh, I wouldn't worry 'bout that. Things got a way o' workin' out.

Chapter Thirty

Hatching a Plan

"A quiet man is a thinking man.
A quiet woman is hatching a plan."

Unknown

The town was quiet when Langford and Davis got back to Oakwood. Except for Moore's whining about how he was treated in Mississippi and the damage to his patrol car.

"I got a good mind to round up some o' the boys and go after those Mississippi hicks in the dead o' night," the deputy postured.

"Stifle it, Jimmy," Davis replied. "You ain't got no business goin' after nobody. Sounds like your big mouth got ya in trouble mostly. Those people over there got their own ways, an' you ain't none the worse for wear. Your pride'll heal in a few days."

"Besides," Langford added, "this is still a murder investigation and your little Mississippi escapade is part of the federal record. Any shenanigans from you 'boys' might bring more feds down here than you can handle."

"Hmmph!" Moore snorted. "I'm goin' home and get some rest. Been through one helluva ordeal no matter what you two seem to think."

"That's a good idea, Jimmy," Davis said. "Come back well-rested and clear-headed in the mornin'. In fact, sleep in if you want and come in at noon."

Moore left in a huff and Davis shook his head at Langford. "Gotta get me a better class o' deputy one o' these days."

"I'm sure the pool of potential applicants isn't too deep around here."

"Now that's a fact." Davis said, stretching. "I'll stay here again in case any trouble starts. You'd best go get some sleep too, Langford."

Langford headed for the door. "Pleasant dreams, sheriff."

"Only one thing I'm dreamin' of lately and I ain't sure I'll ever see her again. Lock up on your way out and just hang onto the key, will ya?"

Langford nodded his head and left. He decided to visit Irene Thorpe and the kids at the safe house to check on their welfare and to bring them up-to-date.

Agent Madison met Langford at the front door. Irene Thorpe shouted as she ran from the kitchen, "Thank goodness you're here!"

"Why?" Langford asked. "What's wrong?" His voice showed the apprehension her comment caused.

"We're all about to go stir crazy for one thing. But worse than that, the kids are talkin' about leavin' here and huntin' for the woman that saved the girls. They're all upstairs probably plottin' right now."

Langford stopped a moment and reconsidered his message, quickly deciding not to mention Pansy or her testimony. "Don't worry Mrs. Thorpe, my agents are here to prevent anyone from getting out as well as getting in. There's one posted outside as well as the one in here."

"You should never underestimate determined young folks, Agent Langford."

"I'll have a chat with our men and make sure they're aware, then I'll bring you and the kids up to date on our investigation."

Langford signaled for Agent Madison to follow him into the den. Madison closed the door behind him. "Getting pretty boring around here, sir," Madison said, "but we're all hanging in there."

"As you heard, Mrs. Thorpe just informed me that the kids are planning to take matters into their own hands, so be sure to keep a close eye on them. They're good kids but they've been through a lot, so try to handle them carefully but firmly."

"Yes, sir. I've heard them whispering but I agree they're good kids. I'll be alert for anything that might signal some trouble."

"Good. Now for your information, we're lookin' for the woman who saved the girls and hope her story matches what the kids have told us. But we can't rule her out on the Harper killing until we talk to her. Once we find her, which shouldn't take too long now, we'll hold her in protective custody at the sheriff's office while we round up some of the suspects. Hope to have this whole thing wrapped up in a day or two. So, hang tight and I'll be in touch. I'll brief Agent Browning on my way out."

"Yes sir. We'll await word from you. Good luck."

Neither of them noticed the closet door ajar across the room.

Langford called the kids downstairs so he could reassure them and Irene of progress without divulging Pansy's story.

"Hope you got good news for us," Maggie said warily, holding baby Willis in her arms.

Michael and Annalee stood behind Maggie, their expressions hopeful. Langford noticed that their fingers were laced, but they quickly dropped hands when Irene came up beside them. "I know you're all about to go crazy being held here, but I'm glad to tell you it will only be for a couple more days at most. We're in the process of rounding up some suspects and once that's done, you'll be free to return home."

"What about the Harper killing?" Michael asked suspiciously.

"We're workin' on that, son, and we hope to have that answer as well so you can all be cleared. Please be patient just a little bit longer."

Irene Thorpe spoke up. "And for goodness sake, kids, don't try to do anything on your own!"

"She's right, you know," Langford said. "If you were to try to do anything now you could upset our whole investigation. We know who all the major players are, and we are in the process of wrapping things up. Please just let us do our jobs."

"It feels kinda like we're imprisoned here anyway," Annalee said softly.

"Yeah," Maggie added, "not like we could get outta here if we wanted to."

"That's bein' done for your own protection, you know," Langford said. "I know these past few days have been hard on you. It's been hard on Mr. Thorpe and Mr. Roberts, too, being away from their families. Think about them too. You wouldn't want to put them in harm's way or jeopardize things at this point. So just sit tight and I'll be back in touch very soon. Promise?"

"Yeah," the three kids all mumbled together.

"Thank you, Agent Langford," Irene said softly. "It's reassuring to know this will all be over soon."

After Langford left, Maggie handed the baby off to Irene. "Mama, I can't seem to get this little boy to sleep for his nap. Guess I don't have the same touch you always had. Would you mind tryin'?"

"Of course not. Come here, little Willis," Irene said, taking the child in her arms. "I'll rock him over here and I bet that'll do the trick." She sat down in the rocker and began to sing to her grandson.

"Thanks, Mom. I love how you always know what to do." Maggie touched her mother's shoulder. "Think I need a nap of my own," she added yawning.

"Go ahead, honey, you need your rest. I've got this little guy."

"Thanks, Mom," Maggie said, as she walked over to the stairs.

Once upstairs, Maggie slipped into Michael's room where her brother and Annalee awaited her.

Maggie looked at Michael. "Glad you needed a pencil at such an opportune time. Well, what'd you hear?"

"They're onto the woman that found you girls," Michael said.

"So why can't we get outta here?" Annalee asked.

"Like Langford said, they're still roundin' up the ones that hurt you and also whoever killed Harper. But they haven't ruled us out, nor the woman that saved you."

"So, who's the gal that helped us and where's she?" Maggie asked.

"Didn't say her name either. Just said they'd be holdin' her in protective custody down at the sheriff's office."

Annalee thought for a second. "Don't suppose it would hurt nothin' for us to go pay our respects, d'ya?"

"Oh, let's just wait now," Michael replied. "We can wait another day or two, can't we?"

Maggie chimed in, "Well, it ain't exactly like we'd be interferin' with nothin', just thankin' her for helpin' us. Maybe helpin' her out a little at the same time."

Michael looked skeptically at his sister and Annalee. "Now just how do you propose we do this, walk straight out the dang front door?"

"Yes," Annalee smiled. "Or maybe the back door would be easier. Anyhow, we'll put a little somethin' into the afternoon tea, which we won't drink. But we'll make sure Agent Madison does. And we'll give Miss Irene a small dose, so she won't be too far under to hear Baby Willis if he wakes up. Say about 3:00 A.M. when the inside agent is fast asleep, Maggie takes a nice cup of coffee out to the other guy because she was up with Willis and thought the agent might like some joe."

Maggie shrugged. "Sounds simple enough. Michael, what d'ya think?"

Michael sighed. "I guess there ain't no talkin' you two outta this, so I'm game.

Maggie raised her eyebrows. "And just what goes into the tea and coffee, Annalee?"

Annalee smiled. "Just a little concoction Miss Salina showed my mama one time."

Chapter Thirty-One

Mr. and Mrs. Davis

"A house divided against itself cannot stand."

~ The Bible
Matthew 12:25

Sheriff Davis dreamed of his wife again just as he had for weeks now, ever since she left. Often, they were nightmares where she was grabbed by a lynch mob and he was held back from helping her. Or she was on the ground being beaten with clubs. Or the worst one of all, when she was violated by a gang then doused with gasoline and set on fire. He often woke up in a cold sweat, trying to shake the images from his mind.

But this night she was back beside him, gently pushing the hair from his forehead. It was like old times when they were easier with each other. He took her hand to kiss her palm just as he had done so many times in the early days. "I'm sorry," he whispered aloud.

But it wasn't him whispering. She quickly pulled her hand from his grasp and said it again, "I'm sorry. I'm so sorry, but I couldn't just leave them there."

Pansy stood up beside Langford, both of them looking down at Davis as he shook his head to loosen the cobwebs. He swung his legs over the side of the cot and rubbed his eyes. "It IS you. You're really here." He stood to reach for Pansy, but she backed away.

Langford interceded. "Vivian Beauford showed up on my doorstep before dawn this morning with your wife in tow. Mrs. Beauford said she trusts we will do right by Pansy and I intend to. We've got some business to take care of before any family reunions."

"Sure. Yeah. Business first," Davis replied, clearing his throat and straightening his posture.

"Let's go into your office, Sheriff. We can close the door, and no one will know she's here."

"Righto. I'll make us a pot of coffee."

After pouring three coffees, Davis then sat himself behind the desk. Pansy took a seat facing him and Langford leaned on the corner of the desk. There was palpable tension in the room. Davis awkwardly shuffled papers without looking at his wife. For her part, Pansy kept her eyes on her fingernails or the floor. Langford broke the silence as he cleared his throat and began his interrogation.

"Mrs. Davis..."

She looked up uncomfortably, but courage showed in her eyes as she said, "You can call me Pansy."

Sheriff Davis visibly flinched.

"Okay then, Pansy, I'm sure Mrs. Beauford informed you of the Leland Harper killing. We're gonna need to know where you've been the past week."

"I went from my sister's place in Memphis down to Hernando, Mississippi, to visit an old friend."

"The Indian woman, Miss Salina?"

"That's right. I was only there one night when your Deputy Moore showed up makin' noise about takin' me in for questionin'. He'da delivered me to the devil on a silver platter so Miss Salina decided to delay him 'til I could get back here and tell my story."

"And just what is your story?"

Pansy looked at her husband then quickly down at the floor. Finally, she met Langford's eyes. "It was Jack Beauford and Leland Harper that killed that Negro boy and hurt those girls. Them an' their kids an' Buck Dudley an' Roy Johnson an' their kids and let's not forget Jimmy Moore. They dumped 'em at our place for Jonathan to deal with. But I got to 'em first and helped 'em get away."

Langford looked at Sheriff Davis. "Is this true? Were you going to do the Klan's dirty work for them and dispose of those kids?"

"No! No, I wasn't gonna do that. I admit I done more than I shoulda to cover their tracks in the past. But I draw the line at killin' kids no matter what color they are. I planned to get back as soon as I could and help those kids, if they was still alive. But, like she said, Pansy got to 'em first."

"And you didn't know anything about this 'til they brought them to your place?"

"No sir, I didn't. I'da tried to stop 'em somehow, I swear."

Langford stood and stretched, pausing to think of the message he'd have to deliver. Then he turned to Davis and breathed a sigh. "You know you're gonna have to answer for withholding information in this investigation."

"Yeah, I ain't worried 'bout that. There's others I'll have to answer to once they find out Pansy's back and I ain't done nothin' to keep her quiet."

Langford looked at Pansy. "And we really can't rule you out as a suspect in Harper's murder. Not 'til we talk with the Indian woman to verify you were with her when it happened. Don't know when she'll be available."

"Yeah, I know. It's ok. Go ahead and lock me up. I got nowhere else to be."

"Sheriff, I want you to keep Pansy here in protective custody. Keep her in the back, out of sight. I'll send over an agent just in case."

"And just where are you headed, Langford?" asked Davis. "Seems to me you might need my assistance as much as Pansy needs guardin'. I know these boys and their hangouts. We can put your man in here and I'll go with you."

"What about Deputy Moore? He's due in here about noon, isn't he?"

“Yeah, maybe we should pick him up on the way. See where his loyalties lay. And long as he’s with us he ain’t gonna get word to nobody that we’re comin’.”

“Good idea, Davis. I’ll go get my agents and give you two a chance to talk.”

Pansy Davis looked across the desk at her husband. “Would you really have helped those kids?”

“So help me God,” he replied, holding up his right hand. “You got no idea how this stuff has twisted up my gut the last few years.”

“You never said nothin’.”

“I didn’t want you to know a lot of stuff for your own good.”

“I thought your silences were just where we’d got to in the marriage. So, you ain’t mad at me for helpin’ those girls?”

Jonathan Davis came around the desk and took the chair next to his wife. “Pans, I can’t rightly say I was happy ‘bout it, just cause o’ what kinda trouble it might bring you. But we both know you did the right thing.”

“Can bring you trouble, too.” She said. “Surprised it ain’t already.”

He reached out and took her hand in his. “Don’t you worry ‘bout me. I can take care o’ myself. An’ I gotta say I think that Langford fella seems to know what he’s doin’.”

There was an awkward silence between them for a moment and Pansy took her hand out of his.

"You gotta know you hurt me Jonny. When I lost the baby, I wanted to run away from you so bad, but I didn't have a way nor the courage. Since then I just been existin'."

Jonathan stood up and paced nervously. "I know," he said, facing her. "I relived that night over a thousand times, tryin' for a different outcome. I can't blame it on the liquor, but that's what brung it on. I never meant to hurt you and I sure as hell never meant to kill our baby. But that's what I done, and it'll haunt me 'til my dyin' day."

"Haunts me too," Pansy said softly. "Maybe we shoulda talked about all this years ago. Maybe then I wouldn'ta started hatin' you."

"You still hate me?"

"I dunno. I seen the old you, the one I loved, here this mornin'. But how can I trust it?"

Just then there was a tap on the office door. "Sheriff Davis? Agents Coughlin and Randall here. Langford sent us. He's waiting outside for you."

Davis stood and reached out his hand to his wife. "We'll keep talkin' bout this when I get back, okay? Give me that much?"

Pansy took his hand and rose from her chair. She gave him a quick kiss on the cheek before going through the door.

"Take good care of this woman, agents," Davis said. "She's my wife and she may be in danger."

"We've been fully briefed, Sheriff," Agent Coughlin replied. "She's in good hands."

To Pansy, he asked, "You play gin, ma'am? My partner here is lousy at it."

Pansy chuckled. "I'm a little rusty, but what else we got to do?"

Chapter Thirty-Two

Both Sides of the Law

"At his best, man is the noblest of all animals;
separated from law and justice
he is the worst."

~ Aristotle (384-322BC)
Ancient Greek philosopher and scientist.

Deputy Jimmy Moore was quite surprised to see Agent Langford and Sheriff Davis at his door when he looked through the window to see who was knocking. He considered for a second looking around the room to see if anything needed hiding, then he opened the door wide.

"Mornin' y'all. Whatcha doin' here? I ain't overslept cause you told me not to come in 'til noon. So, who's mindin' the store?"

Langford stepped inside and began to look around while Davis engaged Moore in conversation. "Mornin' Jimmy. Me and Agent Langford here got some business to tend to and we thought we'd take you along. Got some new information on who mighta hurt those kids."

"Like what?" Moore asked, seeming to be a little nervous. "What d'ya need me for?"

Langford spoke up. "We're gonna pay a little visit to a couple friends of yours and we thought maybe you could help us get our foot in the door, so to speak."

Moore was anxious now. "What's he talkin' 'bout, Sheriff?"

"Oh, don't worry, Jimmy, me and Langford here had a nice long talk earlier. Right after we talked with Pansy."

"Pansy? I heard she might be comin' back."

Davis grabbed Moore by the throat and shoved him up against the wall. "Who'd you hear that from? Who knows she's here? Answer me, dammit!"

Langford grabbed Davis' arm and Moore slid to the floor holding his neck and smirking. Langford hated sneering criminals, especially if they lived under the cloak of law enforcement. He picked up the deputy by his collar and threw him on the sofa. He jumped on top of Moore and thrust his knee into the deputy's crotch. He pulled his gun from its holster and held the barrel up to Moore's jugular. "Be a shame for you to get killed in self-defense during a federal investigation, deputy," he said evenly. "I suggest you give us the names we want now."

Davis stood by in stunned silence; he stared in disbelief as he heard Langford cock his pistol.

"Okay, okay, you crazy bastard, let me up and I'll tell ya!" Moore pleaded.

Langford backed off with his gun still trained on Moore. Moore swung his legs around and sat up on the couch, grimacing in pain. "Buck told me they was trackin' her down and somebody thought they spotted her at the Beauford place, but they wasn't sure."

"When was this?" Langford asked.

"Just last night. Buck come by for a beer after I got home."

"And just what did Buck plan to do?"

"I dunno. He said he might have to pay a call to the Beauford place, but he'd talk to Roy today first."

"Let's go, Agent, "Davis said, heading toward the door. "Roy Johnson's place ain't far from here. Jimmy, you're comin' along."

Moore protested, but Langford dragged him out the door. Once inside the car, Langford radioed for dispatch to call one of his agents at the jail and instruct them to check on Vivian Beauford.

Deputy Moore sulked in handcuffs in the back seat. He turned his anger on Sheriff Davis. "It's one thing to have a fed diggin' into this, but you Sheriff, you're a local boy. You know how things work down here. Hell, you been coverin' for stuff long enough to know you ain't gonna get outta this unhurt, maybe not even alive. Your old lady neither."

Davis reached into the back seat and squeezed Moore's face in his hand. "You leave Pansy outta this. She done what she thought was right. That's more than I can say for the rest of us." He shoved the deputy's head against the seat.

Langford spoke to Davis. "Come on, now. Take it easy, Sheriff. You know Deputy Moore is probably just a little rattled, wondering if we're gonna tell his friend Buck who squealed on him. That right, deputy?"

"Hmmph!" snorted Moore. He then settled back and looked out the window. Langford looked in the rearview mirror. He was certain Moore had that smirk on his face again and it worried him. He pressed the accelerator.

"Nobody home at Beauford's place," Agent Randall said, coming through the door to the Sheriff's Office. At about the same time he realized the door had been unlocked, he was clubbed from behind and fell to the floor unconscious.

Taking charge, Buck Dudley instructed Roy Johnson to drag Randall to a cell in the back. "Just tie him up and throw him in with the other one. They ain't goin' nowhere," he chuckled, "We'll finish 'em later."

Pansy sat tied to a desk chair. She hung her head, wondering if this was how she would die.

Roy Johnson walked up behind Pansy, grabbed her hair and yanked up her head. "Pay attention, Pansy! I wanna see the look on your husband's face when he comes in that door and sees us blow your head off. The shock won't even wear off before we do the same to him."

"You know the FBI's all over this mess, Roy. Won't matter what you do to me but what d'ya think they're gonna do when they find out you took out a couple o' their agents?"

"Well, the way I see it, it was all on your old man. Yessir, he come in here, saw those agents gettin' a little too friendly with you, and killed all o' ya. Then felt so bad about it he couldn't live with hisself."

"Why you wanna kill Jonathan? Ya know it's me that squealed on ya. He's only helped ya out in the past."

"Well, it sure wasn't us that killed Leland, so it had to be either you or him. Either way, we got scores to settle with both o' ya."

"I didn't do it and neither did Jonathan. But you're gonna believe whatever your ol' warped minds wanna believe. Either way... he deserved killin'."

Not liking what Pansy had to say, Dudley smacked her upside the head. Blood spurted onto her shirt and she could feel it trickling down the side of her face. She didn't know whether Dudley and Johnson were aware that Langford was with her husband, so she hung her head, deciding to keep quiet and hope for the best.

Vivian Beauford had seen the FBI man snooping around her house. She had hidden behind the curtain when she heard him knock on the door then peeked out at him as he left. She didn't recognize him and since he drove an unfamiliar sedan, she figured he was part of Langford's group. After pondering about why he might have come looking for her, she decided it might be best to check on Pansy's welfare.

Something didn't feel right when she drove up to the courthouse and looked over at the annex. There was the same sedan she'd seen at her place. Other vehicles were parked out front, as well, but no patrol cars. Vivian sat in her car a few minutes considering her next move. She decided to enter the back door of the sheriff's office, which could only be reached through a tunnel under the courthouse steps. But first, she pulled a pistol from under the front seat and tucked it into her waistband. Then she retrieved a switchblade from her purse and dropped it into her pocket.

Roy Johnson's wife was no help to Langford and Davis. She claimed she didn't know where he was or when he'd be back. Neither did she know whether Buck Dudley was with him.

Deputy Moore carefully listened to the exchange through the opened window of the patrol car. When the others got back in the car, he snickered.

Langford looked in his rearview mirror, only to see that same smug look on Moore's face. Suddenly it dawned on him what Moore knew that they didn't. "Damn!" he said to Davis. "We gotta get back to your office—they're goin' after Pansy."

Moore let out a howl of laughter, and Davis turned on him with a right cross that shut him up and knocked him over. Davis turned forward rubbing his knuckles and brushing bits of teeth off his sleeve. "Step on it," was all he said.

Vivian slipped quietly in through the back door of the jail and stood listening. At first she heard nothing. Suddenly the sound of a smack out in the front office startled her. She started to move forward but stopped when she heard someone moaning. Turning to her right, she saw a pair of feet sticking out of a cell. She tiptoed toward the feet until she could see two bound bodies on the floor, one slowly moving its feet and moaning, the other silent and still. She slipped into the cell, kneeled and felt for a pulse on the first body. There was none. Vivian hung her head, crossed herself and moved to the next man.

Langford radioed headquarters in Little Rock and asked them to call the sheriff's office in Oakwood. When he was advised that the call went unanswered, Langford asked for back-up to be sent as soon as possible.

"What's our plan, Langford?" Davis asked, staring straight ahead.

"I was hoping you had one," came the reply.

There was only moaning in the back seat.

Just outside of town, Langford pulled into a grove of trees out of sight of the road. He opened the back door and drug Moore from the car. Davis joined him and held Moore upright against the car.

Langford poked his finger into Moore's chest. "This is the way it's gonna go down, Deputy. We're gonna walk up to the sheriff's office and try the door. If it's open, you're goin' in first. We'll be right behind you with guns drawn and you just fall to the floor out of the way. If the door's locked, you're gonna knock and tell them it's you and to let you in. Then the same scenario. Got that?"

"Why should I help you? I could get killed!"

"Oh, you can get killed right here in the trees if that's how you wanna play it, Jimmy," Langford said evenly. "But you help us out and I'll put in a word for the authorities to go easy on you."

"Davis, you gonna let him do me this way? You okay with usin' me like a human shield?"

Davis turned and spit on the ground. "Human shield or body in the trees, don't make no difference to me, after the way you sold out Pansy. You'd best take Mr. Langford's offer. There won't be another."

Langford pulled his gun and aimed it at the deputy. Moore flinched then shook his head. Another tooth fragment and some blood flew from his mouth.

"You... you're the law, you're not supposed to treat folks this way, dammit!"

Langford cocked his gun.

"Alright, alright, I'll do it! Can't be any riskier than bein' with you maniacs."

Chapter Thirty-Three

Convergence

"The future depends on what you do today."

~ Mahatma Gandhi (1869-1948)
Indian activist and leader of the Indian independence movement against British rule.

Winston Roberts was trying to concentrate on the book he was reading when his phone rang. "Hello?"

"Roberts? It's Thorpe. I just got a call from Michael. Those kids are up to somethin' and they need our help. You in?"

"What about those guys we been avoidin'? You think it's safe?"

"Michael heard Langford talkin' to his agent. Seems they got things pretty well under control and should have it wrapped up soon. So again, are you in?"

"You bet I'm in. I been goin' crazy over here all alone wonderin' what was happenin' with my little girl."

"Me too. I'll pick you up at 1:00 A.M."

"I'll be ready."

The kitchen clock read 2:00 as Michael and Annalee slipped quietly out the back door. Maggie met up with them in the back yard, after taking coffee to Agent Browning. "How long's he gonna be out?" she asked.

"Oh, maybe all day, and maybe into night," Annalee replied.

"Long enough," Michael said.

"Okay, now how do we get into town and to the sheriff's office from way out here?" Annalee asked. "Anybody thought o' that?"

"Got it covered," Michael answered. "Follow me and stay quiet."

They walked along silently through the countryside for some time. Topping the rise of a hill, they saw a car parked up ahead on a gravel road. Michael put his finger to his mouth. As they got closer Maggie stopped short.

"Michael, what the hell have you done?"

"Sis, we needed help. Can't think o' nobody I'd rather have in our corner."

"But what if it put him in danger?"

"You heard Langford. I honestly don't think anybody's worried 'bout keepin' an eye on our Dad anymore."

"Your father?" Annalee asked incredulously. "You called your father to help us?"

"Not only that, but he was gonna pick up yours to help, too," Michael replied.

"Daddy?" Annalee couldn't believe her ears. "Do you mean they're together? Do they know we plan to spring that woman even if she did kill Harper, who we know ain't no loss to nobody?"

"Oh, they'll find out in time, it's no use spoilin' the surprise," Michael replied.

Maggie and Annalee started running toward the car. Michael rushed after them.

Eddie Thorpe jumped out of the car and ran to hug his daughter. Winston Roberts leaped from the passenger side and gathered Annalee into his arms. Michael stopped to catch his breath but Eddie pulled him into the embrace he still shared with Maggie.

"How's your mom doin'?" Eddie asked anxiously.

"She's holdin' up okay, I guess considerin'," Maggie answered.

Michael shook Winston's hand and thanked him for coming along.

"No thanks needed. We're all in this together, son."

"We'd better get a move on if we wanna get this done under the cover o' darkness," Michael said to the group.

"Now, that sounds a little ominous to my ears..." Winston commented.

Vivian Beauford heard loud angry voices out front. She stopped to listen, trying to distinguish how many men were there. Agent Randall stirred beneath her touch as she checked his pulse.

"Try to stay calm," Vivian whispered. "I'll get you outta here as soon as I can, but I can't do it alone. Just stay quiet for now."

Randall labored to speak. "There's two men," he uttered. "Guns 'n clubs... don't go out there."

"Shush now. Just rest. I'm gonna try to slip out the back where I came in and go for help."

"Langford..." Randall whispered.

"Yes, son, I know him. I'll call the FBI. Don't worry, I'll get you help."

Vivian patted Randall's shoulder then straightened up to a crouch. She listened intently and heard back-and-forth conversation between the two men out front.

Should I go now? she wondered. *Should I wait to see if help arrives? How the hell did I get into this mess anyhow? All I planned to do was kill myself after Joey died. Then Pansy shows up and she's my one friend. And maybe, just maybe, it's the debt I owe for doin' what I done.*

Vivian patted the gun in her waistband, took a deep breath and slipped through the hallway toward the back door.

Langford considered waiting for the back-up to arrive, but he knew the nearest agent station was in Little Rock. It would take them a while to arrive, providing the call was handled quickly. He couldn't be sure that someone wouldn't light a match to this local powder keg at any moment. No, it had to be now and it had to be him. Him and Sheriff Davis, a man he had mistrusted up until just recently. He certainly hoped his instincts about the sheriff proved right.

"Davis, you ready for this?"

"Yessir. I got too much at stake on the other side o' that door."

"Deputy Moore?" Langford called into the back seat. "You remember our plan and what's at stake for you, right?"

"Yeah, yeah, all I can say is you two better be crack shots or it's my ass they're gonna be moppin' the floor with."

"Relax, Moore, we'll save your ass or at the very least die trying," Langford said.

"All the same to you, I'd just as soon do it the first way," Davis replied.

Langford set his jaw and pulled back onto the roadway. "Well let's get this over with."

"Ok what's our plan when we get there?" Winston asked Eddie.

"Well if she's just bein' held in protective custody there's probly only gonna be a deputy there, so I figure we just go right in the front door and tell 'em why we come."

Michael spoke up from the back seat. “Suppose he won’t let us talk to her?”

“Oh, he shouldn’t give us any trouble, but I bet we can persuade him to give us five minutes with her at least.”

“Daddy?” Maggie said. “Would it be alright if me and Annalee go in first? We’d really like to thank her personally for savin’ our lives.”

“Winston, you okay with that?” Eddie asked.

“Don’t see why not, except I’m thinkin’ we all go in together and then the girls go talk to this woman on their own from there. Just present a united front ‘n all.”

“Good idea,” Michael added.

“Yeah, good idea, Daddy,” Annalee chimed in.

“Okay then,” said Eddie. “We’ve got just another couple blocks.”

Vivian Beauford didn’t see the hand that grabbed her as she reached for the doorknob, but she felt the club strike hard against the side of her head. She began to lose consciousness almost immediately but not before spinning around and plunging her switchblade into Roy Johnson’s jugular as her gun fell to the floor and discharged. They fell together against the back door, him mortally wounded and falling on top of Vivian, still clinging to life.

“Hold up!” shouted Eddie, as the group stepped out of the car. “That sounded like a gunshot.”

"It sure as hell did, Thorpe," Winston said. "Ain't no black man needs to be nearby when a gun goes off in the dark o' night."

"But it sounded like it come from the sheriff's office. Doncha think we oughtta check it out?"

Michael and the girls were already running toward the door.

"Stop kids! It may not be safe!" yelled Eddie.

Winston was already running after the kids and Eddie followed.

The four of them burst through the sheriff's door at once.

Buck Dudley didn't have any time to check out the gunshot in the back. Just as he turned toward the sound, the front door spilled five people into his office. He instinctively fired at the black man, dropping him on the spot.

"Daddy!" Annalee yelled, rushing to her father who lay moaning in the corner.

Pansy shook; she was still bound and gagged in a chair facing the door. Her eyes were wide with fright. She could not control her shivering body nor the tears spilling down her face.

"Stop shootin', dammit, just stop the shootin'" Eddie shouted with his hands in the air, visibly shaking. "We ain't no threat to you, Dudley!"

"How do I know you're not?" Dudley shouted. "Ain't nothin' goin' right in here. Just sit down on the floor right there by your buddy, you and the kids both."

Michael had already rushed to Annalee's side, trying to comfort her and check on Winston. Eddie and Maggie sat down beside them keeping a wary eye on Dudley.

"This man needs a doctor!" Michael shouted at Dudley.

"Ain't callin' no doctor for no nigger," Dudley spat. "Got enough problems here as it is. Fact, git over here gal," he said to Maggie as he dragged her by the arm to stand beside him. He held his gun against her head. "Now I got me a hostage, case any o' you wanna try somethin' stupid."

Eddie pleaded with Dudley. "Don't hurt her again, Buck. We'll be calm. We'll do whatever you say. Only please don't hurt my little girl anymore."

Langford had a bad feeling as they pulled up across from the sheriff's office. Something wasn't right. But it was too late to change plans at this point, and he didn't know how much time they had left. *You can't un-ring this bell,* he thought to himself.

"You ready?" he said again to Davis.

Davis nodded and exited the car, pulling Moore from the back seat. The three of them headed toward the sheriff's office on the other side of the street.

As planned, Moore tried the door only to find it locked. He tentatively looked at the others. Davis motioned for him to knock. Moore knocked three times.

Dudley whispered for Michael to unlock the door.

"No! I'll do it," Eddie said, lunging for the lock, then stepping back.

As the door slowly opened, Dudley looked up to see Deputy Moore on the other side.

"Boy, am I glad to see you Jimmy!" Dudley shouted, shoving Maggie aside and turning his gun on Pansy. "We gotta get this over... what the hell?"

Moore suddenly dove for the floor while Langford and Davis rushed in with guns drawn. "Drop it, Dudley!" Davis shouted. Dudley turned on them, not sure who to point his firearm at.

"Do it now!" Langford added.

Dudley hesitated. Moore started to crawl over to him. Eddie stomped on the deputy and pinned him to the floor with a sickening crack of bones.

As Dudley turned his aim once again on Pansy, Davis shot him square between the shoulder blades, the bullet piercing his heart and killing him instantly. The sheriff then rushed to his wife, removed her gag and began to untie her.

"Hurry, call an ambulance!" Pansy shouted. "That man over there is shot, and there's a couple agents in the back they hurt pretty bad, too."

"You folks okay?" Langford asked Eddie and the kids.

"We're okay," Eddie replied. "Please just take care of Winston here."

As Davis called for help, Langford rushed to the back. There was a bloody heap of flesh laying in front of the back door. Hard to even determine where one body began and the other ended due to the amount of blood. Langford was finally able to drag Roy Johnson off Vivian Beauford. Finding no pulse, he rolled him aside and lifted Vivian's head in his arms.

"Mrs. Beauford? We got an ambulance on the way, try to hang on."

"Nah, can't hang on..."

"Please, Mrs. Beauford, it'll just be a few minutes!"

Vivian was struggling to breathe now. "Ya ever hear o' just desserts?"

"Yes, you took him down, Mrs. Beauford. You got him. Just hang in there and we'll get you fixed up."

"No. Not him ... me."

"What are you talking about?"

"...deathbed confession... I killed Harper... an' his kid... was me done it."

Langford was stunned. He looked up at Davis who had checked on the other agents. Davis shook his head and held up one finger.

"Mrs. Beauford, Sheriff Davis is here now. Are you sure you want these to be your last words? Are you sure you want to confess to stabbing Leland Harper and leaving his son to die in the house fire as you've told me?"

Pansy came in from the other room and fell beside Vivian. "Please hang in there Viv. Help's on the way. We'll get you fixed up and then you can talk if you want to."

Vivian gave a faint smile. "Pans... I killed 'em both. f' my Joey... this my penance. Vengeance mine, says t' Lord... Jus' let me go'n face my God."

Chapter Thirty-Four

Closing One File

"The reward for work well done is the opportunity to do more."

~ Jonas Salk (1914-1995)
American medical researcher and virologist.

Agent Langford sat at the sheriff's desk finishing up paperwork. Davis walked in and set a cup of coffee before him on the desk.

"Thanks, I'll need that," Langford said, stretching and sighing.

Davis took a sip from his own cup. "Your agent, Randall? How's he doin?"

"He's gonna be okay but it's gonna take a while. Thanks for askin'. How's Pansy?"

"Near as I can tell she's gonna be okay, too. Like you said 'bout Randall it's gonna take a while."

"Look, I know you're worried about this federal rap hangin' over your head but I'm gonna put in a good word for you that any obstruction of justice was out of concern for your wife's welfare, who was a material witness in the case. All things considered, I'm hoping you get off with probation. Unfortunately, it's not up to me."

"I'll take my medicine, whatever it is. You been pretty straight with me. There's one thing I'd like to ask you, though."

"What's that?"

"The way you went off on Deputy Moore. Would you o' killed him or was that all an act?"

"If you have to ask then what does it matter? Either I'm a highly trained professional who's good at bluffing or I'm a psychopath with a gun and a badge. In this business that's sometimes a fine line; the day I don't know the difference is the day I walk away."

"Oh I knew you was bluffin' all along," Davis shrugged. "Just wanted to hear ya say it."

Langford closed up his file and stood to gather his things. "Been a pleasure, Sheriff Davis. Don't think I can say it started out that way but I can say sincerely that I'm glad you were on my side." He extended his hand.

Davis shook Langford's hand and reached for one of the boxes Langford was trying to balance. "Pansy and I may have a second chance after all this and I wanna thank you for that, Langford."

"No thanks needed, part of the job. Good luck to both of you, Sheriff. Now if you'll excuse me, I got a long trip ahead of me and a few folks to say good-bye to before leaving town."

At the hospital, Langford stopped in to see Agent Randall who was sitting up in bed while a woman fed him breakfast. His head was bandaged, and his arm was in a cast. Half his face was purple and yellow, and one eye was still swollen shut.

"Looks like you're in good hands, Agent," Langford said with a smile.

"Sir," Randall replied with a crooked smile. "I'd like you to meet my wife, Lorna." And to his wife, he said, "Honey, this is Agent Langford that I told you about."

"How d'you do?" Lorna asked.

"Pleased to meet you, Mrs. Randall. Sorry our boy here had to take such a beating."

"She knows it goes with the territory, sir," Randall said.

"Doesn't mean I have to like it," Lorna said with a scowl. "You need to take some time off after this dear."

Langford nodded his head. "She's right, you know. You're on paid leave until further notice and that's an order. And thanks for everything, Agent Randall. You're a good man."

Over in the colored side of the hospital Langford found Winston Roberts' room. Annalee was sitting on the side of the bed reading to her father. Winston looked up when Langford knocked on the door frame.

"How's the patient?" he asked Annalee.

"Stubborn as ever and uncooperative," she replied.

"Now don't let her fool you, Agent, I been a model patient cause I wanna get outta this place."

"Don't blame you a bit there. The doc tells me your shoulder ought to be good as new in a while. Good thing that bullet went clean through."

Annalee glared at her father with a smirk on her face. "Yeah but in the meantime, will you please tell this man to obey his doctor's orders and get some rest? And to obey his nurse too, who just happens to be me?"

Winston sighed. "Guess I got my orders, Agent. Rest and nap and read. Lord that's all they'll let me do."

Langford grinned. "Well if you wanna heal up, you gotta follow those orders, Mr. Roberts. I'm betting that Annalee will bring little Willis over to see you once you start getting better."

"Now THAT'S the goal I'm shootin' for," Winston answered with a chuckle.

Langford stepped closer and offered his hand. "Pleasure to meet you folks and I'm hoping if I ever see you again, it'll be under much better circumstances."

Eddie Thorpe opened the door wide when he saw Agent Langford through the window. "Come in, Agent, come right on in, we was just talkin' bout you," he said as he stuck out his hand.

"Uh oh," Langford said, shaking Eddie's hand. "That why my ears been ringing?"

Irene Thorpe came into the living room, wiping her hands on her apron. "Oh, it was mostly good, Agent," she laughed. "We didn't always understand your methods, but we all agreed that you did a good job and we thank you."

"No thanks needed, ma'am, I WAS just doing my job. Wanted to come and say good-bye before I leave town. It's been a pleasure knowing you folks and I wish all of you the best."

"Agent," Eddie began, "I gotta tell you that this was an ordeal alright, but I certainly think I'm a better man for it after all is said and done."

Just then little Willis cried from the crib in the corner.

"And look at the booby prize!" Eddie said with a laugh, as Irene gathered Willis into a tight embrace.

"Edward Thorpe!" Irene scolded. "Don't you dare talk about this precious child that way! Just like Maggie said, he's our little miracle, the one good thing that came out of all that bad."

"Now, that's a fact," Eddie said sheepishly.

Irene looked at the clock. "Michael and Maggie will be sorry they missed you, Agent. They just went over to the hospital to visit Mr. Roberts and Annalee."

"Well, I just came from there, so we must have passed on the road somewhere. Anyway, I need to get going. You folks take care and best of luck to you."

Eddie walked Langford to his car. "So do I call you if there's any more trouble or can I trust Davis to take care of it now?"

"I think you can trust Sheriff Davis, Mr. Thorpe. He's a better man now, too. But if you need me you've got my number."

CHAPTER THIRTY-FIVE

1968

Little Rock

"Those who make peaceful revolution impossible,
make violent revolution inevitable."

~ John F. Kennedy (1917-1963)
American politician;
35th President of the United States.

ONCE WINSTON WAS home from the hospital, Annalee took good care of him. And Michael took good care of her. The two were growing closer, a fondness borne of mutual affection and shared experiences. Winston wasn't sure about it. This was new untested territory in the midst of a changing world.

But he was also very fond of Michael, especially in light of the boy's help and protection of both Annalee and him following the shooting. And he liked the way Michael stood up for his sister during her trying time in Memphis and beyond. There was no doubt that Michael was of good character and could be trusted. It was the character of others that had Winston worried.

Michael and Annalee sat in the front porch swing late one night after Winston had fallen asleep. The August night was hot and muggy as they fanned themselves and swatted bugs.

"Lordy I wish this weather would break," Michael noted. "Seems to make everybody cranky and short-tempered. 'Cept you, o' course, sweet Annalee." This last comment was punctuated with a kiss on her cheek.

Annalee took his hand and looked deeply into his eyes. "Michael, there's somethin' I wanna talk to you about. You don't have to do it if you don't want to, but I feel compelled."

Michael straightened up with his back against the swing. "Sounds serious. Tell me."

"I know you know what's been goin' on up in Little Rock. I got an old friend from school that wants me to come to a rally up there."

"A rally? You mean a demonstration or somethin'?"

"Not exactly. It's more of a march from the black neighborhood down to the courthouse and then a gatherin' there to talk about the boy that was killed in the jail—and to demand justice."

"Like I said, a demonstration."

"But it's supposed to be peaceful, Michael. There's an organization up there, the BUY—Black United Youth and they're puttin' it together, so it's organized. Michael, all I did was weep when Dr. King was killed. I just wanna stand up for somethin', you know what I mean?"

"I do understand, Annalee. I know you wanna help your people and I admire you for that. But you know how volatile things are up there right now. Just cause it's supposed to be peaceful don't mean it will be. Does your daddy know about this?"

"No and don't you say nothin' to him. Michael, this is somethin' I feel I need to do. But it ain't your fight and I'll understand if you don't wanna go along."

"Well, when is it?"

"Friday."

"Then I guess I'll pick you up on Friday 'cause I ain't lettin' you go by yourself. And Annalee? Don't never say this ain't my fight cause if it's yours, then it's mine. We come through too much together to draw a color line now."

She leaned in to kiss him on the lips. "That's what I love about you, Michael Thorpe. With you, there is no line."

It was the first time either of them had said the word "love." Michael drew her to him and prolonged the kiss. Suddenly he pulled away. "I gotta get home before things get outta hand. Good night… my love."

The next morning, Michael whistled as he went through the door, headed for his job at the lumber yard. He stopped in his tracks when he saw his pick-up. His beloved truck was slathered with the words, NIGGER LOVER, on each side. He threw his cap on the ground, waved his arms and shouted to the heavens, "It's 1968 you dumb shits, get your heads outta your asses!"

Eddie Thorpe came running from the garage when he heard his son yelling. He, too, was stopped in his tracks. "Holy shit! I can't believe it! Michael, you got any idea who in hell did this?"

Michael just looked at his father, shaking his head.

"Well, pull it round back and we'll sure get that paint off o' it. It won't be pretty for a while but we'll get a new paint job soon's we can."

Michael stood with his feet planted, staring at his truck. "Could this o' been us a while back, Dad? Were we this hateful?"

Eddie sucked in his breath, then let it out with a sad kind of sigh. "I ain't never deliberately done nothin' against the coloreds but I have given plenty o' lip service, son. Not since I been grown. But there was a time when I was about your age that I fought a colored man just 'cause I thought he disrespected me. And I was stupid drunk or I'da never done it then."

"It runs deep don't it?" Michael asked sincerely.

"Yeah," Eddie replied. "It surely runs mighty deep and it ain't usually questioned 'til somethin' happens that smacks you upside the head."

"Like with Maggie and little Willis."

Eddie just nodded his head and cleared his throat. "Pull on 'round back and we'll get this taken care of. Got some paint remover in the shed."

On Friday afternoon Michael drove to the Roberts home after work. Annalee came through the screen door as soon as he pulled into the dirt driveway. She stopped and gave him a quizzical look when she saw the raw stripped side of his truck.

As he opened the door for her, Michael said simply, "Just a little paint splash, nothin' to worry 'bout. What d'you tell your daddy?"

"I told him we were goin' for a bite to eat, then a double feature at the drive in, so not to wait up for us. Mrs. Parker next door's gonna bring supper over and help him get tucked in later. Now what the heck really happened to your truck?"

Michael backed into the street and proceeded to tell Annalee what had happened as they drove toward the outskirts of town. "So I guess it ain't any more dangerous drivin' up to Little Rock than bein' right here in Oakwood. Maybe even less since we'll be anonymous there."

Annalee put her hand on top of his on the gear knob. "I'm sorry. Maybe I'm bein' naïve about all this. Already you been put in harm's way cause o' me."

Michael patted her hand, then shifted into high gear as he sped onto the highway. "You seem to forget that I got a little nephew at home who's the OTHER apple o' my eye. Doin' this as much for him as for you, no offense."

"Oh, none taken. I couldn't compete with that boy even if I wanted to," she answered with a smile.

As dusk settled over Little Rock, a crowd gathered near the Dunbar Community Center in the heart of the black neighborhood. Following the instructions of Annalee's friend, Michael parked on the far end of Wright Avenue, hoping to avoid any trouble. By the time they walked to the community center, the crowd had grown to several hundred. As they left for the Pulaski County Courthouse where the rally was to be held, Michael felt somewhat relieved to see several other white people joining the march. He and Annalee were unnerved by the heavy police presence all along the route. They had agreed not to join hands for fear of provoking someone's anger, but soon the marchers were arm in arm all across the street anyway.

At the rally they noticed National Guardsmen lining up on the crowd's perimeter. Swallowing their apprehensions, they each tried to concentrate on the speeches. Michael had never known such fear and dread. He questioned his own motives as he felt a shaky tension throughout his body. Was he here just to impress Annalee or did he really want to set an example for little Willis? Was even THAT too narrow a focus when a whole race was being treated unjustly? Did he really belong here? Or, was that last thought just a convenient escape clause playing with his fear of what was to come?

Annalee seemed to sense the change in Michael as she read into his nervous dilemma. She grabbed his hand between their bodies and whispered into his ear that they could leave if he wanted to. He shook his head and mouthed "I'm fine for now, let's stay a little longer." He hoped his expression convinced her that he meant it even though he wasn't sure of his own conviction.

Some people began to move away, and Michael took Annalee's hand, slowly and gently moving her toward the edge of the crowd. There were enough people dispersing now that Micheal felt they wouldn't be alone in the street. They followed those leaving ahead of them, heading south on Broadway, figuring it must be a shortcut back to the community center.

They walked along silently, digesting exactly what the speakers had said and wondering what came next. Suddenly they heard raised voices then the sound of glass breaking and people shouting. Michael stopped cold, not sure what to do. Then he grabbed Annalee's hand and raced down a side street, hoping to skirt whatever trouble lay up ahead. They continued that direction with a few others who had made the same decision.

Soon there were sirens, more glass breaking, louder shouts and curses, even a gunshot. Just as Michael and Annalee entered the black neighborhood, they saw jeeps racing toward the commotion. As they rounded a corner hoping to weave their way back to Michael's truck, they saw National Guardsmen pulling into vacant lots where they loaded their rifles and fixed their bayonets.

Michael looked quickly at Annalee. "We gotta get outta here fast!" She had never seen Michael's face look quite so white. They ran through alleys and across lawns, sure that they were running for their lives. Finally, they saw Michael's truck up ahead of them as police lights flashed and sirens wailed behind them.

As they left town, Annalee kept looking out the back window as state troopers roared by them in the opposite direction with lights flashing and sirens screaming. "Holy shit, Michael, I never seen so many police lights all lit up at once! And look, there's a fire—and another one flarin' up!"

Michael tried to tune in a Little Rock radio station to see if he could get the latest news. Between the static and the newscaster's frantic reporting, they were able to gather that the state police had cordoned off eighty square blocks and the National Guard was called into service amidst the chaos and bedlam.

"Whoowee, we got outta there just in the nick o' time," Michael declared. "Five more minutes, one wrong turn, and we'd be shot or locked up by now."

"And this is the danger on our side o' the line all the time, Michael."

"Yeah, I'm beginnin' to see what you mean. And I'm still right by your side. But at the same time, I wanna protect you from all this."

"We can't hide from it. I'm afraid it's always gonna be a fact o' life."

"Well, I know one way I can protect you better."

"Yeah, how's that?"

Michael pulled the truck to the side of the road and turned to face Annalee.

"Miss Annalee Roberts, will you do me the honor of marryin' me?"

"Of all the crazy white boys in this world, you gotta be the craziest, Michael Thorpe!"

"S'that a yes or a no?"

She flung her arms around his neck, wanting never to let go. "Oh, it's definitely a yes! But how d'you think marryin' me's gonna keep me better protected?"

"Well, we'll be livin' together and I can just keep a better eye on you, that's all. Not that I'm gonna try to run your life or nothin,' 'cause I know you're pretty independent. Annalee maybe we will never change the world, but it'll make me feel a whole lot better just havin' you close."

"Me, too, Michael, me too." She pulled away a little and looked at him. "Now which one o' us is gonna break the news to our long-sufferin' parents?"

"Oh, I think we'd best do that together, safety in numbers 'n all that!"

Chapter Thirty-Six

1969

Bells and Flashing Lights

"Love recognizes no barriers. It jumps hurdles, leaps fences, and penetrates walls to arrive at its destination full of hope."

~ Maya Angelou (1928-2014)
American poet, singer, memoirist, and civil rights activist.

On a hot Saturday afternoon in August, people approached the steps of the Oakwood Lutheran Church. They came from both directions, women dressed up in pastel summer dresses and men wearing suits of gabardine and seersucker. Whites generally came from the left and blacks approached from the right. They nodded politely then proceeded up the steps and into the church. The last white man going up the steps turned to address the couple coming up after him.

"Hot enough for ya?" asked the man, of the Negro following him on the stairs.

"Yessir, it surely is a scorcher," the man replied.

Across the street from the church, a few angry young white men were gathered, mumbling among themselves and sneering toward the church. One picked up a rock and pulled his arm back to launch it at the church. His arm was caught mid-air by a hand belonging to someone much stronger than him. James Langford, in plainclothes, flashed his FBI badge with the other hand while clamping down on the young thug's arm with a vice grip.

"Wouldn't do that if I were you, son. Could lead to more trouble than you're prepared to deal with."

The young man turned on Langford with a sneer. "What're the feds doin' back here again? We integrated a long time ago, ya know!"

Langford let go of the boy's arm as the rock dropped. "Personally, I'm headed into that church as an invited guest. Now the rest of those men parked over yonder, well, let's just say they're here to observe firsthand that southern hospitality you're all so famous for."

One of the boys looked at the row of dark sedans parked along the street to their left. "Come on, Jimmy, let's get outta here. We don't need no FBI breathin' down our necks. A few nigger lovers over there ain't worth bringin' the law down on us."

"Better listen to your buddy there, Jimbo," Langford said. "You boys need to find a new hobby."

Jimmy swaggered away, spitting over his shoulder in false bravado. "Yeah, well y'all can try to force 'em down our throats but ain't nothin' gonna change round here."

Langford smiled as he donned his hat and turned toward the church. "That's where you're wrong, my friend, that's where you're wrong."

Inside the church the organ was just beginning "The Wedding March," as Langford took his seat in the back of the half-full sanctuary. The groom stood up front at the end of the aisle and a single bridesmaid smiled across from him. The smattering of guests rose as the bride approached on her father's arm. She wore a floor-length white lace wedding gown with a long veil that trailed behind her. At the front pew near the aisle stood a small woman with long, straight gray hair, wearing a white buckskin dress. Her brown aged hand with silver rings on all five fingers reached out to take a white rose extended by the bride as she passed.

Michael beamed at Annalee as he lifted her veil and she smiled back at him. They joined hands and turned to face the minister. Annalee handed her bouquet to her bridesmaid, Maggie. The two young women exchanged affectionate looks. The minister asked for the rings and Michael turned to the ringbearer at his side. Five-year-old Willis, adorable in his tuxedo, held up the pillow to Michael who patted his nephew's head.

In the front pew on the groom's side Irene slipped her arm through Eddie's and whispered in his ear as she gazed with tears in her eyes at the bridal party. "Mighty nice lookin' family you have there, Mr. Thorpe."

Eddie lovingly patted his wife's hand and nodded, swallowing a lump in his throat. Then he looked across the aisle at Winston Roberts seated beside Salina. The two men exchanged a solemn look then a nod and a knowing smile.

After the ceremony, everyone headed to the basement for the reception. The bride and groom and their parents formed a receiving line for well-wishers while Maggie and Willis stacked wrapped packages on a table at the back of the room. The guests mingled, each feeling the impact of black and white together seemingly effortlessly, most of them by now already acquainted. Winston Roberts introduced Salina to Eddie and Irene Thorpe.

"I am pleased to see these two youngsters taking their vows of marriage, Mr. and Mrs. Thorpe. Also, to see your guests enjoy themselves without rancor or awkwardness."

"Well, I guess those folks that don't approve either weren't invited or stayed away," Eddie suggested.

Irene took Salina's hand. "Maggie told us what a help and comfort you were to her during Little Willis' birth, Miss Salina. You have our eternal gratitude for bringin' that precious little boy into the world."

Salina paused, and said, "Well it has certainly been my honor and privilege, Mrs. Thorpe. 'Specially seeing how that boy is a special gift."

"Indeed, he is and please call me Irene. Can I interest you in some cake and punch?"

As the two women moved away, Eddie and Winston were left to make idle chit-chat, something neither was very good at. Eddie finally broke the ice.

"Say Winston. It's alright if I call you Winston?" Receiving a nod of the head, Eddie continued. "Michael and me been talkin' 'bout takin' little Willis fishin' one o' these days up on Ouachita Creek, after the honeymoon's over and all that. Would you care to join us?"

Winston inclined his head, as though he were contemplating the offer. "You know, it's been some time since I been fishin.' That's one of the favorite things me and Willis used to do together. Since then... well, I ain't had much interest in it for a while now."

"Well I betcha Willis would love for you to come along with us."

"Guess I can't live in the past all the time. Maybe I do need to make some new fishin' memories with that grandson. Yessir, I'd be pleased to join you fellas."

"Great! I'll give ya a call when we got a time picked out, probly' late summer, early fall."

"Sounds good. And thanks for the offer, Eddie."

After a while Annalee slipped away to change into her traveling suit. She and Michael made the rounds thanking their guests and saying good-byes. They were off on their honeymoon to St. Louis and then the Ozarks, compliments of Winston.

Michael's pick-up, repainted a bright candy-apple-red the previous year, awaited the honeymooners in front of the church. Relatives and guests threw rice at the couple as they departed. Little Willis squealed with delight when the tin cans that he and Maggie had tied to the rear axle and hidden underneath tumbled, clanged and banged down the street behind the pick-up. Little did he know that Michael had stashed a knife in the glove-box just in case. He stopped outside of town and freed his truck from its noisy attachment.

Darkness fell as the newlyweds drove toward Little Rock where they had a room reserved, compliments of Eddie and Irene. Annalee snuggled up against Michael who placed his arm around her and kissed the top of her head.

"How you doin', Mrs. Thorpe?"

"Cozy and contented thank you very much. And you, Mr. Thorpe?"

Before Michael could answer, he noticed a pair of headlights coming up fast behind them. He accelerated and shoved Annalee onto the floor.

"Get down! I think somebody's followin' us and I'm gonna try to lose 'em."

"Michael be careful! Don't try to be a hero!"

"I'm gonna turn off and see if they follow us. It might be nothin' but just stay down 'til we know."

Michael sped up and turned sharply onto a dirt side road, spraying dust into the air behind them. For a moment, he thought he'd lost them. But then faint headlights shone through the settling dust.

"Stay put Annalee. We still got company."

As he accelerated as fast as he dared on the narrow road, flashing lights appeared behind him in the dust. Not having met the new county sheriff, Michael didn't know whether he could trust whoever was in the car behind him. It could be a trick. But he didn't have many options. He didn't know where the road led, and it seemed to narrow before him. There were no side roads. He was lost and unable to get his bearings. His gut told him he had to stop, if for no other reason than to protect Annalee. He had his knife and the rifle from his gun rack in the window behind him. He could fend off one or two if he had to.

"Annalee stay where you are. There's flashin' lights behind us and I gotta stop. There's no other choices at this point." He scrambled in the glove box and handed her his hunting knife. "Take this and anybody tries to harm you, you gut 'em. I got my rifle and I'm gonna hop into the bushes to see who comes outta that car. I'll get anybody before they get you but hang onto that knife just in case. Trust me. I love you!"

"I love you, too, Michael. Please don't take any chances!"

With that he came to a sudden stop and leapt from the truck in a dust cloud. Annalee sat curled up in front of the passenger side of the cab, making herself as small as she could and listening, silently praying. She could hear her own heart thumping in her ears. Another vehicle pulled to a stop behind them. She heard someone close a vehicle door then footsteps coming toward her. She squeezed her eyes shut and tried to keep her pounding heart from being heard

Annalee listened to the loud tapping on the driver's window. "Anybody in there? It's Agent Jim Langford, FBI."

Annalee peered out and saw a familiar photo and badge pressed against the driver's window. By the time she could uncurl her body and get out, Michael yanked open the passenger door and took her into his arms.

"It's okay baby, it's okay. It's our ol' buddy from the FBI!"

Langford shone his flashlight on their faces and broke into a huge grin. "Thought you two might need an escort to Little Rock so we followed you. My colleagues intercepted some thugs back a ways that had followed you, too."

"Agent Langford I was fixin' to blow your damned head off, you know that?" Michael shouted.

"Yep, I saw you bail out—knew you were here waitin' for me. That's why I didn't sneak up on ya, but announced myself. I figured you'd give ME the benefit of the doubt before you fired."

"And how'd you figure that?"

"Gut instinct. You're not a killer, Michael and it'd take a few seconds to resolve to kill, even to protect your wife."

Annalee spoke up as she and Michael walked around to greet Langford. "Well, 's far's I'm concerned, you were in the right place at the right time, Agent."

"That's what we shoot for, so to speak. Now you want that escort or not?"

"Damn straight we do," answered Michael as he shook Langford's hand, then helped Annalee back into the truck.

Chapter Thirty-Seven

1971

Willis

"It's the children the world almost breaks who grow up to save it."

~ Frank Warren (1952-2002)
American football player: New Orleans Saints.

It had taken Eddie Thorpe a while to adjust to the new dynamics of his family. At first he was cautious and suspicious of anyone commenting on his adorable grandchild. He was distant with the child initially, which only seemed to draw Willis to him more. The gruffer Eddie spoke, the more Willis laughed, as though his Gramps couldn't possibly be wary of him so he must be teasing. As Willis grew into a toddler and then a young child, he followed his grandfather everywhere.

Eddie tried to ditch him from time to time, but Willis would have none of that. Irene fawned over the boy, waited on him and cared for his every need when Maggie was working her job at the bank. But it was Eddie, who tried to ignore him and disciplined him firmly, to whom Willis took a shine. In his eyes, Gramps could do no wrong.

Willis seemed to be an old soul in a child's body. He had dealt with bullying and racism his entire young life. Now at almost eight, he tried to take it in stride when some white kids at school called him Mulatto and Oreo and worse. Maggie taught him to stand up for himself but to resist the temptation to fight. She schooled him in black history as well as white. When he was a toddler, she told him who his father was and that he died before Willis' birth. She did not tell him how his father died, deciding that would come later if at all. For now, she tried to focus on raising him to be strong, proud and compassionate.

The first time Willis came home from school with a bloody nose, Eddie was aghast. He wanted to know who was responsible, but Willis wouldn't tell him. Eddie marched into the principal's office the very next day, vowing to take matters into his own hands unless the principal disciplined the offender. He was told that the school did not condone violence and they would look into the matter, but without Willis' cooperation in naming his attacker, there was little to be done since no teacher or official saw the altercation.

From that day on, Eddie and Willis were practically inseparable. When Eddie was working, Maggie drove Willis to school on her way to work and Irene picked him up afterward. But on Eddie's days off, he did both, often swinging by the Tastee-Freez ™on the way home for a little treat to share with his grandson.

Then in September when he was about to start third grade, Willis boldly informed his mother and grandparents that he thought he should ride the bus like everyone else in the neighborhood. He told them he didn't want to be isolated or protected and he'd rather be treated like all the other kids. Maggie reminded him that while their closest neighbors had befriended him, there would be other kids riding the bus, possibly some who might want to harm him. Eddie and Irene echoed Maggie's concerns, but Willis stood his ground.

"I ain't afraid," he assured them. "Even if it means gettin' teased or beat on, I wanna be like the other kids."

"I suppose we can't keep you in a bubble forever," Maggie said.

Eddie placed his hand on his grandson's shoulder. "I'll tell you this much Willy, anybody tries to lay a hand on you, you tell 'em you got a mean ol' grandpa at home that'll make 'em wish they hadn't."

"Thanks, Gramps," Willis replied, "but violence ain't the way."

There had been no problems until recently, when a new kid from Mississippi moved into a subdivision at the edge of the bus route. Tommy Clarke taunted Willis constantly. Kids who had befriended Willis were intimidated by Tommy and went along with the teasing to avoid being one of his victims. Soon it seemed that Willis had no friends left. He sat alone on the bus and kept to himself at school.

Then the phone calls began. Irene answered the first one and dropped the receiver in utter disgust. After that, Eddie answered the calls when he was home. The adult voice on the other end of the line, sometimes male and sometimes female, shouted racial epithets and profanity until he hung up. When Eddie wasn't home the phone went unanswered unless it rang twice and stopped then started again, which was the signal they had worked out with Michael and Annalee.

One night during dinner after one of the phone calls, Willis apologized to his mother and grandparents. "I'm sorry I brung this on all of you."

"Willis Emmett Thorpe, don't you EVER apologize for being who you are." Maggie replied. "And it's 'brought' not 'brung'," she added as she took him into her arms.

"It isn't your fault, sweetie," Irene said. "Some folks have empty hearts and no manners."

"Most of all, Willy," Eddie began, "You hold your head up high and remember you're half Thorpe and half Roberts, and can't nobody take that away from you. Don't matter what color your skin is, son, you have a strong mind and a good heart. That's things those hateful folks only wish they had."

The smells of roast chicken and cherry pie greeted Michael, Winston and Annalee as they entered the back door of the Thorpe home late one Sunday afternoon. Inside the kitchen, they found Maggie helping Irene with last-minute details.

Winston handed Irene a bottle of wine. "Thanks for having us, Irene."

"Oh, it's our pleasure, Winston," she replied. "I'm so glad Michael picked you up."

Annalee leaned over Maggie's shoulder taking in the aroma of the gravy being stirred.

"Oh, that smells so good, Maggie. Smells like our kitchen used to when Mama was cookin', don't it, Daddy?"

"It sure does, baby. Brings back sweet memories, all right."

Annalee set a salad dish on the counter just as Maggie turned to hand her the gravy whisk. "You're just in time, Annalee, as I gotta run to the little girl's room. Keep stirrin' that great-smellin' gravy for me, ok?"

"Winston, why don't you and Michael go on into the living room and watch baseball with Eddie and Willis," Irene suggested.

Eddie was talking excitedly to his grandson as Winston and Michael came into the room unnoticed. "Now that's the kinda ball your Uncle Michael woulda hit if he'd of made it to the big leagues, Willy. He was good enough too. He'd a got a scholarship for college and been picked up by St. Louis or somebody."

"There you go dreamin' again," Michael teased.

"Uncle Mike!" Willis shouted as he jumped up for a bear hug. The two fell onto the floor and playfully wrestled around with grunts and laughter.

Eddie pointed to the empty recliner beside him. "Sit yourself down, Winston while those two knuckleheads go at each other. Wanna beer?"

"Don't mind if I do," Winston replied, reaching for the bottle Eddie pulled out of a cooler beside his chair.

Eddie held out the opener and said, "Allow me."

"So who's winnin'?" Winston asked.

"Well it ain't the Cardiac Cards, I can tell ya that," Eddie answered.

"Oh my, those Reds are humiliatin' 'em good, ain't they?" Winston chuckled when he heard the score.

"Speaking of humiliatin', ya gotta look at this!" Willis shouted as he straddled Michael, pretending to pin him to the floor.

"Okay I'm callin' 'uncle' so to speak. I give—you win," Michael gasped, out of breath.

Irene carried the chicken to the dining room table. "Come and get it, you guys."

Everyone gathered around as Maggie and Annalee placed the side dishes on the table. Once seated, Irene asked Eddie to say a blessing.

"Aw Reeny, you know I ain't no good at that," he protested.

"If you don't mind," Winston said, "I'll be happy to bless this gathering."

Suddenly a rock crashed through the front window, startling everyone into momentary silence. Eddie ran through the front door, followed closely behind by Michael and Winston. Willis tried to run after them, but Maggie grabbed him.

"Mama let me go! I know it's about me again, ain't it?" Willis cried.

"You don't know what it's about, Willy, now just calm down and let the men of the family handle this."

"Aunt Anna it's cause we're black, ain't it?" Willis said to Annalee.

Annalee gathered Willis into her lap on the sofa. "Willy, it could be, I ain't gonna lie to you. But we don't know that. And we got no call to feel bad even if it is. It ain't our fault if some folks have hate in their hearts instead of love."

Irene walked over and took the rubber band off the rock where it held a note. She read the note then crumpled it and tossed it in the trash. Maggie retrieved the note and gingerly smoothed out the paper.

"Could be evidence, Mama. We can't just let this go unreported."

"Are they ever gonna stop?" Irene asked plaintively.

The men returned shaking their heads. "Nobody in sight," Eddie said.

Winston and Michael silently took a seat at the table. Eddie began to carve the chicken. The others didn't speak.

Irene broke the silence. "Winston, I believe you were about to offer a blessing, weren't you?"

"Let me do it. Please?" Willis said standing and bowing his head. The others just smiled at him and closed their eyes.

"Oh, dear Lord," Willis began earnestly. "Thank you for this family and thank you for this food and thank you for the love we feel for each other and please take the hate out of other people's hearts. Amen."

Winston cleared his throat to speak. "That's a mighty fine blessin', young man," he said.

"Don't know that I've heard better," Eddie added.

Maggie and Annalee, seated on either side of Willis, reached over and squeezed him in tight hugs. Irene smiled at him and blew him a kiss from across the table.

"Aw let the kid eat for goodness sake," Michael said to lighten the mood.

After Willis went to bed that night, Maggie showed the note to the others. Each of them read it then passed it on.

"It's somebody that knows all of us or knows about us, or knows about our history," Michael said to the group.

Maggie frowned. "But Willy said the only boy he's ever had trouble with on the bus is a new kid from Mississippi."

"It ain't KIDS that's been callin' and spewin' vile language at us," Eddie said.

Irene added, "This is a small town. Word gets around. Some old gossips are probably only too happy to fill in new neighbors on the sordid history of the town. But there are plenty of others that were here back then, too."

Winston had been quiet, contemplative, listening to the others. He finally spoke. "Just when you think it's over, that maybe some progress has truly been made, somethin' like this happens. It hurts my heart that our little Willis has to deal with it too."

"You know, Winston," Eddie began somberly, "there was a time when I didn't want my own kids to get mixed up in the whole race thing. I didn't think it was our fight. I didn't know any Negroes and I didn't want to. Now I got me a half-Negro grandson that's the light of my life. And my fine daughter-in-law and first Negro friend who I consider part of our family. Look at how I benefitted by 'dealin' with it."

Annalee reached out and took Eddie's hand. "You've come a long way, Gramps," she said with a smile.

"All I'm sayin' is, we're all in this together." Eddie replied. "Whatever happens to one of us at this table happens to all of us."

Bright and early Monday morning, Eddie and Michael stopped in at the Sheriff's office to report the rock-throwing incident. Sheriff Davis had left the office for a job in Memphis, where he and Pansy had agreed to start over. The new sheriff had come to Oakwood only two years prior. Eddie had had no occasion to meet the man and he sized him up over the desk. He was quite sure the new sheriff had Indian blood.

"What can I do for you gentlemen this morning?" the sheriff asked politely.

"Name's Eddie Thorpe. And this here's my son, Michael." Eddie placed the rock and the wrinkled note on the sheriff's desk. "This was thrown through our front window at Sunday supper yesterday."

The sheriff took the note and smoothed it out. He frowned as he read it then picked up the rock and looked it over. "Musta made a mess o' your window, a rock this size. Any idea who mighta been responsible?"

"Oh, there's a lotta folks round here that, let's just say, don't like the make-up o' my family," Eddie replied.

"Not sure I understand," the sheriff replied.

Michael leaned forward. "Well then let's just cut to the chase, Sheriff. I'm sure you know there's still Klan activity 'round here. We need to know whether we can trust you before we go any further."

The sheriff narrowed his eyes at Michael, paused and then turned to Eddie and back to Michael. "Son, my job is to uphold the law. I got no loyalties to anybody or anything else, just the laws o' Garland County and the State o' Arkansas. Now I leveled with you and I'd like for you to level with me. Why did this happen to you and who do you suspect?"

"I got one grandson," Eddie said. "He's half-black. At first, I didn't even wanna look at him. But he crawled right up into this ol' boy's heart and made hisself right at home. Couldn't love him any more if he was my own son. No offense, Michael."

"None taken, Dad, you know I love him every bit as much as you."

The sheriff looked at Michael and said gently. "I heard you was married to a black woman, Michael. This must be your son we're talkin' about."

"No sir. My nephew. My sister's son."

Eddie sighed deeply. "Okay I guess we need to explain some history to you, Sheriff, so this'll all make sense to you. Might also help you understand who may be likely to throw rocks at us. It's a long story."

"I got all day, gentlemen," the sheriff said, as he leaned back in his chair.

Eddie laid out the pertinent history, highlighting the grisly reality of what happened to Willis Thorpe and Maggie and Annalee.

When Eddie was finished, the sheriff leaned back in his chair with his hands clasped behind his head, staring at the ceiling, catching his breath, then closing his eyes for a moment. Finally, he sat up straight and looked straight at Eddie and Michael.

"I'm gonna tell you boys somethin'," he began.

Oh, here it comes, another good ol' boy, Michael thought.

Eddie looked skeptically at the sheriff.

The sheriff continued, "In my mind, there ain't no eight-year-old kid deserves to be bullied or scared outta his wits, period. Don't matter whether he's black, white, brown or purple. Neither do good, law-abidin' folks deserve to have their window smashed by a rock with hateful words wrapped 'round it. I've seen this stuff all over the South. I came over here from Mississippi and it ain't any better there."

"So, you'll help us find out who did this?" Eddie asked.

"You have my word on it," Dan Bridges replied.

As they were leaving, Eddie and Michael almost ran into an Indian woman who was entering the office. She was dressed in a plaid shirt, cinched with a leather belt over a cotton skirt. Her shiny black hair fell in a long braid down her back.

"Excuse us, ma'am," Michael offered as they stepped aside to let the woman enter.

The sheriff proudly introduced her to his visitors. "Eddie and Michael Thorpe, I'd like you to meet my wife, Naira."

"I'm pleased to meet you," Naira said with a warm smile.

"Pleasure's ours, Mrs. Bridges," Eddie replied, still a little stunned.

As the sheriff walked the Thorpe men outside, he whispered to them, "You see, gentlemen, I got some idea of what y'all been dealin' with."

Chapter Thirty-Eight

Oreos

"Achievement has no color."

~ Abraham Lincoln (1809-1865)
American statesman, lawyer, and
the 16th President of the United States.

Winston and Eddie were in the stands for Willis' Pop-Warner League football games every time they weren't working. They sat together watching their grandson learn the game on the Oakwood Rascals team.

One day, Michael joined his father and father-in-law in the stands much to their surprise. Willis saw him and waved his arms, to which Michael gave him a thumbs-up.

"Well," Eddie said, "Can you tell me what we owe this pleasure to, son?"

"Oh just in the neighborhood and thought I'd come by. Annalee is at the house with Mom and Maggie doin' some kind o' needlework.

Winston noticed a grin at the corners of Michael's mouth. "Seems there may be somethin' on your mind, Mike?"

Michael grinned broadly then. "Yeah, I thought you two might like to know that you're gonna have another grandchild."

"Well I'll be damned!" Eddie said, slapping Michael on the shoulder.

"No wonder Annalee's been actin' so strange lately," Winston said with a chuckle. "When's the big day?"

"Sometime early summer," Michael said. "That's what we're lookin' at 'til we know more."

"My, my, won't Willis be happy to hear that?" Winston said.

"Oh, he'll be jumpin' for joy," Eddie agreed.

"Thought we might take him out for ice cream after the game and tell him all together," Michael suggested.

Rather than being excited at Michael's news, Willis looked glum as he sat quietly sipping his milkshake. "Congrats, Uncle Mike," was all he said when Michael made his announcement. Though puzzled, the others decided not to press the issue with him, thinking he just needed to adjust to the thought of a new cousin sharing his spotlight.

On the way home, Eddie decided to test the waters. "So, what d'ya think about havin' a new cousin to grow up with?"

"S'ok, I guess," Willis answered.

"Now you know ain't nobody gonna love you any less, doncha?"

"Gramps, I'm eight years old," Willis replied. "O' course I know how loved I am. It ain't about that."

"Then what's buggin' ya my little man?"

"It's just that that baby's gonna be an Oreo just like me."

"Whoa, whoa!" Eddie said. "What the hell does that even mean?"

Willis rolled his eyes at his grandfather's ignorance. "It means half-black, half-white, a mulatto like me Gramps."

Eddie thought he was in over his head, but he had started the conversation. "Willis, I never heard you talk like that before. Is that how you see yourself or is that how the other kids treat you?"

"Both I guess," Willis answered.

"But your family don't treat you any different. Don't we love you enough just the way you are?"

"Yep just the way I am Gramps. When you gotta add that on, it should tell you somethin'."

"But, son, none of us can help who we are," Eddie said earnestly. "Hell, I'm just an uneducated country boy tryin' to make it to retirement. I got nothin' special about me at all. But you, now you got 'special' written all over you."

"Why? Cause I'm a mix-blood person that you don't see many of?

Eddie pulled to the curb and turned to face his grandson...

"***Willis***: after your daddy who was a fine man, a fine athlete, a guy that did good things.

Emmett: after a bright young boy that was a symbol for the rights o' his race.

Thorpe: one in a long line o' hard-workin', God-fearin' folks that try to do the best they can.

Yeah some of us are hard-headed and slow to learn. But Willy, ain't nobody I met in my whole life taught me more 'bout love and compassion and fairness than you have."

"Grandpa, do you think things will ever change? You know, when I'm older will my being part-Negro matter so much to folks?"

Eddie did not feel equipped to answer this question. He had only recently come to accept black people, thanks mostly to Willis. "I really don't know, bud," he sighed. "You're talkin' 'bout hundreds o' years o' folks feelin certain ways, handed down to 'em from their folks, never questionin,' never seein' the other side o' things."

"And thinkin' they're better 'n us cause our people used to be slaves, huh?"

"Damn, boy, you tryin' to make your ol' grandpa feel guilty? I know Willy that I ain't treated black folks right sometimes. But I'm changin.' Hell, times are changin' for that matter. Why, I betcha by the time you're grown up, there won't be none o' this racist stuff goin' on a'tall, the way things are goin.'

Willis pondered this for a moment, then said softly, "Well at least my new cousin will have me to turn to when the goin' gets rough. But I sure hope it's a boy, 'cause I don't know nothin' bout girls!"

Eddie laughed. "Well most of us don't, partner."

Chapter Thirty-Nine

The Fishing Trip

"God never did make a more calm, quiet, innocent recreation than angling."

~ Izaak Walton (1593-1683)
English writer. Best known as the author of "The Compleat Angler."

The big fishing weekend had arrived. Michael was to pick up Winston then come by for Eddie and Willis. It was still dark when Eddie roused Willis for breakfast. The boy was beside himself with excitement and anticipation. All during breakfast Eddie was bombarded with questions.

"We gonna eat what we catch, Gramps?"

"Damn straight we are. No use catchin' 'em if we don't eat 'em."

"Eddie, language!" Irene scolded. "Now I hope you guys are gonna watch your mouths with Willis along on this trip."

"Oh, we'll be on our best behavior, Reeny. Right, Willis?"

"Damn straight!" Willis shot back, feeling rather pleased with himself.

"Young man!" Irene said, hands on her hips and at a loss for words.

"Sorry Grandma," Willis said softly, hanging his head and grinning sideways at Eddie.

Irene filled the thermos with coffee. She wrapped the sandwiches in waxed paper before loading them into the metal cooler, along with some fruit and snacks. "Now you've got tuna salad, peanut butter and jelly, and cheese. That should keep you from starving."

"What about cookies Grandma?" Willis asked.

"Yep, plenty o' chocolate chip cookies for you too, Willy. And there's some milk in the cooler along with the soda for you and beer for the men."

Just then there was a tap from Michael's horn in the driveway. Eddie and Willis gathered up their supplies.

"Looks like as usual you thought o' everything, Reeny," Eddie said as he kissed her on the cheek.

Irene grabbed Willis in a hug. "Doncha let those guys corrupt you, Willis. You come back my sweet, innocent boy, you hear me?"

"Aw Grandma," Willis grinned.

Maggie came shuffling out of her bedroom in her robe and slippers. "Why does fishin' always have to start at the crack o' dawn?" she asked.

"Mama!" Willis shouted as he ran to hug his mother. "I thought you was prob'ly gonna sleep right through us leavin'."

"How could I sleep with all this commotion? And it's WERE not WAS."

"See Grandma? I could use a little corruptin' with Mama always makin' me talk right and do right."

"Oh no you don't," Maggie replied, as she gathered him into a tight bear hug. "Don't you use those guys as an excuse to say bad words or do dumb stuff. It'd be better if you rubbed off on them, not the other way around."

"The hell you say!" Eddie retorted. "Come on, Willy, it's best we get on the road so's we can get away from these self-righteous women!"

Maggie let Willis go and patted her father on the shoulder. "Now Daddy, you be takin' good care of my boy, okay?"

"He couldn't be in better hands and you know it, Sis. We'll see y'all tonight. Don't wait up for us 'cause if the evenin' fishin's good we may linger some."

The Ouachita mountains were beginning to show their fall colors on the high ridgelines, but the air was still warm in the foothills. As Michael drove across the narrow bridge that spanned the creek, Willis became enthralled with the scenery.

"Man, this is nature like I ain't never seen it before!"

"Remember your language," Michael said. "If you go home sayin' ain't I'm sure my sister will blame it on me."

"Well I ain't gonna tell!" Willis shot back, laughing.

Michael gave his nephew a playful punch in the arm, then noticed something in his rear-view mirror. Below in the creek and just behind them, a graceful doe and two small fawns had come for a drink. Michael slowed the pick-up to a stop and pointed. "Look there, Willy, a mama deer and her babies getting' a drink."

"Wow," Willis whispered, totally captivated by the scene. "I shoulda brought Mama's camera."

"We'll try to remember that next time," Eddie replied. "I shoulda known there'd be stuff you wanted a picture of on this trip."

"Where we gonna stop?" Willis asked.

"Just up ahead a little ways and off to the left over a hill. The creek bends around some rocks and there's a great hole over there that we usually have good luck with," Michael replied.

Winston sighed, "I can't believe it, fellas, but that's exactly where my Willis and I used to come, too."

"Gosh I'm sorry, Win," Michael said. "We could go scout out another place if this is too hard on you."

"Yeah we ain't locked into nothin'," Eddie added.

Winston thought for a second. "Naw, it's okay. It's gonna bring back some good memories but I'll also be makin' some new ones with my grandson. Gonna be a good day."

Willis crawled over Eddie to sit on Winston's lap. They rode like that the rest of the way, neither saying a word.

Michael showed Willis how to bait his hook with the live crawfish while Eddie and Winston scouted good spots to throw in a line.

"Now remember," Eddie called back over his shoulder, "dime for the first, dime for the most and dime for the biggest."

"You just watch, we're gonna clean their clocks," Michael whispered to Willis. "Remember, when you feel somethin' hit your line, yell out "Fish on!"

No sooner had those words left Michael's mouth, than Winston yelled them out.

They hurried to Winston's side to watch him land his catch. Willis studied his grandfather's actions. There wasn't much of a fight and soon the fish was flopping in the grass beside them. Willis jumped back and laughed, clapping his hands with joy.

"Aw it's just a smallmouth," Winston groaned. "There used to be lots o' rainbows up here, sure hope they ain't gone and disappeared."

"Can we eat it?" Willis asked anxiously.

"You betcha," Winston replied. "Smallmouth bass ain't as good as trout but they ain't bad eatin."

So, Winston won the first dime and there were calls of "fish on" several more times through the morning. Michael helped Willis land a trout and the boy was delighted. The men all hustled over to admire his catch while Willis beamed with pride.

"Okay my little man," Eddie began. "It's gettin' close to lunch time so what d'ya say we go find us a place to clean these guys?"

"You mean we gotta wash 'em?" Willis asked. "They just come outta a pretty clear stream, Gramps."

"No, that ain't what I mean, Willy," laughed Eddie. "We gotta gut 'em and get their insides out before we can eat 'em. Come on, it's fun!"

Winston started a cook fire, while Michael grabbed his cast iron skillet, some lard and the rest of the food from his pick-up. Meanwhile, Eddie found a good-sized tree stump. He carefully took Willis' fish from the basket."

"Okay Willy, here's your guy. I'll show ya how it's done. Lay him on that stump on his side"

Willis followed his grandpa's orders, shaking a little in anticipation of what he was about to do.

Eddie began, "Take this here fish knife and poke it through this little spot right here," indicating the soft spot on the fish's underside above its tail.

"Like this?" Willis asked nervously.

"That's right, son, just watch your knife, then poke it right in there, and slice him right up the middle to his gills."

Willis gulped and closed his eyes for a second, then ripped the fish open.

"Good job!" Winston said. "You're a natural!"

Willis smiled, proud of himself. "Now what?" he asked.

"Here comes the fun part Dad told you about," Michael said with a grin.

"Just reach right in there like this," Eddie said, demonstrating with a fish he had cut up the middle. "Get a good hold on those innards, like this, and just rip 'em right down and pull 'em outta there."

Willis thought this was about the most disgusting thing he'd ever seen, but he didn't want to be a chicken in front of his uncle and grandpas. Holding his mouth tight against the gag reflex he felt in his throat, he mimicked his grandfather and flung the entrails into the bushes as fast as he could.

"Atta boy!" Eddie exclaimed. "Now we can fry these boys up and have a real good meal. "

Willis was still recuperating from the gutting process. He wasn't sure he could eat the fish after pulling that slimy mess from its stomach. But again, he didn't want to appear weak, so he rubbed his hands together in feigned anticipation.

When it was all said and done, the fish tasted pretty good. Willis had four cookies afterward, washed down with plenty of milk, without disturbing his gag reflex whatsoever.

Michael began to clean up after lunch. "Okay, so much for the mornin', let's see what we can land this afternoon."

"Are we gonna eat 'em all again?" Willis asked apprehensively.

"Naw," Eddie replied. "We got ice in the other cooler to take this mess home with us. So catch another nice trout to show your mama and grandma, why doncha?"

They fished into late afternoon, when they began to hear thunder rumbling in the distance. Clouds began to roll in overhead.

"Looks like we better pack it up," Eddie said. "Don't wanna be caught in no storm. I seen this creek when it's angry and it ain't pretty."

"Yeah you got that right," Michael chimed in.

"I hear that," Winston added. "A downpour can turn this creek into a ragin' river in no time."

They quickly packed up their gear and cleaned up their campsite. Just as Michael started up the truck, raindrops began to dot the windshield. "Good timin'," he observed.

As they slowly made their way over the rough road, the raindrops fell harder and faster. Eddie turned to see the concerned look on Willis' face as the rain fell harder. He tried to take his grandson's mind off the storm.

"So little man, what d'ya think o' your first fishin' trip?"

"About the most fun I ever had, Gramps," Willis said without taking his eyes from the windshield.

"Now don't you worry none 'bout this storm, kiddo, we'll be outta it before ya know it. Soon's we cross that bridge and head downhill, we'll be back in the sunshine I betcha."

Winston patted Willis' leg. "Pretty good mess o' fish you caught there, son."

"Thanks," Willis said softly.

Michael was having trouble seeing through the downpour. His old truck's wipers strained to keep up with the sheets of rain now cascading across his windshield.

"The bridge is just ahead now, Willis," he assured his nephew. "We'll be outta this rain before you can say Jack Spratt."

And sure enough, they came around a bend and there was the bridge. Willis breathed an audible sigh of relief.

"What the hell?" Michael said as he slowed to a stop in the middle of the bridge, facing a pick-up stopped at the other end.

"Aw, that idiot oughta know this is a one-lane bridge," Eddie declared. "Why's he just sittin' there 'stead o' turnin' round? Flash your lights at him."

"What's goin' on, Gramps?" Willis asked fearfully, as he and Winston leaned forward to see for themselves.

"Okay now he's backin' up," Michael said with a sigh, as he slowly drove forward. "Thought for a minute there we were gonna have to push him outta the way."

Eddie chuckled. "No offense, son, but I think you'da been outgunned."

Winston kept an eye on the other truck as it continued to back up. "Looks like he's gonna let us pass. Surely he don't plan to go on up in this storm."

Willis stretched to get a better look. "Hey, that looks like Tommy Clarke's dad's truck. I seen him pick Tommy up at school one day. I was waitin' for the bus and they drove by and spit at me."

Eddie and Michael exchanged side glances.

"You say anything to Tommy about our fishin' trip, Willy?" Eddie asked.

"No, we don't talk to each other. But he mighta heard me talkin' 'bout it. I guess I bragged about it some."

"Did that include where we were goin', Willis?" Michael asked.

Willis didn't have a chance to answer his uncle.

Just as they reached the end of the bridge, the other truck came roaring at them full-speed and slammed into Michael's pick-up. The candy-apple-red truck spun around and flipped over the bank, landing on its side in the swollen creek. The other truck gunned its motor and sped off in the rain.

Michael was the first to emerge, climbing out on the side of the truck that now partially jutted above the water. He reached back and yelled for Willis to take his hand. Willis was screaming incoherently. The rushing water all around them made it almost impossible to hear each other.

"Willis!" Michael shouted. "Pull yourself together and grab my hand now!"

"I'm pushin' him!" Winston yelled from inside.

Finally, Michael grabbed hold of the boy's hand and pulled him out.

"You're next, Winston!" Michael shouted.

"Naw, I gotta see 'bout Eddie, Mike! He's under water!"

Michael lay down on the truck and shouted to his father. Willis lay beside him crying and shaking. Meanwhile, Winston got hold of Eddie and pulled his head and torso above water, but Eddie's legs were stuck under the seat. Winston pulled and pulled, but it only rocked the truck.

"Stop!" yelled Eddie, sputtering and spitting water. "I'm okay, just stuck! Don't rock the truck no more or it might flip over!"

"But we gotta get you outta there, Dad!" Michael cried.

"You listen to me, Mike! Somebody's gotta go for help! Can you and Willy make it to the bank?"

Michael looked around, disoriented. He wasn't sure which direction they were facing at first. He collected himself and watched the current of the stream to get his bearings. Behind him was a big fallen pine tree that protruded into the creek. Water rushed around the end of it, but several branches hung farther into the roaring creek. If he could jump far enough and grab onto one of those branches, he thought he could pull himself up onto the bank. Willis would have to ride on his back.

He shouted to his father, "Yeah, we can make it, Dad, but I ain't leavin' you here! We'll get you outta there first!"

"Mike!" yelled Winston. "I got your dad! I'm gonna keep workin' to free him, soon's you and Willis are in the clear. Now go! I won't leave him!"

"No!" cried Eddie. "All o' you get the hell outta here and get me some help, that's the smartest way! Winston leave, dammit!"

"Eddie, I'm stayin', dammit! Now the sooner we get those boys outta here, the sooner we can work on that seat!" To Michael, he yelled "Go, Mike, go!"

Michael took a second to steady himself. He knew what he had to do, but he didn't like it. He put his arm around Willis.

"Willy, this is life and death, man, and you gotta trust me! We gotta go get help and you gotta hop up on my back to do it. Now we can make it, but only if you trust me and hang on, okay?"

Willis' eyes had grown as big as saucers, but he swallowed and nodded his head, speechless in the situation.

Michael figured Willis was in shock and he knew they had to hurry. "Get up on my back, piggy-back style and hold onto my shoulders—not my neck, my shoulders, as tight as you can! Wrap your arms around underneath mine and hold on for dear life!"

Willis obeyed silently but Michael knew his fear; he could feel his nephew shaking.

"It's gonna be okay, buddy, we're gonna be just fine! You trust me?"

"Yeah..."

Michael yelled into the truck, "Ok, we're headin' out now—help'll be comin' soon!"

"God speed!" yelled Winston.

"Be careful, Mike!" Eddie shouted.

"Hold on, Willy, here we go!" Michael cried.

He leapt as far as he could and they hit with a resounding splash that sent them underwater for an instant. Michael hadn't realized how much the creek had already risen but he knew now. When they surfaced, he had a grip on a long branch from the fallen tree. He tried to pull them up onto the tree, but it rolled slightly.

"Willy, we can't pull up this way. You gotta climb up my back, get onto that tree and shinny up to the bank. I'll come after you, but the two of us together is rollin' the tree, we gotta do it one at a time. Now go!"

Willis crept tentatively over Michael, pulled on the branch, and landed on his stomach across the tree.

"Good job!" Michael yelled. "Now climb on up that tree to the bank!"

Once Willis was safely on the bank, Michael was free to yank on the branch. The old pine tree gave a little but then settled back as he jumped up on top of it. He scampered as fast as he could to the bank and pulled Willis with him up to the roadside.

"We made it!" Michael shouted toward the partially submerged pick-up, knowing they couldn't hear him over the rushing water.

Back at the truck, Winston tried to take the seat apart to free Eddie. He didn't realize how badly Eddie was hurt until he heard him groan.

"Hold on, man! I'ma get you outta here!"

"Win, I ain't gonna make it. My leg's busted pretty bad—you'd have to drag me if you COULD get me unpinned. You go now. Ain't no use, man—you save yourself!"

"Don't you talk like that, Eddie Thorpe! Took me this long to get my first white friend and by God, I ain't leavin' you behind!" He yanked again on the back of the seat, hoping it would give way. It budged just a little and Winston put his shoulder into it.

"Ahhh!" Eddie screamed.

The seat had moved just enough for him to free one leg, the broken one that shot pain through his body as he moved.

Winston reached for Eddie's other leg, just as the truck shifted. Now he was pinned by the seat, as well. Water rushed in through the shattered rear window and rose quickly inside the cab.

Eyes wide, the two men looked at each other in panic, just as they had when they first laid eyes on each other years before.

"You a prayin' man, Eddie?"

"Well, I guess there ain't no atheists in foxholes or sinkin' trucks, Win."

Michael and Willis were exhausted by the time they reached the bait shop. They had been half-walking, half-running in the rain for five miles. Willis lay down in the mud outside the store. Michael rushed inside.

"Help's comin', little man," Michael said gently to Willis, as he gathered him into his arms and brushed the mud from his face.

Willis turned his face into his uncle's chest and sobbed.

CHAPTER FORTY

Amazing Grace

"It takes courage to grow up and become who you really are."

~ e.e. cummings (1894-1962)
American poet, painter, essayist, author, and playwright.

ANNALEE COULD NOT recall seeing white folks at the Crossroads Baptist Church before. Besides Michael, Irene and Maggie in her pew there were more. Too many to be seated since the church was filled with black church members. So they stood outside. When the service for Winston was over, the white folks outside formed a gauntlet. Quietly, reverently, they then marched behind the family and black parishioners to the Negro graveyard up the hill.

When the 21-gun salute sounded at the graveside service, Annalee shook and doubled over with the sobs that had been building for days. Michael held her and stroked her hair while his own tears slowly fell on her shoulder. Maggie had an arm around her mother and wrapped Willis close on her other side.

Annalee composed herself to receive the precisely folded flag commemorating her father's service in the Korean conflict. Willis came over to embrace her and whispered in her ear, "I didn't even know Grandpa was in the army, Auntie."

She hugged him tight and whispered back, "There's a lot about your grandpa you didn't know, Willy, and we'll have to make up for that."

From the graveyard, they returned to the church, where a feast was laid out in the basement. There were rows of tables laden with fruit, meat, side dishes, homemade rolls and desserts. The minister blessed the food and the socializing began.

Irene could not believe how warmly this group of strangers welcomed her and her family and friends. She had been numb to all feeling since sobbing her heart out the night Eddie died. Now as these warm-hearted people hugged her, brought her food, offered their condolences, she began to relax into her grief instead of closing it off as a separate chamber within herself. Soon enough, it would be time to lay Eddie to rest tomorrow and the thought of that final good-bye lodged in her throat and tore at her heart.

The plan was to walk down Main Street from the courthouse to the church. From there they would drive out to the cemetery. Eddie, who had often cursed JFK's politics and policies, was nonetheless impressed by the funeral procession following his casket in 1963. He had asked Irene at the time to do that when he died if he went first. She hadn't thought another thing about it until the unbearable planning began. While Michael and Maggie disagreed, Irene stood firm that she would honor their father's wishes. Michael worried that it would be too hard on Annalee, in her condition, but his wife surprised him by saying she thought it a fitting tribute.

And so the next day, they gathered at the post office just beyond the courthouse. When the minister raised his arms, the crowd stood silent and listened to his prayer. Then they followed the family into the street. Blacks and whites together, they marched in silent respect. Somewhere in the midst of the group, a strong black soprano voice began to sing *"Amazing Grace."* Others joined in. Some began to hold hands. Irene stumbled and Michael caught her. From that point, they walked arm-in-arm with each other and Annalee and Maggie. Willis stepped alongside, not wanting to hold someone's hand and appear to be a baby.

Sheriff Bridges marched his prisoners out to the sidewalk in front of his office. The two men were cuffed with their hands behind their backs.

"Kneel," he ordered them.

"What the hell?" snapped Buddy Clarke.

Bridges struck his bully club across the back of Clarke's knees. "I said kneel."

Clarke fell to his knees, stumbling forward, and couldn't get up. Bridges pulled him upright to his knees. Clarke's cousin, Rupert Thomas, decided to kneel without the sheriff's help.

"Now you boys will be payin' your respects as this procession goes by. Keep your mouths shut and your eyes on the folks. Maybe even do a little soul-searchin' while you're at it."

Willis felt numb. He couldn't come to terms with the fact that he'd lost both his grandpas at once and would never see them again. He couldn't accept that anyone could hate them so much. His heart ached. The only thing that kept him from curling into a ball on his bed was that his family was hurting too. He spotted the sheriff and his prisoners on the sidewalk. The other marchers were too lost in the moment to notice him breaking ranks.

"This them?" Willis asked the sheriff.

"It's them," Bridges replied.

Willis looked the two men up and down. He had seen Clarke before, but not his cousin.

"You hate blacks, too?" Willis asked Thomas.

Thomas just glared at him.

Willis turned to Clarke. "I know you do, cause you spit at me one time when I was waitin' for the bus at school. Your boy carries your hatred, too."

Willis stared at the men until his face crumpled and tears began to stream down his face. "You never even knew my grandpas," he began plaintively. "Why'd you wanna go and kill 'em? They never done nothin' to you."

The men would not meet Willis' eyes. He wiped his face on his shirt sleeve, then continued. "My grandpas taught me how to fish. On the day they died. That's what they died for, showin' their grandson how to fish. Ain't you proud you killed that kind o' threat?"

"Pickaninny!" Clarke caustically said to Willis' back as he walked away. Bridges butted him in the shoulder with his club.

Willis came back to look at Clarke. He remembered his promise to his mother that he would never be the one to start violence. He ached from the desire to punch or kick this man. He seemed to emit a long, low growl, but it was the sound of him mustering up all the saliva in his mouth, which he then launched straight into Clarke's face before he walked away.

"Aw, damn, Sheriff!" Clarke whined with his face dripping. "Gimme somepin, wipe this off!"

Sheriff Bridges reached into his pocket and pulled out a large white handkerchief. He took pains to slowly unfold it. Then he wiped his brow and returned the handkerchief to his pocket. "Sure is hot today," he said, "best get you boys back inside."

As the sheriff pushed his charges into the jail, Clarke furiously wiped his face on his shoulder. "You may get us, Bridges, but there's plenty more where we come from."

"Plenty more where they came from, too. But here's the difference. You're fightin' against them from hate and ignorance. They're fightin' FOR somethin', their own dignity and for their very lives. That takes a kind o' courage the likes o' which you boys'll never understand.

About the Author

Sharon Hart Strickland was born and raised in the St. Louis area, where she spent the first twenty years of her life. Filled with a fascination for the Great American West, she spent the next decade living in and exploring Oregon, California, and finally Idaho, where she fell in love with a native son and put down roots. Sharon has been writing throughout her life and has honed her natural skills over many years, through collegiate creative writing classes, and as a long-time professional administrative assistant, office manager and certified paralegal.

As a member of the Idaho Writers' League, she has won awards for her short stories and poetry. Sharon and her husband, Rick, live in their dream house, built with their own blood, sweat and tears, on a hillside in Idaho. They are active in church and community musical endeavors, and family events. They have been blessed with three children, four grandchildren, and two adopted dogs. *The Kiss* is Sharon's second book. Her first, *The Third Step,* was published in 2013.

OTHER BOOKS BY THE AUTHOR

The Third Step

In the Wild West of the late 1800s, a pretty, pragmatic twenty-year-old named Polly is making ends meet as a lady of the night at Belle's Place, a brothel in Pendleton, Oregon.

At the same time...-in a labyrinth of tunnels underneath the house, Ben, a Chinese immigrant, toils in his uncle's laundry and accepts his lot as an unwelcome stranger in America who dares not appear above ground after dark.

Against all social codes of the day, these two outcasts begin a fragile love affair. The Third Step, an enthralling work of historical fiction by Sharon Hart Strickland, breathes new life into Oregon's Pendleton Underground of the late 1800s in a story of forbidden love between two social outcasts, and the colorful characters who inhabit their world.

Based on historical fact and characters, The Third Step begins when Polly arrives at Belle's Place, a brothel in Pendleton, Oregon, to work in the only profession she knows. When she accidentally runs afoul of a prominent client, she becomes caught up in a series of events that change her life forever.

Belle's bouncer, a stoic Native American name Quinton, is implicated in the events and must flee for his life, while Belle tries to cover everyone's tracks.

When Polly is secretly nursed back to health in the laundry by Ben, the feelings that develop between the two of them fly in the face of the local society's rigid rules.

A work of high drama leavened with gentle humor, The Third Step spins a tale of the Old West that is rarely chronicled in history books, but factually based and full of the courageous characters that were drawn to life in the West.

There's the beautiful madame Belle; Ben's wise uncle, Lu Chung, who runs the laundry; Father Perigan, a de-frocked priest who holds services in the brothel's unlikely chapel; as well as hypocritical townsfolk, a prominent and arrogant judge, the Native American bouncer, and a mysterious state senator, among others. As Polly regains her strength, Ben has a reason to step beyond the subterranean world where he has been forced to live.

Lovers of history will get a rare glimpse of the rough-edged and often discriminatory landscape of the American West, as Ben and Polly navigate a hostile climate in Pendleton and beyond. This powerful, poignant work delivers a fascinating tale that is rich in historical detail, colorful characters and good, old-fashioned romance. Anyone looking for a page-turning, wildly imaginative American tale will relish this trip out West where the conditions are harsh, but love, honor, and redemption can still prevail.

https://www.amazon.com/Third-Step-Sharon-Strickland-ebook/dp/B00H3PESIU

Print Length:266 pages
ISBN:1491247851
Publication Date: December 4, 2013
Language: English

Digital Version ASIN B00H3PESIU

-

THANK YOU IN ADVANCE...

IF YOU ENJOYED The Kiss, I would greatly appreciate it if you would spread the word about it.

You have the power to do that in two quick ways:

Recommend the book to your friends and/or the whole wide world on social media. Shouting from rooftops is particularly appreciated!

Review the book. Take just five minutes to write an honest review and it can make a huge difference and would mean the world to this author. As you likely know, it's the single best way for your fellow readers to find books they'll enjoy, too. This is not a laborious process like you endured in junior high English class... it is just a quick note of what you liked about the book, and what you feel other readers may experience. You see, our readers' opinions are what help us grow as writers, and predicate how our work is perceived in the industry.

To me—as an author and a reader—the goal is always to find a good author-reader match. By sharing your reading experience through recommendations and reviews, you become a highly appreciated matchmaker!

AMAZON:
https://www.amazon.com/dp/0578453932

Scroll down until you see:

Review this product

Share your thoughts with other customers

Write a customer review

www.ingramcontent.com/pod-product-compliance
Lightning Source LLC
Chambersburg PA
CBHW062013170626
46813CB00001B/136

* 9 7 8 0 5 7 8 4 5 3 9 3 4 *